The IVORY CARIBOU

Caroline McCullagh

iCrewDigitalPublishing.com
Chula Vista, California

The Ivory Caribou
Copyright © 2016 Caroline McCullagh

Printed in the United States of America
Published by iCrew Digital Publishing
Website: icrewdigitalpublishing.com
e-mail: icrewdigital@gmail.com
Book Design by DJ Rogers, justwritedesign.com

ISBN-13: 978-0692724347
ISBN-10: 0692724346

iCrew Digital Publishing is an independent publisher of digital works. We support the efforts of authors who wish to self-publish in the digital world.

All rights reserved. No part of this publication may be reproduced or transmitted in any form or by any means, electronic or mechanical, including photocopy, recording, or any information storage or retrieval system, without permission in writing from the copyright owner.

This is a work of fiction and all characters and events mentioned are imaginary.

For Alice, who is generous in her praise

ACKNOWLEDGEMENTS

Thanks to my many friends who over the years have given me the two things an author needs most: critiques and encouragement, especially Byron Earhart, Dave Feldman, Richard Lederer, Syd Love, Muriel Sandy, and Lola Sparrowhawk.

Thanks also to my publisher, Rick Lakin at iCrew Digital Publishing and DJ Rogers at justwritedesign.com who designed the cover and the interior.

Also by
CAROLINE McCULLAGH

With Richard Lederer
American Trivia
American Trivia Quiz Book

Coming Soon
Twenty-Six Eskimo Words for Love

Visit www.CarolineMcCullagh.com

Other voices on
The Ivory Caribou

In The Ivory Caribou, Caroline McCullagh has created an enduring love story between a sixty-year-old woman and a man of unusual ethnicity. The author's real love, though, is of anthropology, history, and language. She is a luminous storyteller and wordsmith of the highest order.

Richard Lederer, author of
Anguished English and *Amazing Words*

I haven't had this much fun reading prose in a while. The story moves well, the characters are deftly drawn and the plots are so easily interwoven you won't believe your mind.

Jim Bennett, Poet, Reviewer and
author of *Cold Comes Through*

Best Book I've Read in a Long Time! I decided to read the first few pages over lunch, yesterday, and now I know what people mean when they say "I couldn't put it down!" The time I spent immersed in this book was WELL WORTH IT

Lynette M. Smith, All My Best Copyediting
and Heartfelt Publishing

CHAPTER One

You'd think a death would change everything, but the sun still shone, and Carola still kept my kitchen spotless.

She stood filling her cup when I said, "I dreamed about him again last night."

Her hand stopped in midpour. The teapot thumped on the oak table.

I added sugar and milk to my tea in an effort to ignore her steady stare.

"Anne—"

"No, not again. Sometimes I long for the days when you were just the cleaning lady." I picked up my cup with what I hoped was an air of finality.

Her back straightened. "I don't care. I have to say it. Start living again. Robby's been gone more than a year. Is this what he wanted for you—sadness and dreams? You're letting him down."

"No, I'm not."

"I will not watch you kill yourself with grief." She snapped her mouth shut, walked over to the sink, and started loading the breakfast dishes into the dishwasher.

Her words stung as sharp as a slap to the face. Now her silence—louder than her words had been—separated us.

I set my cup down. "Don't be angry."

Her response was the clink of dishes.

The radio on the tiled counter, tuned to a Tijuana station, played softly. Mariachi music drifted through the room with the scent of the red roses on the trellis just outside the open French doors. The tick-tock of the antique regulator clock on the wall measured our silence.

She finally turned. "I don't want to be angry, but I am . . . and worried."

I held my hand out to her. "I'm so sorry. I don't want to make things difficult for you."

She returned to the table and took my hand in hers. "I know. But nothing will change unless you change something. He always took care of you, but he can't take care of this, no matter how long you wait, no matter how much you dream."

"Oh, Carola. Everyone says I have to move on, but I don't know how. My father used to say, 'When times get tough, you just put one foot in front of the other and keep going.' I've tried, I really have."

"I know it's difficult, but why don't you go out with someone? What do you have to lose?"

Maybe she's right. Men ask me out. I'm complimented. I'm almost sixty, but everyone says I look younger, in spite of my used-to-be-brown, salt and pepper hair. They seem to like my figure, even though my hips are too big and my breasts are too small. At five-five, I don't intimidate even shorter men. And I get compliments on my dark brown eyes.

We hadn't been in denial. Robby was forty-six and I was twenty-four when we met. We knew when we married that I'd probably be a widow someday. We thought I'd be able to manage, but I hadn't known it would be like this.

I guess I'm waiting for him. I go through the motions of life, and I wait and wait for him to come back. I think I hear his car in the driveway or his key in the lock. When I go out, I see men, and, for an instant, I think I see him walking in a door down the block or passing by in a taxi. When the phone rings, I always expect to hear his voice. I never do.

I don't know how to be alone. When Robby worked, when he was away on trips, he was always "there," somewhere. I was never really alone. Now I am.

I shook my head. "I don't want another man."

She moved and put her arm around me.

I leaned into her soft warmth and wept.

After a while, she handed me a paper napkin from the holder and took one for herself. We blotted our eyes and she sat.

"You need to start something," she said.

"What?"

"I don't know what. Just something."

I nodded. "I'll think about it."

"You're like the Energizer Bunny, Anne. Once you're moving, there's no stopping you, but it sure is hard to get you moving sometimes. You need to start something today. Why don't you work on the genealogy?"

"The genealogy?" I shook my head. "No. We did that together. I can't."

The more I thought about it, though, the better it seemed. I'd have a mission, a quest. I could finish the genealogy. It could be my last gift to Robby . . . and then I could go be with him. I've been thinking about that for a long time. I can't see any way of going on without him anymore. It's just too hard.

I know it might break Carola's heart. She's been my housekeeper for more than thirty-five years, and she's been my best friend and confidante for most of that time. I trust her as I trust no one else in the world. But I won't tell her that doing the genealogy won't be a way of saying good-bye to Robby.

So I started.

When we finished our tea, I went into the den.

I had the radio there tuned to the local classical station. Carola and I have become a little territorial over the years. I get the rest of the house, but she's the boss of the kitchen and the small sitting room where she watches *General Hospital* every afternoon that she's here. When we're in those two rooms, we listen to her stations. Everywhere else, we listen to mine.

I switched the radio on just as an orchestra started to play the overture to *Marriage of Figaro*. That had been Robby's favorite opera. It seemed like an omen, a message that I've made the right decision.

I pulled a large notebook labeled "Brendan O'Malley" off the lowest bookshelf. I'd say I dusted it off, but nothing around Carola would dare be dusty. I spent the rest of the morning reading the notes on the project Robby and I had not completed before his death.

Each page held memories—happy then, sad now. We'd spent many hours researching, trying to find out about his father, Brendan. I remembered the excitement of finding a clue, a document, sometimes even a photo. I thought genealogical research would be boring, but it was like a treasure hunt.

Brendan had been born and raised in Pittsburgh. His father owned a bank and was one of the movers and shakers of that era— his name appeared in many newspaper stories of the day.

We found out where Brendan went to school, how well he did in different subjects, and what his political and religious affiliations were, but then, when he reached the age of twenty-two, the records just stopped. We couldn't find anything more about him until he reappeared in public records nine years later.

Of course, we thought about him being in prison, but even prisoners show up in the census rolls.

Before Brendan dropped out of sight, he'd worked as a banker in the family business, but when he reappeared, he identified himself as a farmer on the marriage license he filed with Robby's mother, Isabelle.

The few photos we have of him were taken after that nine-year gap. He looked old beyond his years, tired, ill. He died at the age of thirty-two, before Robby's first birthday.

When Isabelle remarried, Robby had been strongly discouraged from asking about Brendan. He was expected to accept Isabelle's new husband as his father, but the man had been cold and uninterested in a lonely little boy. In later years, Robby thought it was because he'd been an unwelcome reminder that Isabelle had loved someone else. He had grown up "knowing" that life would have been better with his own father. Searching for information about him, which had started as a pleasurable hobby, ultimately became almost an obsession.

The focus of that obsession was a leather-bound pocket notebook that had come to Robby as part of his inheritance. Brendan's small, neat handwriting in some sort of code filled its yellowed pages. We guessed it might have information about the missing years, but we'd never found anyone to verify that, even though we hired linguists and code specialists to help us.

And now I couldn't see any loose ends I could pull to unravel his secrets.

I felt so let down.

Carola and I walked around the garden after lunch looking at the begonias Ernesto, Carola's husband, had spent the morning setting out in the shaded beds.

Usually spring in San Diego is mild, but the air was still now, and the sun stood high in the cloudless sky, making it hot for this early in May. I was almost too warm in my dark blue slacks and a long-sleeved blue plaid shirt. Carola was more seasonably dressed in black slacks (to make her hips look slimmer) and a yellow short-sleeved knit top.

A scrub jay scolded us for invading his territory, but we didn't let that interrupt our conversation.

"Maybe there aren't any records in Pennsylvania because he went someplace else," Carola said.

"We looked in all the states."

"World War I happened about then. Maybe he was in the army or something."

"We checked military records."

"What about another country?"

I shrugged.

"What if he went out of the country? Where would he have

gone?" She bent down to pull several small weeds, walked to the compost pile, and tossed them on. Years ago, in a moment of candor, Ernesto told me that he always left a few weeds or something else undone for her to find. When I scolded him for being deceptive, he simply said, "It makes her happy."

We stopped again, this time in the sunshine at the edge of the kitchen garden, and contemplated the lettuces that had begun to bolt in the spring warmth.

I considered her question. "Maybe Ireland. His parents came from there. Maybe relatives still lived there. We never heard of any though."

"Anywhere else?"

"Canada, I suppose. Brendan's Uncle James lived in Ottawa."

"Where else?"

I thought a moment. "No place I know of."

"Ottawa's a lot closer to Pittsburgh than Ireland is." Carola's voice trailed off. She turned with a smile. "Maybe you should go there. See what you can find."

"Go where? To Ottawa?"

"Why not?"

"Well—"

"Why not?"

"Carola, no."

She talked right over my refusal. "If that doesn't work out, you can look in Ireland."

"Ireland. Carola, wait a minute."

"How soon do you want to go? We can pack now." She turned and walked purposefully toward the kitchen door. "We'd better pack just for Canada though. I think it's wetter in Ireland this time of year. You'll need different clothes. You'll probably want to come home a few days before you go there, anyway, to catch up on the mail and get your hair done. I wonder where we put your passport."

"Carola, stop." I hurried to catch up with her. "You can't be serious."

But she was, and when she gets an idea, she's like a terrier with a rat.

We spent the rest of the afternoon talking. I finally said, "Carola,

I don't have the strength to argue anymore."

She smiled. "It's the right thing, Anne. You'll see."

I'd really known all along that I'd give in eventually. In all the years I've known her, I've never figured out how to distract her when she latches onto an idea.

We decided I'd stay a month. She said I could do whatever research needed to be done, go to some art galleries, some concerts. I don't have obligations in San Diego. The opera season was over, and I'd quit doing volunteer work when Robby was ill.

Two days later, I stood in line at the gate waiting to board the flight to Ottawa.

CHAPTER Two

I'M ALWAYS UNCOMFORTABLE EVEN ON THE BEST OF FLIGHTS, and I hadn't gone anywhere in the almost three years since 9/11. I expected problems. They didn't materialize, but I still felt tense and uncomfortable. I was glad when I finally walked along the jetway into the Ottawa terminal.

I rented a car, but I planned to keep it for only a few days. I wanted to be where I could get around on foot and by cab. I stayed in a hotel Saturday night and spent the next day looking for an apartment.

I found a small place in an upscale neighborhood not too far from the center of Ottawa. Several single-story units sat around an attractive courtyard garden. I hoped the cheerful celadon green living room might bring my mood up a little. A dining area with a table for four abutted a tiny kitchen. The large cream-colored bedroom had ample storage—not that I'd brought much that needed storing. The windows faced east, but heavy drapes would allow me to sleep through the early sunrises of spring. Their pleasing floral pattern in greens, yellows, and pinks might make me glad to open my eyes each morning.

Monday, I arrived at the Library and Archives Canada. I was so early I had to wait until they unlocked the doors at eight o'clock.

As I entered, the people I'd waited with scattered or lined up at the information desk.

The entry hall was bigger and grander than I expected. I wasn't sure what to do. I guess I looked bewildered. I heard a French-accented voice say, "Madam, may I help you?"

He looked about my age and wore a well-tailored dark brown suit with a fine pinstripe. A lively yellow and brown tie over a cream-colored shirt saved the suit from being dull. He also wore a small gold ring in his left earlobe. The discreet nametag pinned to his jacket pocket read "René Benoit."

"Mr. Benoit, I don't know where to start."

"Have you come to research or to tour the building?"

"I've come from San Diego to research. I didn't know you could tour the building."

"I'll tell you what. We'll start with a tour. We have a nice display of historical documents, artwork, photos, and maps." He gestured toward a large archway on my right. "I'll give you a quick run through; you can come back later and really look at them at your leisure. Then we'll talk about your specific research problem, eh?"

I looked around. I didn't see anyone else getting an individual tour. I wondered why he'd picked me. "That would be great, but don't you have work you're supposed to be doing? I don't want your boss mad at you for spending too much time with me."

"That's OK. I am the boss." He fished a business card out of his jacket pocket. It read "René J. Benoit, PhD, Chief Research Librarian, Library and Archives Canada."

In surprise, I said, "Dr. Benoit, do you have time?"

"Yes, as a matter of fact, I do. I was scheduled to go to a long and boring meeting this morning. It's been canceled at the last minute. I'm like a boy with a day off from school." He smiled broadly.

"Really?"

"Yes, my calendar's blank. I'm going to celebrate by doing what I love best. I'm going to help you with your research." He turned and gestured again. I walked ahead of him through the archway.

"What can I call you?" he asked.

"Anne. My name's Anne O'Malley."

"Well, Anne, you call me René."

His "little tour" turned out to be a fascinating view of public areas and behind-the-scenes places where the public normally didn't go.

Tall and lanky, René was one of those men who seemed to be all knees and elbows and yet managed to move with surprising grace. He made me think of Fred Astaire. His ash blond hair shaded into gray. He had a blond's light coloration, brown eyes flecked with gold, and a charming smile. I found out later that morning that he wore wire-rim half-glasses on his angular face when he read. They made him look dry and academic. In reality, he had a lively sense of humor and a hearty laugh, and he loved to talk.

When we finished the tour, we went to the fifth floor. His corner office commanded a spectacular view of the city of Gatineau across the Ottawa River. Double-hung windows muted the sound of any traffic below. His large desk was bare except for a telephone, computer monitor, keyboard, and a large dusky-pink cymbidium orchid in full bloom. When I complimented him on the orchid's beauty, he said he'd grown it in his greenhouse at home.

Bookshelves lined the walls. Files and books in neat stacks covered a library table. A small sofa of buttery-soft black leather, matching easy chair, and coffee table completed the furnishings. The overall feeling was strongly masculine.

He offered me a seat on the sofa. He sat in the chair with easy elegance and crossed his long legs.

His secretary brought in a tray with cups of coffee for him and tea for me.

"Now tell me about the research that brought you all the way from San Diego."

"I'm trying to find out about my husband's father, Brendan O'Malley. He died before my husband, Robby, was a year old. Robby's mother remarried. Contact with his father's family faded. As Robby got older, he felt the loss more acutely. He died in January last year. He really wanted this, so I thought I'd try to complete it for him."

"You're a widow then. I saw your ring. I assumed otherwise."

I looked at my left hand. "I haven't been able to bring myself to take it off yet."

"I'm sorry for your loss."

"Thank you." I took a sip of tea to get past this awkward moment.

"Where have you looked?"

"Looked?" I had to pull my mind back from thoughts of Robby. "Researched."

"Oh. In the Mormon Library and the US National Archives. We even went to Pittsburgh—where his father was born and buried—but we still had a big hole in our information."

"Sometimes you never do fill those holes. Old records are often spotty because of fires, floods, insects. Records are stolen too."

"I'm not ready to give up yet. I'm willing to work hard. This is very important to me."

"Tell me what you've found so far." He prepared to take notes.

I set my cup down and picked up my folder. "Brendan John O'Malley was born in Pittsburgh, Pennsylvania, on August 24, 1890. He lived with his parents until 1912. He was a city boy, born and bred. His father owned a bank. After he completed two years of college, Brendan worked at the bank until he was almost twenty-two, when he disappeared from records in the US. When he reappeared in 1921, he listed his occupation as 'farmer.' He died in 1923 of chronic leukemia."

"Ah. That puts our research back further than I thought. What else did you find?"

"We managed to get copies of his medical records."

He looked up from his paper. "Ha! Talk about luck."

"I know. He died at a teaching hospital that's still in business in Pittsburgh. They archived all their records for future research needs."

"I assume they showed something interesting besides the leukemia."

"Yes. How he became a farmer wasn't the only mystery in his life. He'd recovered from injuries suffered in a plane crash."

"That's interesting. Planes were uncommon in those days."

"But we never found a connection between Brendan and flying."

"That might be a place to start, though. What else?"

"He was an accomplished artist and he played the mandolin."

"Hmm. What did you look for that you couldn't find?"

I closed my folder. "We couldn't find a record of him in the military or any indication he participated in any flying-related activities such as barnstorming or the early airmail service, and we couldn't find any clue as to where he might've learned to farm."

"Why have you come to Ottawa? You must think he was here at some point." He looked up expectantly.

"His obituary listed an uncle in Ottawa. It's a slim lead, but it's something. I don't have anything else."

He finished his coffee and stood. "Well, that does give us a place to start. Let's see what we can track down about that uncle. What was his name?"

"James Patrick O'Malley."

We spent the rest of the morning researching, and we did find some property records for the uncle. At 12:30, René apologized. "The second half of my boring meeting hasn't been canceled, so I won't be able to help you any more today. Thank you for an interesting morning."

"You shouldn't thank me. You've done so much. This has been wonderful. I really feel like I have a start."

"Will you be coming back tomorrow?"

"Definitely."

"I'll look for you," he said.

After a lunch break, I worked systematically through city census and property records. By five, my eyes were tired from peering at the screen of the brightly lit microfiche reader, and I was stiff from sitting so long. I did find out that Uncle James had an extra adult living in his household in 1913. I walked home satisfied with that small step forward.

The next morning, I stood outside the doors at eight o'clock again. I didn't see René, but I couldn't expect him to wait at the door every day. In any case, I had plenty of work to do.

At 11:45, he arrived.

I showed him what I'd done so far.

He made some notes on other references I should check. "I'm sorry I won't have time to help you this afternoon."

"As much as I'd like that, I do remember you have other responsibilities."

"Well, still, I'd have liked to. Could I take you to lunch instead? We could talk about your research while we eat."

I wondered what René wanted from me. He'd sort of picked me up the previous day. I didn't know if this lunch was a date or friendship, and I didn't know how to ask that question. My first instinct was to turn him down, but I thought, *Well, why not? I came here because Carola wants me to have new experiences.*

"I'll go to lunch with you, but you have to tell me one thing first."

He looked puzzled. "What?"

"Why do you wear an earring?"

"It's a secret."

"Oh, I'm sorry."

"It's OK. I'll tell you. It's so that when I look in the mirror, I'm reminded that I'm a librarian by choice. I could have been a pirate." He winked.

I giggled. "I've never had lunch with a pirate or a librarian either."

I had second thoughts, though, as I gathered up my papers and picked up my purse. I didn't know if he was married. He didn't wear a ring, but many men don't. I had to find out.

We walked to the Earl of Sussex Pub, a short distance from the Archives. It was crowded and noisy, but the food on the diners' tables looked wonderful and smelled even better.

We managed to find a booth.

I'd never been in a pub, but I had always imagined that one would be just like this—dark wood, whitewashed walls, wrought iron light fixtures. The only things that hadn't been part of my imaginary pub were the paintings on the walls: athletes skiing, racing on skates, and playing ice hockey. That, I suspected, was a unique Canadian touch. The classic rock on the sound system was almost drowned out by conversation and the clink of utensils on plates as people hurried through their meals to get back to work.

We ordered the pub lunch: steak and kidney pie—that's what had smelled so good—Merlot for him, iced tea for me.

After the waitress left, I said, "Well, tell me about your family. Are you married? Do you have children?"

"No, I've never married. I used to think about it, but it wasn't in the cards. I have a younger sister, Yvonne. She's my only sibling. We don't have any other family."

He pulled out his wallet and took out a photo of him standing in a garden with a woman. She was much shorter than he was, but otherwise, looked very like him and had the same ash-blond hair, cut short in a simple style.

"She's mentally disabled. She attends an adult day care program while I work, but I take care of her the rest of the time."

I handed the picture back to him. "What's that like for you?"

He put the picture in the wallet and the wallet back in his pocket. "It's not bad. She's sweet and loving. She can't be left without supervision, though."

"She can't take care of herself?"

"She's like a three- or four-year-old. She can dress, bathe, and feed herself. She can't read, but she can count money. She helps me with the grocery shopping. She's good at recognizing pictures on boxes and cans. Once in a while, I leave her in the care of a neighbor, but my social life is limited."

"Is that difficult for you?"

"Sometimes. My parents took care of her before. She could have been institutionalized when they died, but I didn't want that for her, and I knew they didn't. So I chose not to marry." He shrugged.

"I'm so sorry. I think that must be sad for you."

"Sometimes I mind, but most of the time it's OK. The thing I miss most, though, is conversation. She's not good at that. At work, I spend a lot of time shuffling paper. I like to talk to people when I can. That's why I asked you to lunch."

"Oh. Well, I'm glad you did."

"Now, tell me about Robby."

"It's strange. He's been gone more than a year now, but I can't seem to get myself to realize it. He's still here for me somehow."

"You're not ready to move on?"

"We were happy together, but I know I need to let him go. I just can't seem to figure out how to do it. My friend Carola pushed me into this trip to see if it might get my life off dead center." I shook my head. "You don't want to hear this stuff."

"But I do. If we're going to be friends, we need to know about each other, eh?"

The waitress brought our drinks. I had a little time to think about what he'd said. Friendship was what he wanted, and I was willing to provide that. I relaxed and enjoyed the lunch.

We met for lunch nearly every weekday after that, even when I researched at other facilities. He called me on the weekends too. There seemed to be a lot to talk about.

René was invaluable. He knew so much more about research techniques than I did. He saved me from spending time on things that would have been dead ends. Instead, he pointed me in the right direction when he suggested I look through Canadian military records. Brendan's obituary said he served honorably in the "Great War," but we'd never found any records in the US. It hadn't occurred to me that that service might have been for Canada.

To my delight, I found Brendan's name in a list of Canadian Army promotions from January 1917. I could hardly wait for lunchtime to show it to René.

"Look." I laid the copies of the microfiche out in a row on the library table. "They gave him a promotion from staff sergeant to warrant officer. But I don't understand why these papers were marked 'Top Secret.'"

He looked startled. "You have something top secret?" He rose and hurried around his desk to look at the documents.

"Oh, no. Not now. They were declassified in 1938."

"Ah, OK." He relaxed as he stood next to me reading the papers. "You're sure it's your Brendan? That's not necessarily an unusual name."

"I'm sure. His date of birth is right."

"That's great. Now you can use his military serial number to find other things, eh? This really opens a door."

"What could he have been doing that a record of his promotion was secret?"

"It's a mystery, but we'll just have to solve it. World War I was going on in 1917, so it has to have had something to do with that."

"Well, I'll see what the afternoon provides," I said, as he set the papers down.

We'd been standing shoulder to shoulder looking at the documents. I started to turn. Before I could say no, he turned to me, put his hands on my shoulders, leaned down, and kissed me gently.

I was so shocked.

When I didn't pull away, he pulled me closer, put his arms around me, and kissed me again—this time harder. Then he released me and stepped back. "I'm so sorry. You were standing so close, and you're so beautiful. I couldn't stop myself. Please accept my apology."

I blushed. "Oh, René. You surprised me."

"You didn't think I'd be attracted to you?"

"When you told me you'd chosen not to marry, I thought you'd given up on all that."

"I've been thinking about kissing you since the first time I saw you." He took me into his arms and kissed me again.

I hadn't kissed anyone since Robby. I didn't really feel single, no matter what I told myself, but I was lonely. His mouth so warm on mine, his body pressed against me—I'd forgotten how good a kiss could feel. Better than good.

Something in me that had been quiescent for so long came to life. I relaxed into his arms with a little sigh of pleasure. When I did, he tightened his arms around me and deepened the kiss. I knew I should stop this, but I couldn't . . . I didn't . . . I wanted . . .

He let me go.

I took a deep breath. "Oh, René. I don't—"

"It's OK. I really won't do that again if you don't want me to."

"I don't know what I want."

"Your body knows."

He was right.

"Is this why you came over to me that first day?"

"Yes. I saw your mouth—so sensuous. Like a magnet."

"But I wear a ring."

"I didn't care. I figured that was his problem, whoever he was."

"When you found out I was a widow did you figure I'd be easy?"

I blushed again.

"No, Anne, not that. I'm a man. You're a beautiful woman. That's all."

I couldn't think of the right response.

Finally, he said, "We'd better go to lunch. Though, maybe you don't want to go with me now."

"I do want to go with you."

We gathered up my papers and walked out of the office together. My heart rate was off the charts. I couldn't look at his secretary. I was still blushing.

I spent the whole lunchtime trying to pretend to myself that I was sophisticated enough to handle something like this. No matter what I told myself, though, I couldn't control the thoughts swirling through my mind. I felt like everyone in the place must know what we'd been doing. Every time I caught someone's eye, I blushed. They didn't even know me, but I felt they were judging me. It didn't feel good.

At the same time, I wondered if that was all. Had he satisfied his curiosity? He'd been so quick to say he wouldn't do it again. Maybe I wasn't what he'd hoped. What should I say? What should I do? What if he wanted to kiss me again? What if he didn't? Oh, Lord!

René and I didn't talk much. He asked me to pass the catsup, and then he offered to share his French fries. I said something about the weather. Conversation drifted.

When we finished lunch, we walked back to the archives. We hadn't mentioned the kisses.

In the elevator lobby, he said, "I'd like to drive you home today."

"Don't you have to pick up you sister?"

"I generally pick her up at six. You go home at five, don't you?"

"Yes. But I don't want to inconvenience you."

He brushed my lips with his finger. "Anne, I want to kiss you again."

"Oh." And without thinking even a moment, I said, "I'd like that." My heart soared.

He leaned toward me.

Two women walked into the lobby to join us.

He sighed and moved away.

A soft bell announced the arrival of the elevator. We all got on.

When I stepped out on the third floor, he said, "I'll find you this afternoon. Wait for me."

As the elevator door closed, I thought, I should have told him no. I can't do this.

I couldn't settle down and focus on my research that afternoon. I kept trying to work out how I was going to tell him I'd changed my mind, but I couldn't focus on that either. I kept thinking about his lips on mine, how his tongue felt in that most intimate of kisses . . . and how much I wanted more.

I intended to call Carola as soon as I got in the door, but I couldn't figure out what I was going to tell her.

Finally, I sat on the sofa and dialed the phone.

"It's me."

I could hear the TV in the background. I'd forgotten about the time difference. She was watching *General Hospital*.

"Anne, are you OK."

Maybe I hadn't calmed down as much as I'd thought.

"René kissed me."

There was a pause. The sound of the TV disappeared.

"Kissed you. What do you mean?"

"Kissed me, that's what I mean."

"On the mouth?"

"Oh, yes."

"I thought you said he wasn't interested in women."

"I was wrong."

"Well, I guess so. What did you do?"

"I kissed him back."

"Way to go, Chiquita! How was it?"

"Carola!"

"Well, I've been married a long time. I've forgotten."

I chuckled. "Tell me another."

"Well?"

"Heaven. He can really kiss."

"Where were you?"

"In his office the first time. Then, in his car."

"In his car! Aah. What does it mean? Did he ask you out?"

"No. I don't really know what it means. Carola, I shouldn't have done it. How am I going to tell him it was a mistake?"

"You don't like him?"

"That's not it. I do like him. But I'm not ready."

"Tell him that. If you're not ready, you're not ready. That's all."

We talked for an hour. I couldn't think about anything else the rest of the evening.

After that, René drove me home every day, but I never told him I wasn't ready. He didn't come into my apartment, partly because he had to pick up his sister and partly because I didn't know what might happen if he did. But we stopped in a wooded area in a park. We pulled over on a seldom-traveled road. It felt a little like high school again—parking in an out-of-the-way place. I didn't ask if he'd been there with other women. He never volunteered any information.

We kissed, and the kisses became more passionate.

When I was in his arms, I didn't think about Robby.

When I got home, I felt so guilty.

Brendan's military serial number led me to his record of enlistment in March 1915. He was twenty-five. His induction physical made no mention of injuries from a plane crash. Those must have come later.

The enlistment papers included his home address and next of kin. He'd listed his parents as his next of kin, but he didn't list his parents' address in Pittsburgh or any address in Ottawa as his home. Instead, he'd written a single word—Ungavaq.

"Ungavaq? René, where's that?"

"It's not a suburb of Ottawa. It could be the name of a town or a village. Let's get an atlas. If it's not in a current atlas, we'll get one from the 1910s or '20s."

He walked to a shelf and brought back a huge book of maps. He flipped pages to check the index and then to find the relevant map.

"Here it is," he said, "on the western shore of Ungava Bay in northern Québec." He moved over so I could see where he was pointing.

"It looks tiny."

"It isn't near anything except this village farther north called Seal Haven. Ungava Bay is an extension of Hudson's Bay. That's Inuit territory."

"Inuit? What's that?"

"Think Eskimo."

"I feel like Alice in Wonderland. Each time I think something makes sense, instead it gets 'curiouser and curiouser.'"

"Yes, another mystery. Your next step should be to find his service record and discharge papers. They'll have a lot more information."

I plowed back into the files, but I found nothing more. The documents that should have been there just weren't.

On Monday of my fourth week in Ottawa, we sat in a red-plastic upholstered booth in our favorite coffee shop. I'd ordered chicken salad. He'd ordered a hamburger and French fries. The waitress set the plates down with a clatter, refilled our water glasses, and left us to enjoy our food.

"I'm considering another month in Ottawa, but I don't know which way to go with the research."

As he reached for the catsup, he said, "I don't think you have much choice. I think you have to go to Ungavaq, eh?"

"Go there? It's like the other side of the moon. How would I do that? There aren't even any roads on the map."

He drenched the fries with catsup and pushed the plate over so I could have my share. I'd never think of ordering French fries because of the fat and salt, but I wasn't above cadging them from him.

"It's doable," he said. "I'll bet there are bush pilots who go up there on a regular basis. They have to get their mail."

"Mail?"

"Yes, mail."

"I'd never have thought of an Eskimo village having mail delivery."

He laughed. "You're thinking of *Nanook of the North* or something. This is the twenty-first century. They're called Inuit now, and they write letters."

"Would I ride with the bush pilot?"

René thought a moment. "Probably. As soon as we get back to the archives, we'll call the post office and find out how the mail is handled for Ungavaq."

It turned out that mail to the north was a sometime thing. In the winter, everything depended on the weather. In the short summer, mail was delivered every Friday. Now, during the second week of June, regular delivery had started for the season. The mail arrived at the nearest city, Blackwell, on commercial flights and was transferred to a small plane owned by Northern Air. Then the bush pilot took over.

"You really think I should go there?"

"Sure. Why not? The only thing is, it wouldn't be cheap."

"That's not a problem. What would I look for there?"

"It's pretty small. There won't be a library or a history society, but there'll be a village teacher. He or she will probably know the history of the area. And there'll be old people. They're the ones you really want to talk to. If Brendan was there long enough to think of it as his home, there'll be stories."

"What could he have been doing?"

"He might've been a trader or a medical officer. He might have been in the Mounties and handled law enforcement there. That's certainly the kind of post a person without seniority would get stuck with. People would have gone up there for lots of different reasons. There's no guessing. You'll have to go ask."

"This Friday?"

"If you're going, why not?"

"Well, yes, why not?"

"There won't be a hotel. It's possible they do a round-trip in one day. Then you wouldn't have to worry about where to stay. If you do the round-trip on Friday, you might want to spend Saturday at the Blackwell Library to see what they have."

René emailed Northern Air. Someone named L.G. Chandler wrote back that the company regularly carried mail, supplies, and passengers to Ungavaq. The round-trip did take one day, the pilot generally stayed on the ground in Ungavaq about two hours before going on to Seal Haven, and there would be room for me on Friday.

"I guess I'll be back Sunday or Monday at the latest. That's the day my rent is due. I'd better pay for another month."

"Good. I'm selfish enough to be glad you're staying."

I thought about the implications of his compliment. Our relationship had developed from a friendship to a flirtation to something more, as yet undefined. He hadn't asked for anything else yet, but I was sure he would. I did find him very attractive, but every time I thought about going to bed with him, I thought about Robby. It didn't feel right. If nothing else, this trip would set that decision aside for a few days.

CHAPTER Three

ON THURSDAY AFTERNOON, I WALKED THROUGH THE OTTAWA Airport carrying my boarding pass to Blackwell. René had dropped me off. I had his passionate kiss on my lips and in my mind.

I'd told Carola about my trip. She'd been pleased, but I still had my doubts. I don't usually do things on the spur of the moment, but the trip to Ottawa had been last minute, and this trip was too.

I thought I'd have time in the waiting area at the gate to sit and think, but a man sat next to me and interrupted my concentration. He carried a briefcase, so I thought, *businessman*. His rumpled suit and tie pulled askew suggested that business hadn't been good. I didn't pay much attention to him, but I couldn't miss the odor of beer wafting in my direction. I figured he'd had a beer with his lunch, but it didn't take me long to realize that he'd probably had beer instead of his lunch.

He leaned toward me. "Hiya, Honey. You travelin' to Blackwell?"

We were in the crowded waiting area for the Blackwell plane. "Yes."

"Well, things are lookin' up. I didn't think there was gonna to be any good lookin' women on this flight, eh?"

I didn't answer.

"Your husband travelin' with you?"

He'd noticed my ring, at least. "No."

"Oh, waitin' for you in Blackwell?"

"No." And as soon as that word came out of my mouth, I kicked myself for being a fool. It would have been so easy to say yes.

He leaned even closer and leered. "A woman like you shouldn't be by herself. I'll keep you company, eh."

Frost in my voice. "That's not necessary."

"No problem. We'll have a good time. How 'bout I buy you a beer while we're waitin'?"

"Thank you, no." I'd begun to think about a retreat to the ladies' room. As I looked around, another man walked up. He was about my age and quite good looking, with dark hair and a neatly trimmed dark beard. He wore a white shirt, open at the neck, and black slacks.

"Well, Sarah," he said. "What a surprise. I would never have imagined bumping into you here. Are you flying home?" He winked.

I hoped I wasn't going from the frying pan into the fire. "Mr. Smith, this is a surprise. Yes, I'm flying home." I turned to the drunk. "I think you'll have to excuse me, now. We'll have to have that beer some other time. I haven't had a chance to talk to my parole officer in a while. In fact, I've missed our last two meetings, so I suppose I'm in a bit of trouble."

"Mr. Smith" said sternly, "Yes, I think you'd better come along with me now, Sarah. If you cooperate, I won't have to put the cuffs on you this time." I rose, picked up my purse and bag, and left the drunk with his mouth agape.

When we got a few feet away, the man said, "You are wicked. I hope I don't really look like your parole officer."

"Oh, no. He's much better looking."

He tried to stifle his laughter until we were farther away.

"Thank you for rescuing me."

"I watched what was happening. I hoped he wasn't your husband. I'd have looked like a proper fool in that case. But your body language made me guess he wasn't."

"No, I've never seen him before. What's your name? I don't suppose it's Mr. Smith."

"I'm Guy Lavelle."

"I'm Anne O'Malley."

"Well, Mrs. O'Malley, let's sit over here until they call the flight. After that, I think you'll be OK. He'll have an assigned seat. They may not even let him on board, he's that drunk, eh?"

In fact, the gate personnel didn't allow my beer-drinking friend on board. I sat in a window seat in an empty row. Guy changed his seat to sit next to me. After the plane took off, I had a difficult choice to make. I could hardly stop looking at the scenery, but I had this very nice man sitting next to me. Carola would have been pleased. Canada seemed to be full of good-looking men who wanted to help me with things.

"Why are you going to Blackwell?" he asked. "Do you have family there?"

"Actually, I'm going through Blackwell to Ungavaq."

"Well, you *are* going to the back of beyond."

"Have you ever been there?" I asked.

"No. I don't think there's much up there. It's just a little village. Why are you going?"

"Well, it may be a wild goose chase. I'm working on the history of my late husband's family. His father may have been in Ungavaq at some point. I want to talk to the old people and see if anyone remembers stories about him."

"There aren't many more than a hundred people there, I don't think. That shouldn't take you long."

For most of the trip, we flew over forest. As we neared Blackwell, though, the scenery changed. In the distance, I could see range after range of snow-covered mountains and glaciers. Below us, the trees were gone. Large patches of snow lay scattered on the ground.

"This view is spectacular."

"Yes. Dramatic," he said. "There aren't any more trees between here and the North Pole."

Tundra stretched below and ahead of us. From our altitude, it looked almost like bare ground, but Guy told me the marshy soil was solid with low-growing plants. Here and there, lakes dotted the land

and reflected the sunlight like mirrors. Ribbons of meandering water connected them.

When we landed, bright sunshine greeted us. The pilot announced clear skies and a temperature of fifteen degrees. I still had trouble converting Celsius to Fahrenheit, but I finally worked out that it was fifty-nine, not too cold, but definitely not warm. We taxied toward the terminal past shrubs and grasses bent in the wind.

Guy's wife, Elise, was there to meet him. He introduced us and told her how we met. Before they left, I asked for directions to Northern Air. He pointed out a small counter at the far end of the concourse.

"It's been a pleasure, Anne," he said. "You tell Sarah to keep out of trouble."

"I will. Thanks again."

I turned and walked toward the Northern Air counter.

"I'm looking for L.G. Chandler."

"You must be Mrs. O'Malley. I'm L.G. Chandler, but please, call me Laura." The petite, neatly dressed woman who greeted me didn't fit my notions of what the employee of a bush airline would look like. I'd guess she was in her early forties. She had large brown eyes and short curly brown hair. I asked her later, and she said the curl was natural. She wore a sort of dress-for-success blue pantsuit and a white blouse. She had no makeup on, but she did wear rings on just about every finger and big gold hoop earrings.

Laura directed me to my hotel—arranged by René—and asked me to be back no later than seven o'clock the next morning.

I didn't have a good night. Northern Air's web site had shown that the plane to Ungavaq was a four-seater. I've never flown in a small plane. When I tried to imagine the trip, I just thought about throwing up inside the plane as it swooped up and down through the sky.

I went from breakfast to an all-night drugstore Laura had recommended. She'd advised me to get sunscreen and bug repellent. I decided to get some motion sickness pills too.

The temperature was in the low forties, the air crisp. I'd had to do some shopping at clearance sales in Ottawa to get warm clothes. I hadn't brought any from San Diego. I wore maroon wool slacks, a pink turtle neck shirt, a cardigan sweater, a warm jacket, and sturdy walking shoes. I felt warm enough, but not too warm.

I arrived at the Northern Air counter with my overnight bag in hand. I didn't plan on staying overnight, but René told me that, even at the best of times, the weather was uncertain, and I should be prepared for a change of plans.

Laura waited for me, more casually dressed this morning in jeans, a bulky yellow pullover sweater, and boots. The extravagant jewelry of the day before had disappeared. She put on a leather jacket and a wool cap and led me through a door to the tarmac. I didn't see a plane. She took me to a small panel truck and said, "Get in." We drove about five minutes to a river where a number of floatplanes were tied up like boats in a marina. We walked to a small but solid-looking red and white plane—one of two sitting there. She stepped out onto the pontoon and gestured to me to follow. I stepped next to her and she showed me where to put my hands on the short ladder built into the plane's structure. "Go ahead, climb up."

"Will the pilot be along soon?"

"That's me. I'm the pilot. Go ahead, get in, and we'll get going. I've just been waiting for you."

I wondered if this petite, pretty woman was competent to fly a plane into the Canadian wilderness. I hesitated for a moment, then started climbing. I wasn't backing out now.

I watched her as she moved all the way around the plane, balancing on the pontoons and inspecting. She untied the lines that held the plane to the dock, coiled them, and climbed into her seat, stowing the coils under the seat as she sat. She went over a checklist on a clipboard, then taxied the plane away from the dock.

I'd thought I wouldn't mind the takeoff, but the faster the plane went, the more nervous I got. My hands were clammy, and I broke out in a cold sweat. Riding in the front of the plane and looking out the window at the water speeding by is very different from looking at the seatback in front of you.

When the pontoons came off the water, I began to think I couldn't handle the wave of fear building in me.

Laura banked the plane to the right and crossed the river's edge.

I looked out the side window at the ground receding below me, and I was terrified. This certainly didn't feel like the big planes.

When we finally leveled out, though, I managed to get myself under control.

Laura had been concentrating on the takeoff, so I didn't think she'd seen how white my knuckles were. I didn't tell her. I certainly didn't want to tell a woman—and a younger one at that—I couldn't manage something she could. I just hoped the worst was over.

The rest of the flight turned out to be uneventful—no swooping and no throwing up. At times, Laura concentrated on the plane. At other times, we talked.

She started the conversation by saying, "I guess the takeoff made you a little tense."

Ah, she had seen.

"Lots of people feel that way if they haven't been in a small plane before," she said. "You'll get over it."

"You're right. I've never been in a small plane before."

"Well, this old plane and I'll take care of you."

"The plane's old, or are you kidding?"

"This is a Cessna 185 Skywagon built in 1981, one of the last off the line."

"Isn't that awfully old?"

"No, this plane's going to fly forever. It was my dad's. It's the one he started the business with. Now I take good care of it, and it takes good care of me."

"You do the maintenance?"

"Sure."

"How fast are we going?"

"A little over 240."

"Kilometers or miles per hour?"

"Kilometers. That's about 150 miles per hour. We're up to cruising speed. I'll keep it here for the rest of the trip."

"Don't you get bored doing the same trip week after week?"

"Never. It's always different. And I get to meet so many people, like you. Why are you going to Ungavaq?"

"I'm researching my father-in-law's life. It looks like he might have gone there around 1915." I told her about my project.

She'd never thought about tracing the genealogy of her family, so we talked a while about how she might get started.

"My parents came to Blackwell during a boom time and stayed on to start Northern Air. They saw Québec as a paradise for hunters and fishermen and knew there was money to be made transporting them. I grew up in the business. Don't tell anyone, but I flew this plane the first time when I was eleven. I've been flying solo since I was a teenager. I never thought of doing anything else. Now my father's retired. He turned the business over to me. He still comes in to help when things get extra busy."

Our conversation was strange at times. At one point, Laura said, "You certainly didn't bring much luggage, eh? I flew Jack back last week. He practically filled the plane with his stuff."

Jack who? I wondered. "No, only an overnight bag."

"You realize I come to Ungavaq only once a week."

"Yes," I said, not seeing the connection. "Every Friday."

"Yes."

"Do they have a little airport there?"

"No."

"Where do we land?"

"On the bay. That's what the pontoons are for."

I intended to ask Laura who Jack was, but the tower at Blackwell called with an updated weather report, and she switched her attention to the radio. What they said was technical, but I took it to mean clear skies all the way. I forgot to ask my question.

As she handled more radio traffic, I gazed out the window. We flew much lower than the commercial flight to Blackwell over tundra like an exotic grey and green oriental carpet. Streams and one large river cut across it. Laura told me that they ultimately flowed into the bay.

Finally, in the distance ahead, I saw it—Ungava Bay. It stretched ahead and to the right as far as I could see—the icy home of seals, walruses, polar bears, whales, and uncounted millions of sea birds and fish.

We followed the shoreline north, and passed over what I was surprised to see was a big herd of caribou traveling the same direction we were. Less than a half-hour later, I saw a cluster of fifty or more low buildings adjacent to a protected inlet—Ungavaq!

As we approached, I could see one- and two-story wooden buildings—some raw and unfinished-looking, others painted in earth tones, and some even red or blue.

Barrels of fuel oil sat next to each building. Almost all the houses also had racks where, Laura told me, fish hung drying. Small boats bobbed at their moorings at a short dock. A path led from the dock to the nearest house and then through the village. I didn't see any cars or anything that looked like a road.

We flew over people, including a group of children playing. Many waved. Laura waggled the wings in response.

Dogs tied near the houses looked up. I could tell they were howling.

We headed out over the inlet.

"Here we go," Laura said. "Don't get nervous. Landing's a little tricky here because it's always windy, but I've been doing it for so many years I could do it with my eyes closed." She headed the plane toward the water in what seemed like a nose-dive.

I sure hoped her eyes were open. I'd been blasé about the idea of a water landing when Laura first mentioned it, but not anymore. At the last minute, she executed a steep banking turn, and landed with a solid thump not too far from the dock.

I managed to get my fingers unclenched before she looked at me.

"You must really be glad to get here, eh?"

I assumed she thought I was glad to get on the ground, or water, to be exact. "Oh, yes." I said, with more enthusiasm than I meant to show.

As she taxied toward an open space at the end of the rows of boats, she pointed out two kayaks and an umiak, the traditional women's boat. They bobbed next to outboard motor boats of various sizes and vintages.

She turned off the engine and undid her seatbelt. "I'll be here for a while. We'll offload the plane, have some tea and chitchat, and then I'll head to Seal Haven. Are you going back next week or do you plan to stay longer."

"Oh, no. I thought you'd pick me up on your way back from Seal Haven today."

"You mean you don't want to visit a while? They'll expect you to stay a week at least."

"Who?"

"Why, all your relatives."

"What relatives?"

"All your relatives here in Ungavaq."

With that, she opened her door. "Hi. I brought you a visitor," she said to the man who'd walked down to the dock from the nearby house as we taxied in. Laura picked up the two coils of rope from under her seat. She put one heel on the ladder, grabbed the edge of the door, and swung herself down onto the left pontoon. She tied the end of one of the ropes to a bracket on the fuselage and tossed the other end to the man. He tied it to a cleat on the dock. They did the same at the back before he gave her a hand onto the wooden platform.

I sat in total confusion. Had I said something to Laura to make her think I had relatives here? I couldn't remember anything. Well, maybe René had in his email, or maybe she'd misinterpreted our talk about genealogy.

I undid my seatbelt and clambered out over her seat. The plane rocked gently in the swell, so I didn't try to copy her acrobatics. I turned to face the ladder and climbed carefully down. When I'd just set my feet on the pontoon I felt a pair of strong hands lift me and set me down gently on the dock. I turned and found myself face to face with the man who'd greeted Laura.

He was a broad-shouldered Inuit dressed in a green plaid wool jacket, Levi's, and heavy boots. He stood only three inches or so taller than my five-feet-five, but his big work-hardened hands dwarfed mine. His thick black hair, touched with gray at the temples, was combed straight back almost to his collar. The lines on his clean-shaven face showed he spent a lot of time outdoors. I wouldn't call him handsome, but his strong, pleasant face had a ready smile. That smile kept me from noticing immediately that he had tattoos, two parallel lines that went the full width of his face across his nose.

I started to thank him, but stopped, perplexed. He looked familiar, but I couldn't think where I might've seen him before.

Now, Laura looked confused. Then, she laughed. "Oh, it didn't occur to me the two of you might not have met before. Anne, this is Jack."

We both said, "Hi."

There was another awkward pause.

Laura tried again. "Anne O'Malley, this is Jack O'Malley. I guess he's your cousin or something, eh?"

A look of surprise came over Jack's face. I don't know what my face looked like, but suddenly I realized why he looked familiar. In that broad Inuit face, I looked into Robby's hazel eyes. I finally registered what Laura had said and realized there could be no doubt—he was some kind of relative.

CHAPTER Four

*S*UDDENLY, I FELT ODD. I STARED AT JACK'S INUIT FACE AND those incongruous eyes, and for a moment, I couldn't tell if I'd imagined them.

He'd been looking at my face as I had looked at his, and he seemed to recognize something in my face too.

He put his hand out and touched my arm gently. "You look a little wobbly."

"I feel light-headed all of a sudden. Maybe, the flight . . ." But I knew that wasn't it.

He put his right hand under my elbow. "You hold on to me if you think you might fall. You just need to relax a minute and breathe some fresh air."

The cool breeze on my face did feel good, but I still reached out and put my other hand on his arm to steady myself. My hand trembled.

After some time, he said, "There, you look better. Your color's coming back. You'll be OK."

I smiled and took my hand off his arm. "Thank you."

He smiled back and released my elbow.

"We'd better start over. Welcome to Ungavaq. So you're a cousin."

"I don't know."

"I thought almost all my relatives lived here, but you're certainly welcome. Come up to the house. We'll figure things out."

Laura climbed back into the plane. She handed boxes to Jack. He stacked them on the dock. When she climbed out again, she brought the mailbag with her. He took it and led the way along the length of the dock and up the gravel path to the small wooden house nearby.

As we walked, Laura said, "Good news. We saw caribou. They're about eighty miles south and coming this way."

"That is good news," Jack said.

I don't know what I expected, but the living room was just like a living room you'd see any place—sofa, chairs, coffee table, end tables, a big multicolored rag rug like the ones my cousin in Arizona used to make. The thing that really stood out, though, was a whatnot shelf next to the door we'd just come in. It held beautiful ivory carvings—a polar bear, a walrus, a man in a kayak, and others, some large, some tiny.

The room smelled of fresh-baked bread. Through an open door, I could see loaves cooling on a rack in the kitchen, and I could hear the tick-tock of a clock someplace.

An elderly Inuit put her sewing project down on the coffee table and rose from the sofa to welcome us as we entered. She was shorter than I, slender, and wizened, her straight gray hair cut to just below her ears. Her face was similar to Jack's in shape and proportion, and she had his same smile. She moved easily as she crossed the room.

She also had tattoos, but they were much more elaborate than Jack's. Five lines started on her lower lip and diverged as they ran to her chin. A large double "V" ran up from the bridge of her nose to flare in curves back to her hair. Pairs of horizontal lines decorated her cheeks, and lines went from the outer corners of her eyes horizontally to her hairline. Tattoos covered the backs of her hands too.

"It's a beautiful day, Maata," Laura said.

"Yes, beautiful," the woman responded.

"*Anaana*," Jack said, "this is Anne O'Malley. Laura thinks she's a relative. Anne, this is my mother, Maata O'Malley."

Mrs. O'Malley looked as surprised as Jack had, but she smiled and extended her hand. I reached out to her. We shook hands gently.

"Mrs. O'Malley, I came hoping someone in the village knew stories of what happened in the early years of the last century. I never imagined finding people with my same name."

"Yes, what a surprise your name is also O'Malley," she said softly.

Our conversation was interrupted. The front door opened, and people came in. They greeted Laura, and Jack introduced them to me. Each one smiled and gently shook my hand. Even the men's handshakes were gentle—no bone crushers here.

I couldn't remember all the names, but I did remember Jack's sisters: Miqo, Allaq, and Saarak. The older women, including Jack's sisters, had tattoos like Maata's, but the younger ones didn't. The people settled into chairs or squatted or sat on the floor. The children, Mrs. O'Malley's great-grandchildren, played quietly.

I told them about Robby, our work on family genealogy, and my decision to continue the work after Robby's death.

When I mentioned Brendan, Jack's face lit up, as did Mrs. O'Malley's. "Brendan O'Malley was my husband's father," she said.

"How could that be? Robby didn't have any brothers," I said.

"I don't know, but it's true."

This set off a murmur of conversation. We became involved figuring out my relationship to each person there, down to the smallest baby. I had become family.

This flood of family pleased and scared me at the same time. I saw Laura beaming with delight. Only Jack seemed to be aware of my confusion. He smiled, but he had a concerned look in those familiar eyes.

"Anaana, tea pleases people when they gather together," he said.

"Tea is always pleasant," Mrs. O'Malley responded. She and Allaq rose and went into the kitchen.

He rose too. "Anne, come with me."

He helped me with my coat, guided me out the door, across the porch, and down the two steps that led to the gravel path. Some of the younger children followed us for a way, but soon became distracted with a game.

Jack shortened his steps to match mine. Our feet crunched in unison on the gravel.

The damp wind chilled my hands. I put them in my pockets.

"I thought a short break might be helpful," he said.

"Thank you. This has been quite a surprise. It isn't what I expected. I thought I'd have a couple of hours of conversation with some old people who might be able to give me some clues to the past. Now, suddenly, I have all these relatives. I have you. I don't know what to think or do."

"All you have to do right now is drink some tea. You'll have plenty of time to talk to people." His calm voice made it seem so simple.

"I'll be leaving with Laura when she goes back to Blackwell."

"That's not necessary. Mother will have assumed you're staying. No Inuit would think a two-hour visit was adequate."

"I don't want to impose."

"Life in a village has a sameness from day to day. Visitors are a welcome change." He gave me that smile that seemed always to be so near the surface.

I stopped. "Do you mean that?"

He turned to face me. "Sure."

"I only brought an overnight bag, in case the weather turned bad."

"A storm might have lasted several days."

"In June?"

"Yes."

It seemed he really did want me to stay. There was no reason I couldn't. It would give me more time to research.

"Well," he said, "That's settled. We can borrow clothes from my sisters. They can find something to fit you. If not, they'll be glad to do some temporary tailoring."

"Your sisters are seamstresses?"

"Among the best." His quiet pride was obvious.

"I never learned to sew."

"Where you come from, it wasn't a skill essential for survival. You may not know much about Inuit culture."

"I know nothing about it."

"This climate is unforgiving. In the old days, a man couldn't survive if he didn't have someone to sew for him."

"You say someone. You mean his wife?"

"A man married as soon as he was a competent hunter if a woman was available. Otherwise, he stayed with his parents, and his mother sewed for him."

"So women were valued."

"They were especially prized and gave their husbands high status if they were good seamstresses. A woman married as soon as she was mature enough to bear children. Bearing children was her most important responsibility, but she and her children couldn't survive without someone to hunt for them. Her husband couldn't hunt if he didn't have proper clothing. They had a partnership of necessity."

"Did they love each other?"

"Love often developed."

I thought about that—so different from what I was familiar with. "So your sisters are valued by their husbands."

"Yes, and loved. Sewing skill is still highly valued today. They're geniuses with sewing needles."

We started to walk again.

"You might be right that I could wear your sisters' clothes. I'm similar to them in size and build. But don't you think they'll mind you volunteering them that way?"

He shook his head. "No, of course not."

"Well, OK."

"Good."

"Your father wasn't there today."

"No, he died three years ago—in a hunting accident."

"Oh, I'm sorry. . . . Did he remember Brendan?"

"No. My grandfather left before my father was born. But there are stories about Brendan. You'll have time to hear them."

We'd walked to the edge of the village. Our approach startled dozens of small brown animals that ran in all directions.

"Look, rabbits!" I said.

"No, not rabbits. *Ukaliq*—Arctic hare. We don't have rabbits here."

"Ah."

We stopped to gaze at the astonishing sweep of land and water in front of us. Plants in every shade of gray and green covered the ground. Tiny flowers bloomed everywhere. Boulders covered with patches of red, orange, and green lichens dotted the low growth. A beach of water-smoothed rocks led down to the bay's edge, where wavelets broke at regular intervals. The chilly wind was stronger now. I could smell the salt tang of the water. The hares reappeared in an area farther away from us to continue eating the low-growing plants.

"Why don't trees grow here?" I asked.

"We're too far north. We're standing on permafrost."

"I've heard that word, but I don't really know what it is."

"The ground is permanently frozen."

I touched the toe of my shoe to the ground off the path. It felt spongy. I'd thought I'd felt the ground give as we'd walked along the path. I looked at him quizzically.

"The surface is called muskeg. It thaws in the summer. The frozen ground starts a few centimeters below the surface, and it can go as much as 300 meters down. We don't get much precipitation here. Technically, we're a cold desert. If the permafrost didn't prevent the rain and snowmelt from draining away, there wouldn't be much water available at all. As it is, it's pretty boggy. The plants get water. The tradeoff is they don't get any room for their roots. The roots don't penetrate the permafrost. These plants have been dwarfed—like bonsai."

As we stood there, I realized that something was missing—the constant low-grade ambient noise of a city. I could hear Jack's breathing and mine. I could hear little slapping noises from the wavelets. In the distance, I could hear yips from a dog and some birds calling, but nothing else.

I turned to the left. Looking west, I could see the outlet of a river emptying into the bay. The angle of the sun made the water look like liquid silver. On the bay, in the far distance, I could barely make out the silhouette of an island.

"This is strikingly beautiful," I said.

"Most visitors think it's pretty bleak."

"I love this openness. I lived for two years in a town in a forest. It was oppressive. The trees seemed to close in on me all the time."

He looked at me appraisingly. "You should come back in the fall. All these plants turn to red and gold."

"I'd like to."

I turned, thinking we were going back.

Jack held up his hand to stop me. "I want to say something. On the dock, you saw something in my face that made you feel faint—maybe my tattoos. I frightened you. I didn't want to."

I felt my cheeks get hot. "No, you didn't frighten me." I looked down. "For a moment, I saw my husband in your eyes. They're like his. I'm still emotional about his death."

"Ah. I'm sorry."

"Thank you. You saw something in my face too. You're looking at me now the way you did then."

He didn't say anything.

"What do you see?"

"I don't know. . . . Something. . . ." And he smiled that smile again.

We walked back to the house, with the children falling in step with us as we approached.

There, the table held two large pots of tea and a plate of slices of homemade bread spread generously with berry jam. Maata O'Malley clearly had practice at providing food for groups of visitors.

Jack announced that I'd spend a week with his mother. "Two pieces of good news," Miqo said, "a visitor and caribou."

I heard a buzz of pleased comments.

We had tea and chatted about the latest political news that Laura had brought with the Blackwell newspapers. I wouldn't have guessed that there would be much political interest in such an isolated village, but everyone had an opinion. Allaq refilled the teapots, and we had seconds as we talked.

"Well, I'd better get going," Laura said. "Anne, you'll want your bag."

"I'll get it," Jack said.

The three of us walked to the dock. Jack rescued my overnight case from the back of the plane and loaded the new boxes and a mailbag sitting on the dock.

"Laura," I asked, "would you email René Benoit and tell him I'm staying a week? And could you also phone the hotel, and tell them I won't be using the room tonight?"

"OK."

We waved as she taxied away and took off. I thought, *how amazing. I'm spending a week with people I don't know in the middle of the Canadian tundra. I wonder what Carola will say about this.*

CHAPTER
Five

WE WALKED BACK TO MAATA'S.

She'd told me to call her that. If her husband was Robby's half-brother, she was my sister-in-law. She was quite a bit older than I was—probably in her eighties—but she didn't know her true age because exact dates hadn't been important to the Inuit of her generation.

Jack had been born sometime in the winter of 1945. He wasn't sure exactly when, but he'd had to fill out so many forms in his life, he said, that he'd arbitrarily chosen January 1 as his birth date. That meant we were close in age because I was born in 1944.

At the house, the family had settled in for a visit. I had a photo of Robby in my wallet, and I'd brought several photos of Brendan. They were passed from hand to hand.

When the photos came to her, Maata looked at the picture of Robby. "His eyes are like Jack's."

"I noticed that when I first saw Jack."

"My husband eyes were like that too."

She took a long time looking at the pictures of Brendan.

"Do you see a relationship?" I asked.

"Yes, he looks like Piuvkaq." She handed the photos to me.

"Do you have any photos of Piuvkaq?"

"No, we never had a photograph of him."

"Would you like to keep those photos of Brendan?"

"Oh, yes."

I put them back in her hand. She didn't say anything, but she didn't have to. Two widows—we understood each other.

I began to pay attention to the conversations going on around us. I heard about the daily concerns of family life in Ungavaq. The men talked about the upcoming hunting season—and I found out many of them worked as guides. The women talked about their children and grandchildren.

I understood most of it. They spoke mostly English, sometimes in their language, Inuktitut, and sometimes they mixed words from both languages in the same sentence. Jack or Maata explained the conversations when I had trouble following.

Finally, people started drifting away to do chores and care for the children. More than half the people had gone when Maata decided to serve some lunch. She heated a delicious stew made of caribou.

After lunch, I helped her with the dishes.

She rolled up her sleeves to wash. I saw that her tattoos went beyond her elbows. I asked if they symbolized something.

"No," she said, "They're just patterns that I like. When I became a woman, my mother and my sister made these tattoos. When my younger sister became a woman, I helped make tattoos for her."

"Why?"

"For beauty. For my husband, because I would be married soon."

"Piuvkaq liked them?"

"Oh, yes. Very much."

"How did your mother make them?"

"With a needle and some sooty thread," she said matter-of-factly. "She stitched under the skin. The sinew thread carried the color in. We don't do it anymore. The younger women don't want it. They don't think it's beautiful."

I cringed to even think about it. "I'd be afraid."

"Of course we were afraid too, but it's something you do for someone you will love. To give him pleasure." She had a dreamy smile on her face. I wondered if she was thinking of the pleasure it had given Piuvkaq.

"Did it hurt?"

"A lot. It took months to finish, because we couldn't do much at one time."

"I don't think I'd ever have the courage to do something like that," I said.

Jack talked to his sisters. They didn't mind that he'd said they'd help me. I spent the rest of the afternoon going through clothes with them in their homes. We had a lot of fun. They pulled out things they thought I could use, and they were soon busy sewing to make the necessary adjustments.

My sewing ability stretched to buttons and hems, so I got some good-natured teasing, but they showed me how to do some simple things, and I handled my share of getting me presentable.

Jack took me back to Maata's for supper. After Maata and I cleared the table and washed the dishes, the three of us sat and talked.

I took that time to look at Jack's face in a way that I hadn't before. He'd thought he'd frightened me. I wondered if people were sometimes afraid of him. He was muscular and looked powerful in spite of being nearly sixty. At the same time, he was so gentle, calm, and soft-spoken.

His face was different from the white, black, and Mexican faces I was used to. Scientists think the Eskimoan people originated in Asia, but he didn't look Asian to me either. For a moment, I began to think there *was* something wild in his face, but when I focused on his eyes again, they were so familiar and his smile was beautiful.

Although bright daylight still streamed in through the windows, my watch showed 9:15. I tried to hide a yawn behind my hand, but Maata saw. "Ah, you've had a full day. You should go to bed."

"I shouldn't go so early."

"We don't live by the clock much during the sunlit months. You just sleep when you feel sleepy." She rose and beckoned to me.

That was all the encouragement I needed. I said goodnight to Jack and followed her.

The small window in the bedroom had a roller shade on it. I wondered if the light coming in around the edges would keep me awake, but I soon fell asleep soothed by the gentle murmur of Jack's and Maata's voices from the other room.

When I woke the next morning, I could hear sounds from the kitchen. I dressed and went out to find Maata pouring a cup of strong, hot tea for me. She'd been cutting up a large bloody slab of meat—a haunch of something—with a semicircular knife that almost looked like a nut chopper. She told me the knife was an ulu. She continued to work as we talked.

"I heard you stirring," she said. "Jack will be along in a while."

I sat at the table. "Jack doesn't live here?"

"He just eats here. Men don't cook." She shrugged. "He lives at the other end of the village."

"He's not married?"

"Kaiyuina died nearly ten years ago."

"Oh, I'm sorry."

I heard the sound of boots. Jack came in the front door, hung up his jacket, and walked into the kitchen.

"Good morning," I said.

He smiled. "Good morning. I'm glad to see you're an early riser."

"Yes. Quarter to ten. I don't usually sleep that late. I'm sorry to make you wait so long for breakfast."

Jack chuckled. "I'm always glad for any opportunity to have a second breakfast, late or not."

"I feel a little less guilty."

He saw what Maata was doing. "I see Quipac's back."

"Yes. He had great success."

"Let me finish that for you, Anaana." He walked to the counter.

She stepped away.

Instead of using her ulu, he took a knife from a sheath on his belt, cut easily through the joint she'd been struggling with, and then sliced off a chunk of meat. He ate it as we talked.

I couldn't take my eyes off his mouth. He had beautiful strong white teeth. He bit into the meat and then used his knife to cut off the piece he held in his teeth. When he finished chewing that, he wiped off a little smear of blood that had dripped down his chin and cut another piece.

"You're wearing a Carleton University sweatshirt," he said.

I looked down at the shirt. "Yes, it's Saarak's."

"I thought so. My son, Michael, gave it to her."

"Does he go to Carleton?"

"He did. My daughter, Grace, did too."

"Is that the Carleton in Ottawa?"

"Yes. You want a little something to tide you over? It's caribou." He held the bloody chunk of meat toward me on the end of the knife.

"No, thanks. I just wait for what Maata has planned." I managed not to shudder, but he knew.

"Ah, sorry." He laughed and shook his head.

I had my fingers crossed that Maata wasn't preparing raw meat for breakfast. That was something I hadn't even thought about when I decided to stay. But breakfast turned out to be oatmeal, toast, and blueberries.

"Isn't it early for berries?" I asked.

"That's the advantage of permafrost," he said. "You just dig a hole, and you have a freezer."

"Jack, I finished mending your blue shirt," Maata said. "It's on the back of the chair in the living room."

"Thank you, Anaana. I'll get it later."

I helped Maata clear the table and wash the dishes. After we finished, Jack and I had another cup of tea, while Maata left the kitchen to do something.

"This may sound strange," he said, "but we can treat you as family or a guest. Either is OK with us."

"If I'm going to be family, should I have eaten the meat?"

"Not if you didn't want it." He chuckled at the memory.

"Then I'd rather be treated like family."

"In that case, I'd like to tell you about Inuit etiquette."

"Have I done something wrong?"

"There is one thing. Inuit don't ask questions."

I shook my head. "I don't understand."

"If you pay attention, you'll notice nobody here asks questions."

"What do you do? Well, that's a question, isn't it? Oh, I'm going to be so self-conscious." I could feel the blush starting.

Jack was amused by my confusion. "It's hard. I know. Curiosity is frowned on, so we don't inquire about other people's business. We phrase things as statements rather than questions and even phrase those statements in the third person to distance ourselves even more from any implied curiosity. I'll tell you what, though. I'll make an exception of myself. When you and I are together, you can ask me any questions you want. That'll be OK. When we're around others, try to avoid questions if you can."

"I'll try."

"I watched you yesterday shaking hands. You did just the right thing."

"Laura coached me."

"Good. Americans don't like weak handshakes, but we're different about that. And Inuit don't go in for public displays of affection. People from the south hug and kiss a lot, but we don't do that here, so don't get your feelings hurt if no one offers you a hug or a kiss when it would be appropriate where you come from."

"I feel so ignorant."

"Ignorance can be overcome."

"About kissing," and I was thinking about his mouth.

He looked at me quizzically for a moment. "Ah." He laughed. "Yes, we do know about kissing. It's not just nose rubbing anymore."

"I feel like such an idiot."

"Don't feel that way. You used the right word the first time—ignorant. You can't know something until you learn it. Now, there's something more important than kissing and probably more difficult for you, but it's something you need to learn if you want to fit in. Inuit strongly disapprove of open expressions of emotion, especially anger. You've probably already noticed people speak quietly."

"A person doesn't know why people speak that way."

He smiled and nodded. "Good. That's a good start. We're private about our emotions because, in the past, we lived so closely together in snow houses and tents and under such trying conditions that openly expressed emotion could be dangerous. To defuse things, we often express anger or criticism with ridicule. Now, if I think you need some help, I'll hold my hand like this." He held his hand close to his body with the fingers outstretched and the palm down. "If I do that, try to be aware of your emotional state. Try to back off, no matter what's going on."

"If I get this wrong, what'll happen?"

"People won't criticize you, but they may avoid you. Emotional volatility is actually frightening for them. They won't want to be around you. This is tough. I won't tease you about it. It's difficult, but not impossible.

"When I gave you your choice of being family or guest, I wasn't joking. We have a lot of *kablunas*—white tourists—hunters and fishermen—who come here. We're used to the kabluna way of being, but we don't behave that way, and we don't share ourselves with people who do. No one will be insulted if you ask questions or get openly emotional, but it does make people uncomfortable, and it will emphasize the fact that you're an outsider."

"Thanks for telling me. I'll do my best."

"OK. Good enough." Jack finished his tea and stood. "I'll be back in a minute."

I washed and dried the mugs and put them away. After I hung up the dishtowel, I went into the living room to see where Jack and Maata were.

Maata was nowhere to be seen, but Jack stood with his back to me, singing softly. He was taking his shirt off.

I was so embarrassed. I was going to say something, but whatever it was went right out of my mind when I saw his bare back, shoulders, and arms. They were . . . there's no other word for them but "gorgeous." His skin looked velvety smooth and was light golden tan in color. His shoulders—oh wow! And he didn't look like he had an ounce of fat on him anywhere, just muscle. I don't think I'd ever seen a man who looked like that. No wonder he'd lifted me off the plane so easily.

He picked up the shirt, inspected the mend on the sleeve, and put it on.

I was beginning to feel very warm as I imagined what it might be like to put my hands on his skin, and that made me even more embarrassed.

With a start, I realized how rude I was to stare at him. I gave a little cough.

He turned just as he did the top button so I didn't get to see his chest—just as well, considering the way I'd been staring.

I blushed.

He didn't seem to notice. "Ah, there you are. This is my favorite shirt."

"Yes," I said. "Very nice." I didn't mean the shirt.

We took another walk. This time he pointed out who lived in each house and how they were related to one another. Most of the villagers were related to me through my marriage to Robby.

I tried to pay attention, but my mind kept going back to that moment when I'd walked into the living room. I imagined how it would have felt to run my hand down those beautiful muscles. I had to give myself little mental shakes each time I drifted off.

We passed the school—empty now. The teacher had gone to Montreal until September. Next came a good-sized meeting room, or dance house, as Jack called it, and the village store. Jack had the mail that hadn't been picked up at Maata's. He left it there for the storekeeper to distribute.

When we left there, he said, "You said you didn't know about the Inuit. I could tell you some of our history if you'd like."

"I really would. It might help me understand why Brendan came and why he stayed."

"Let's go for a walk along the shore."

Jack was systematic in what he told me. He knew the history of his people and was proud of them. I almost felt like I was taking "Inuit 101."

I had questions, but I remembered what he'd said. I thought carefully about how to phrase things.

"Someone understands asking isn't polite, but learning new things brings many questions to an ignorant woman's mind."

I caught Jack off guard. He looked at me for a moment and broke out in delighted laughter.

"Even an ignorant woman may learn in many different ways. Perhaps someone would like to practice."

"All right. The name 'Eskimo' has been replaced by 'Inuit,' but a woman doesn't know why."

"That's easy. 'Inuit' means 'the people' in Inuktitut. It's our own name for ourselves; 'Eskimo' was a name imposed on us by others. For other people, though, like the people of Alaska who don't speak our language, the name Eskimo is still correct."

The rest of "Inuit 101" was conducted in a similar manner. Sometimes I got into such convoluted sentences I couldn't find the end of them, and we'd break down in laughter. I'd never had more fun learning something.

"You are talented as a teacher," I said.

He started to say something, paused, and obviously changed his mind. "Thank you. I get a lot of practice. Every fall I help the village teacher instruct the children about their heritage."

During the rest of the week, I had a chance to get acquainted with everyone who wasn't away hunting or fishing, and they had the fun of being entertained by the new arrival. I was practically awash with tea. Coffee wasn't much in evidence.

Jack squired me through these visits. He anticipated areas where I might have problems and prompted me on how to behave.

Before we made our first visit, he said, "Now, there's another thing."

"Tell me."

"Inuit don't interrupt one another. When someone speaks, everyone else waits until they're positive the speaker is done. You may have noticed that."

"Yes."

"It can make the pace of a conversation slow. Sometimes there are long silences until everyone is sure, but that's just the way we do it."

"OK."

The next afternoon, as we walked back to Maata's after tea with Miqo and her husband, Quipac, Jack said, "You're doing well, but there's something you may have trouble with."

"Oh? I don't want to get in trouble."

"Well, you won't be in trouble, but women are supposed to be subordinate to men."

He'd been teasing me that day. I thought I'd give a little back. "Oh. I'm always interested in new experiences. I'll give it a try. Let me know when you want me to start."

Jack chuckled all the way home.

After we got there, though, I had second thoughts. I wondered if he was telling me I was too pushy. I wasn't sure whether he had just teased me or had ridiculed me. I decided I'd better find out. "Sometimes it might be difficult to recognize the difference between teasing and ridicule. It might be that someone hinted in what he said about women being subordinate."

"No, it's not as difficult as you might think. If you're ever in a position to be ridiculed, I don't think you'll be confused. I was teasing. You're doing great. It takes time to learn our ways, though. I know it's not easy to come into a new culture and get everything right. If I see anything I can help you with, I'll tell you. I won't hint."

I hadn't forgotten my reason for visiting the village. Of course, no one had known Brendan, but several people, including Maata, had parents who had known him. They were glad to share what they knew with me.

The Inuit had been nomadic. Certain families usually settled near Ungavaq to trap foxes and hunt seals. These people still lived in the old way, although change had started. They brought trade goods back to the village such as tea, molasses, tobacco, cloth, and guns.

Utak, his wife Kunuk, and their daughter, Ivala, traveled by dog sled to the nearest trading post—where Blackwell is now—to do their annual trading. They had a sled loaded high with fox furs. I didn't understand why they'd take such a long trip in the winter, but Jack explained that winter was the only time they could travel long distances away from the coast. The snow provided the road for the sleds.

At the post, the Inuit met Brendan. He explained through the trader that he'd like to visit the village. They said they'd be glad to have him.

Utak and Kunuk took Brendan into their household. Brendan had a gift for languages, and he learned Inuktitut fairly rapidly. In a short time, he communicated well enough with his hosts that they could teach him how to fish and hunt, how to build a snow house, how to drive a dog sled, and how to accomplish many of the other tasks necessary for survival in the Arctic.

They thought of Brendan as childlike when he first came to the village—he didn't know how to do the most basic things necessary for survival. But I heard stories about when he killed his first seal, the mark of becoming a man, and he soon started to contribute to the economic life of the village.

He intended to stay until his adoptive family took another trip to the trading post the following winter, but he had a bad fall while hunting and broke his leg. One of the women in the village was a bonesetter. She repositioned his leg and splinted it to the best of her abilities, but a trip by dog sled was out of the question. When her parents left for the trading post, Ivala stayed behind to take care of him. Utak carried a letter to give to the trader to mail to Brendan's parents, and Brendan stayed another year.

The second winter after Brendan arrived, he did go with some of the men on a trading trip. He took a stock of furs he'd trapped to trade for supplies. He intended to return to Ungavaq and Ivala with the supplies to live at least another year.

Brendan had not been in contact with the outside world in more than two years. Things had changed. World War I had started the year before, in 1914. Canada, as part of the British Empire, was involved. Brendan was distressed with what he read in the old newspapers. He talked with his Inuit friends. They agreed with his decision to return to Ottawa to find out if the war continued and to join the Canadian Army if it did.

Brendan traded his furs and used the proceeds to send supplies back to his adoptive family. He told his friends he planned to return to the village next winter. They made it clear they hoped he would. With that, they said good-bye. They never saw Brendan again.

They didn't have a concept of the kind of war being waged in Europe, but they did understand that fighting usually led to death. They were saddened, but not surprised, when Brendan didn't return the following winter.

What no one knew at the time Brendan left was that Ivala, the woman he'd been living with—the one who did his sewing for him—was pregnant with his child. She gave birth to his son, Piuvkaq, the following summer—the son who would become Maata's husband and Jack's father.

I really enjoyed my week in the village. When I wasn't visiting, I sewed with Maata and her daughters or walked with Jack. Jack was a tease and fun to be with. I'd asked him if he didn't have other things he had to do, but he said he could afford to take time off. I was glad.

The week sped by. Friday—and the plane—arrived all too soon.

As Laura taxied toward the dock, Jack and I walked down to meet her and help her offload. Jack reached out and took my hand as I stepped from the damp, slippery ground to the dock. He hadn't touched me since that time he'd lifted me off the plane. His hand was strong and gentle. It felt so good. I didn't want him to let go.

As on the previous Friday, we carried things into Maata's house, and people came to claim their mail and supplies. We shared tea again, only this time I helped Maata with the preparations. As we worked in the kitchen, Maata said, "I'd be happy if you could stay longer."

I was delighted. I'd become very fond of Maata, and I'd had more fun in the past week than I'd had in a long time. I began to understand how depressed and lonely I'd become after Robby's death.

I thought carefully about how to answer. Jack no longer had to remind me to avoid questions, but it still took me time to formulate sentences that weren't stiff and convoluted. "At home, people don't visit the way people do here. We have a saying that 'fish and visitors stink after three days.'"

Maata laughed.

"It's different for the Inuit," I said. "I've been here seven days. Still, you say you'd like me to stay longer."

"Yes, we like visitors."

"It's hard to know how long a visit should be."

"Oh, many people think a month more would be a nice visit."

A month seemed a long time, but I remembered Brendan. They'd expected him to stay a year. I had no demands on my time. My bank at home was taking care of my financial obligations, and my trip to Ottawa had been open-ended.

"A visit of a month would be pleasant," I said.

When we carried the tea and bread in, Maata announced, "Anne will stay a while longer." Everyone seemed happy about my decision.

CHAPTER Six

I REALIZED IF I WAS GOING TO STAY, THOUGH, I NEEDED TO go back to Ottawa to update René and Carola, negotiate with my landlady, and pick up some of my things.

"I have some business to take care of in Ottawa too," Jack said. "I'll travel with you, if you don't mind."

I couldn't imagine what kind of business a hunting guide could have in Ottawa, but I was more than glad he was going. Jack was an intriguing man. I wanted to get to know him better.

So it happened that Jack and I walked down to the dock with Laura again.

This time, when Jack loaded the cargo into the plane, he left a large box on the front passenger seat.

"There's room for that in the back," Laura said.

"I didn't want to have to wrestle it into the back and out again. If there's room after we load in Seal Haven, I'll move it."

Laura gave him a questioning look, but she didn't say anything.

I'd been so buoyed up by the excitement of being invited to stay, I hadn't given much thought to having to go up in that plane again.

If I'd been stubborn about letting Laura see my fear, I found I was twice as stubborn about letting Jack see it. Even as I scolded myself for being silly, I forced my hands to unclench and tried to keep my face calm. I could feel the dampness of my palms, though.

Seal Haven was larger than Ungavaq, but otherwise similar. Here, in the village where Jack's wife, Kaiyuina, had come from, almost everyone was related to me through Jack's marriage. For a second time, I had introductions to everyone who came to pick up things from Laura.

We had tea, said good-bye, and up went that damn plane again! This time, without saying a word or even looking at me, Jack reached across and took my hand. I was amazed at how reassuring that was. When we were in the air and leveled out, he let go, again without a word. He did the same thing when we landed on the river in Blackwell.

Laura dropped us off at the airport.

As we walked out on to the concourse, Jack said, "We can catch an Air Canada flight if we hurry."

"OK," I said. "Let's go."

He picked up our pace. Even though I walk a lot for exercise, it was a challenge to keep up with him.

It surprised me that he knew the airline schedule, but I remembered Laura had brought him back to Ungavaq two weeks ago, so he'd made a trip recently. She'd said he filled the plane with his stuff. I wish I'd asked her what kind of stuff. I began to feel I'd misjudged Jack in some way.

As we settled into our seats, I wondered again what his business in Ottawa was, but it seemed too nosy to ask. It might be some kind of village business, since Ottawa was the capital, or maybe he needed a guide's license or something. I thought he'd tell me if he wanted me to know. We filled the time with small talk.

I'd seen Jack in the context of the village. I thought I knew who he was, but when we entered the terminal in Ottawa, it was as though someone had clicked a switch, and he started to show a whole different side.

First, he made an amazing change in his speech patterns. In the village, although he usually spoke English, he spoke it with the same soft, gentle, and almost halting pronunciation that seemed natural to Inuktitut. In Ottawa, as he spoke, the words became more forceful, hurried, even demanding. He sounded like a kabluna.

He took charge of our two small bags and of renting a car. The women at the rental desk knew him. They called him "Jack" and didn't ask him what kind of car he wanted.

I'd been in the restroom when he'd paid for his ticket in Blackwell, but when he pulled a credit card out of his pocket at the rental desk in Ottawa, I knew I needed to reevaluate my ideas about Jack the Inuit.

While he signed the paperwork, I called René. He hadn't left for the day. He offered to pick me up, but I said I had a ride. He was disappointed, but he said he'd be in his office the next day for one of his rare Saturday workdays if I wanted to come by. I said I'd see him in the morning.

In the rental car garage, Jack opened the car door for me. Robby had always done that, and I'd always enjoyed that little courtesy.

We settled into the car. Jack adjusted the mirrors and reset the station on the radio dial.

"Do you like classical music?" he asked.

"That's the first direct question I've heard you ask."

"People away from the village ask and answer questions."

"Do questions make communication easier?"

"Not really. It's just a different style of speaking."

"Well, yes, classical music is my favorite."

He switched it on.

He asked where my apartment was and, without consulting a map, started to drive.

"You know where that is?"

"Oh, I'm fairly familiar with Ottawa."

I'd thought that Jack was, well, not shy, but quiet, reserved, somewhat passive, but that's sure not the way he drove. He was absolutely fearless. He changed lanes when I would never have considered it and drove in the fast lane most of the time. It never felt like he was being reckless, so I wasn't actually afraid, but I was astonished and not a little on edge.

He noticed that I was holding on to the armrest. I didn't think

I was clutching it, but he immediately said, "Would you like me to slow down?"

"I don't want to tell you how to drive, but I'd probably be more comfortable."

He smiled and slowed.

From time to time, he pointed out a building or a point of interest. Other than that, we didn't talk much.

"I'd like to take a short detour," he said. "I do have that errand. It's on our way, but I can come back later if you'd rather get home."

"I'm in no hurry." There was no way I'd refuse a chance to find out more about him.

He took the next exit, which led to our surprising destination—Carleton University. He'd said his son and daughter had studied there. I wondered if he planned to visit one of them, but the campus looked deserted.

Jack parked in a large lot. Ours was the only car there. We walked to the nearest building. He had a ring of keys, and one fit the outer door. We walked down a long empty corridor.

"Where are we going?"

"We're almost there," was the only answer I got.

We finally stopped at Room 124. A sign on the door read "Dr. Jack O'Malley – Anthropology."

"Is this your son's office? I thought his name was Michael."

Jack grinned as he used a key to open the door. He flipped the light switch and ushered me into a small, neat office. A bright Oriental carpet in shades of red and gold covered the floor. It reminded me of what he'd said about Ungavaq in the fall. The room was furnished with a large desk, a comfortable-looking chair, a couple of filing cabinets, and two smaller visitors' chairs. Bookcases lined the walls with books floor to ceiling. A coat tree and small and large artifacts—things that looked like handmade tools and weapons and other items I didn't recognize—filled the otherwise empty spaces in the room.

"You might like to sit here," Jack said, as he ushered me to a visitor's chair.

I sat.

I was at a loss for words.

Jack sat in the chair behind the desk and waited quietly.

"Are you Dr. Jack O'Malley?" A silly question—but I couldn't think of anything else.

He nodded.

"I thought you were a guide, and I thought your name was spelled J-a-q, and I thought it was short for one of those multi-syllable Inuit names. I never thought that it was actually 'Jack.'" The words tumbled out.

He smiled. "Well, it's Jack, and I'm not a guide. I've been teasing you. I couldn't resist. That's why I never invited you into my house. You'd have seen all the books. I almost told you when you made that remark about me being a good teacher. But I'm glad I didn't. It's been too much fun watching you find out."

"I can't believe I didn't see that things didn't add up."

"I have to admit; I took advantage of the fact that you were overwhelmed by everything being so different. Now I'll be fair. Come on. I'll take you home and I'll try to answer your questions."

He stood, but I didn't. I was still trying to assimilate this new information. "Your voice changed," I said.

"Tell me what you mean."

"When we got off the plane. The rhythm of your speech is different."

"Oh. I don't do it on purpose. I just think of that as my teacher voice. I hope it isn't too weird."

"Just surprising."

He nodded. He selected some files and several books, and we left. We walked across the parking lot toward the car. I saw a second car there, and we met a man heading toward the building.

"Hi, Ted."

Ted looked up. "Hello, Jack. I didn't expect to see you before January."

"I'm here for a few days, picking up some things I hadn't realized I'd need. Anne, this is one of my colleagues, Ted Grainger. Ted, this is my aunt, Anne O'Malley, from California."

"Welcome to Ottawa, Mrs. O'Malley. I'd like to stop and talk, but I'm already late. I'm supposed to be on my way home to take my wife out to dinner. Maybe I'll get to see you again before you go home."

"I hope so," I said. "It's been nice meeting you."

"It's strange," I said, after he'd gone, "but being introduced as your aunt makes me feel so old."

"How old are you?" he asked, as he opened the car door for me.

I slid onto the seat. "I turned sixty last month."

"You are older than I am," he said with a mischievous smile. He closed the door before I could respond.

As he got in on the driver's side, I said, with a certain amount of pique, "I'm a few months older than you because you got to choose your own birthday. And, anyway, Jack, you're never supposed to say something like that to a woman."

"Well, I've been corrected by a member of the senior generation. I am truly humbled." He hung his head.

"You'll get more than a correction in a minute," I said, trying not to show him I was ready to laugh.

"But I didn't call you Auntie Anne."

"Still."

He turned to face me. "Well, I guess we can't have you feeling that way. Maybe we can do something about it. We anthropologists are experts at fictive kinship."

"Fictive kinship?"

"Yes. We can just make up a relationship—whatever we want."

"Isn't that lying?"

"No. We have the right to do that as long as we don't try to defraud anyone. Many people call older adults 'uncle' or 'aunt' even if they're not related. You and I can choose the relationship we'd like to have. I have a whole slew of sisters. Suppose I tell people you're my sister. That might make you feel better."

I thought a moment. "It would."

"Then we'll go on to the next order of business—dinner. I hadn't given that any thought. We could go out to eat."

"I'd like that."

"It's Friday night. Let's go someplace nice." He turned the key and started the engine.

"I'd have to get cleaned up and change."

"I'll tell you what. I'll drop you off at your apartment. You can change, and I'll pick you up at eight o'clock. I know a nice Japanese restaurant."

"You like sushi?"

"Well, I do like raw fish," he said.

"Oh, I hadn't thought of that. I love Japanese food."

"OK, you're on."

"Where will you be while I'm changing?"

"Oh, I have a condo over by the river. I'll go over there and shower and clean up."

I gave him a look. "I have to decide to stop being surprised."

Jack dropped me off. I watched as he drove away. Life was taking me in a direction I could never have anticipated. Now, I had to figure out what to do about it.

CHAPTER Seven

I KNOCKED ON MY LANDLADY'S DOOR.

Mrs. Kennedy was glad to see me. Although she was about my age, well dressed, and made-up, she made me think of someone's dithery maiden aunt. When she talked, she often stopped in the middle of a sentence as if she'd forgotten what she was going to say, and she never seemed to know what to do with her hands.

I'd already paid for most of the month I was to be in Ungavaq. I told Mrs. Kennedy I'd keep the apartment for at least the month after that. She said she'd look forward to my return. I thanked her and crossed the garden to my front door.

I couldn't wait to call Carola.

"Well, there you finally are," she said. "I've been calling and calling. I thought you'd be back on Monday. I finally called information and got a phone number for the Archives. René said you were still in Ungavaq."

Carola was talking quietly. That probably meant that she had one of her grandchildren sleeping on her lap. She always seemed to have one or more of them with her, even when she was at my house. Her children and now her grandchildren had always had the run of my house when she was working. I'd enjoyed having them around.

"Ah, you talked to René. What do you think?"

"What a sexy voice. And that accent! Now I know why you let him whisper in your ear. If I weren't an old married lady, I might come up to visit you. But what have you been doing?"

"I'm sorry. I was excited when they asked me to stay, and I forgot to send you a message."

"Who asked you to stay?"

"You won't believe it. Robby had a half-brother."

"What? He never said anything about that, did he?"

"He didn't know, I'm sure. His brother was older, from a first marriage. He was half Inuit. So I'm related to a whole village full of people. They wanted me to stay a week, and now they want me to stay a month."

I waited for Carola to say something. She didn't.

"Carola?"

"Wait a minute. I'm going to put Pablito in the crib. I'll be right back."

I waited. I heard her return and pick up the phone.

"A month. That seems so strange," she said. "Do they want something from you?"

"No. I'm sure they don't."

"It might be that they think since you're American you're rich."

"No. It's not like that. And there's a man—"

"Another man? Not René?"

"No. Someone else. He's Robby's nephew, or half nephew, I guess, but he's my age. His eyes are just like Robby's."

"What's his name?"

"Jack. Jack O'Malley."

"O'Malley? And he's Inuit?"

"Yes, well, three-quarters. I thought he was a hunting guide, but it's turned out he's a college professor here in Ottawa. He was just home for the summer."

"Nothing you're saying makes sense." I could hear the doubt in her voice.

"No. I guess not. It's sort of like a fairy tale."

"What's he like?"

"He's smart. He's fun. He's very strong."

"Is he handsome?"

"Not handsome, but he has a nice face. And oh, Carola, his body's really nice." It gave me a little shiver just thinking about it.

"Anne! You've seen his body?"

"No. I don't mean that. I've only seen him with his clothes on—well, with some of his clothes on."

"I'm not so sure I want any more details."

"So, when did you get to be so prudish?"

"We're getting older, you know." She giggled. "All right. Now let's hear it. How do you know he has a nice body?"

"I accidentally walked in when he was changing his shirt. I only saw his back, but oh, wow!"

"Are you falling in love?"

"Love or lust. I don't know. I'm confused. And he's a relative. I don't think it's right that I'm having feelings for him."

"He's not your relative, he's Robby's relative. I don't see why that would be a problem, but he's a stranger. What do you know about him? Nothing."

"Well, you're not really right about that. I know his entire family. I know where he lives. I know where he works. What more should I know? Besides, everybody in Canada's a stranger. René was a stranger."

"You're certainly capable of making judgments as long as you're clearheaded about it. You've been so lonely, though. I hope you're not overreacting. First René and now this one."

"You're right. It took coming here for me to realize how lonely I was. Now there's this whole big family that seems so happy to have found me. It's almost too much to take in all at once."

"Take things slow, Anne. If it's good, it'll last. You don't need to hurry things."

"But there's something else."

"What?"

"We were sort of joking around. I said it made me feel so old to be called his aunt. He said we could say I'm his sister. I said yes, but do you think that's a message he couldn't be interested in me, that he could think of me only as a sister?"

"It sort of sounds like it."

"He's taking me to dinner tonight."

"Is it a date?"

"I don't know."

"Well, play it cool. Just be his friend. See what happens. I think too much has happened already. You need to let things settle a little."

"You're right. But I am staying a month in the village. I like his mother a lot. She's my sister-in-law. Her name is Maata. There's no way to call from there, but we can write. They get mail delivered every Friday. You just send stuff to Ungavaq, Québec, Canada. The zip code, only they call it a postal code, is J0M 1C7."

"OK. Let me write that down." I heard a drawer open and close. "I'll write to you. Everything's fine here. Thanks for asking."

"Oh, Carola. I'm sorry. Are you mad at me?" I knew she wasn't. On the rare occasions when she is mad, I don't have to ask.

"Of course not. I love hearing you sound happy again. Just don't hurry things. What are you wearing tonight?"

"My blue dress."

Carola had made me pack some dressy clothes. I'd told her I wouldn't need them, but she'd said, "You never know."

"Ah. Well, he'd better watch out. He's about to be blindsided when he sees you in that dress. You behave. Call me tomorrow, and tell me everything."

"OK. Love to Ernesto."

"And from him to you."

"Bye."

I showered and washed my hair. My salt and pepper hair looks silvery when it's clean, gray when it isn't. I have one of those wash-and-wear styles. I just brush the waves in place and wait for it to dry.

While my hair was drying, I took some time to do a pedicure. I've always liked the look of nail polish, but I do so much gardening and other things at home that I can't keep polish on my fingernails looking nice, so I don't wear it on my hands, but I do on my toes. I used one of my favorite colors, Orchid's Dream. I knew he wouldn't see it, but it made me feel glamorous.

I don't normally wear any makeup either, except lipstick, but I'd brought some eye shadow and mascara in case I did have some kind of evening occasion that called for it. I applied them carefully.

I took my dress out of the closet and inspected it. It's soft, form fitting, teal blue. Teal is one of my favorite colors. It goes well with my fair skin and dark brown eyes. I slipped it on and looked at myself in the mirror. Yes, time for Jack to have a little surprise.

He knocked on my door at eight. When I opened it, I was gratified to see his eyes widen. He looked me up and down.

"Wow!" he said.

"'Wow'?"

"Yes. You really look nice."

"Why, thank you, Dr. O'Malley. You clean up pretty good yourself." Jack wore a white knit shirt, a navy blue sports jacket, and gray slacks. I hadn't seen him in anything but jeans and a wool shirt before. He did look nice.

He offered me his arm, and we were on our way.

When we'd settled into the car and he'd pulled into traffic, I said, "I want to apologize. I feel like I patronized you when I complimented you on your teaching. I don't want to withdraw the compliment, but I want to rethink the surprise that generated it. I've been foolish. I have to re-evaluate what I was thinking about you."

"I hope not everything. I thought we were getting along pretty well."

"No, not everything."

"Good. I wasn't fair to you. I should have told you at the beginning. I don't know why I didn't. Sometimes, though, when people know I'm a professor, it gets in the way."

"How?"

He shrugged. "I guess they expect me to be profound or something."

"If you're going to be profound, let me know, so I can be ready for it."

He chuckled. "I can see it's way too late to worry about impressing you."

"Well, the truth is, I'm already impressed."

"In a good way, I hope."

"Yes."

"Good." He smiled.

"Now, tell me about your name. Is Jack really your name or is it just a name you use with kablunas?"

"You know Brendan's father was named John."

"Yes."

"Brendan told my grandmother his father was called Jack by his friends. Just like you, she thought it sounded like an Inuit name and suggested it when I was born."

"So you don't have another name?"

"No, Jack O'Malley, that's my whole name. I don't even have a middle name."

We found a parking place about a half block beyond Fujiyama Restaurant. He gave me his hand as I got out of the car and then offered his arm again.

The small, elegant restaurant was as busy as you'd expect on a summer Friday night. The hostess bowed. "*Yokoso*, Jack." She bowed to me. "Yokoso."

Jack returned the bow, but not as deeply as she had bowed. "Yokoso, Yumiko," he said. I copied him.

"Do you speak Japanese?" I asked.

"Just enough to say hi and good-bye and order sushi. We have a choice: a regular table with chairs or a low table with cushions."

"Well, I may be a member of—what did you call it—the senior generation, but my knees are still flexible. Let's sit on the cushions."

"OK, but if we're going to eat Japanese-style we have to take off our shoes."

"Oh, OK."

We sat in chairs next to the hostess's desk. Yumiko knelt gracefully in front of Jack. She untied his shoes and slipped them off his feet, replacing them with soft cloth slippers. She rose, bowed to him, and moved over to kneel in front of me. She slipped off my high heels.

As she did, I turned to say something to Jack.

He was staring at my feet.

"Is something wrong?"

He shook his head. "No, no, nothing wrong."

I blushed. I was glad I'd taken the time to do the pedicure. I was wearing stockings, but the color on my toenails shone through.

Yumiko placed slippers on my feet, rose, and bowed to me. Then she led us to our table in an area separated from adjacent tables by white paper shoji screens. The low black lacquer table was set with teacups, chopsticks, red cloth napkins, little bowls for soy sauce, and a spray of tiny pink orchids in a white vase. A candle in a small lantern made of oiled rice paper and wood cast a soft flickering light. The peaceful notes of a koto playing a Japanese song filled the air.

"You seem to be well-known in a lot of places," I said.

"People tend to remember me. My face is different from most faces you see around here." He pointed to his tattoos.

The waitress, dressed in a kimono, purple with a pattern of white chrysanthemums, and an obi in shades of yellow, knelt next to Jack. He offered to order sake, but I said, "I don't normally drink. I don't feel like having anything tonight." He didn't drink either, so we settled for the pot of green tea the waitress had set on the table.

She handed me a menu.

"Jack, why don't you order for us? You know what's good here."

"Are there things you don't like?"

"I like it all."

"Chopsticks or fork?"

"Chopsticks are fine."

After the waitress left, we sipped our tea.

"Tell me about yourself," he said. "We've spent a week together and you really haven't said much about your life."

"I think you owe me a story, first," I said.

"It's a long story."

"I don't care. 'Begin at the beginning and go on till you come to the end.'"

"Ah." He nodded. "*Alice in Wonderland.* I can understand you might feel that way."

"Yes, down the rabbit hole."

"I don't know that you'll want to hear a lecture, which might be what you'll get if I get going. It's the peril of socializing with a teacher."

"Go ahead. I'm tough. I can stand it." I sipped my tea again.

"Well, all right. I had an average Inuit boyhood for the time. We were nomadic. We lived in snow houses in the winter and tents in the summer." He paused. "You're surprised at something."

I hadn't said anything, but he could see the look on my face.

"What surprised you?"

"Your family lived that way in Brendan's time, but I assumed you always lived the way you do now."

"We didn't. We're pretty isolated up there by Ungava Bay. Our band was one of the last to be contacted in a formal way. We'd had the occasional explorer through from time to time, but nothing major till the 1960s."

"I'll have to adjust my mental picture again. Go ahead."

The waitress appeared at our table with a bowl of edamame, the bright green bean pods beautiful against the black lacquer surface of the serving bowl. She knelt and with a graceful motion of her hand swept the long sleeve of her kimono out of the way to set the bowl on the table. She rose and left.

Jack continued as we both started opening bean pods and eating the slightly salty beans inside. "In 1955, when I was about ten years old, we met Marcia Black, an anthropologist. She'd just arrived at the trading post. She was looking for an Inuit family she could visit. She stayed with us for a year. She specialized in women's culture."

"I don't understand 'women's culture.'"

"Early on in anthropology, in spite of stars like Margaret Mead and Ruth Benedict, most researchers were men, and they were interested in what men did. They saw women and children as appendages to men—there, but not important." He moved his hand as if brushing something away. "If you define culture as shared understandings about the way the world works, as many anthropologists do, it didn't occur to them that women and even children share sets of understandings that men don't."

"Can you give me an example?"

"Well, sure. I'll give you several. A shared understanding is something as simple as us sharing an understanding that if you flip a light switch up, a light will come on. That's general culture in the Western world. An example of women's culture is correct behavior at a wedding shower. Men don't know those rules. An easy example for children is that they have a rich culture of games. You probably played marbles and jumped rope when you were a child, but except for a few experts, most adults don't remember the rules you knew then—things almost any child could tell you."

"Ah, now I get it." I smiled. I guess I happened to be one of those "few experts." I'd been a first-grade teacher. I knew the rules of marbles and jump rope and many other games. I didn't tell Jack.

"Anyway, Marcia was interested in women's politics—how they handled decision-making when the men were away and how they handled the men when they were at home. Inuit families were independent—there weren't any chiefs or any kind of government—but in any human society, people have goals, and they use politics to achieve those goals. Of course, I didn't understand that at the time."

"So Marcia studied your family?" As I said that, I realized something. Jack had created pauses in his narrative. He adjusted the rhythm of his talking to allow me to ask questions without interrupting. I realized now that he'd been doing the same thing right along, even in the village.

He nodded. "Mine and the others in the village, though when the families went their separate ways during the summer, she stayed with us."

"'Went their separate ways'?"

"The village broke up every summer and came back together when the caribou hunt and fishing were done for the season. We'd meet again at Ungavaq.

"In a way, she repeated Brendan's story. She didn't speak much Inuktitut."

"What did she do?"

"I helped her. I'd take her around, show her things, and name them. She had a pencil and some index cards. She'd write down the words. I couldn't figure out what she was doing, so she showed me the writing and explained how it worked."

"You'd never seen writing?"

"No."

"Not at the trading post?"

"I found out later that, of course, they kept records there, but I never saw them when I was little."

"Ah."

"Marcia had brought a few books. She showed me the words and explained that there were stories in the writing. I wouldn't leave her alone after that. I wanted to learn to read. I didn't know if it was a woman's thing like sewing, but I couldn't resist the desire to learn what seemed to be magic.

"She told me later she had quite a debate with herself about the ethics of teaching me, which is interfering with the culture, an anthropological no-no. Ultimately, she decided she couldn't turn down a child who wanted to learn."

"That wouldn't have been a debate for me, but I'm not an anthropologist. I guess your parents thought it was OK."

"Yes. She took on the task of teaching me during the little spare time she had. First, she taught me to write my name. Then she wrote some simple stories phonetically in Inuktitut with the English words under them—sort of an Inuit Dick and Jane. I learned some English that way. She wrote those stories in the margins and on the few blank pages of her books. She taught me to clean my hands before I touched them, and she trusted me to take good care of them when I read.

"By the end of her visit, I could more or less read out loud from the books she'd brought. Of course, I didn't understand most of what I read. The vocabulary was way beyond me.

"When it came time to go to the trading post, Marcia asked if she might take me with her and bring me back the following winter. My father had always wanted to know more about his father's world, but he'd never had the chance. They sent me as a substitute."

The waitress brought us a fresh pot of tea and said our food would be out shortly. When she'd gone, I asked, "Why did Marcia want to take you?"

"I think there were two reasons. First, she'd grown to like me. We meshed in some way I don't understand. Also, she saw some potential in me she thought wouldn't be satisfied in the village."

"Weren't you scared to go?"

"That's an understatement. But I was excited about having more chances to read. I knew I probably wouldn't get a chance again if Marcia left without me."

"Your parents really gambled. I've read stories about some Eskimos who were taken to New York and put on display, sort of as specimens. I think they died there."

"Yes. They were Inuit from Greenland. Peary took them back to New York in the late 1890s. It's a sad story, but my parents probably wouldn't have known about it. They didn't know much about the world south of the tree line. They'd lived with Marcia for a year, though. They knew she was honorable."

"Was it what you expected?"

"No, although she'd tried to prepare me. We flew with a bush pilot from Blackwell to Montreal. Marcia told me later I was brave, but she misunderstood. I was so frightened I was numb. I couldn't react." He was quiet for a while. He shook his head and continued.

"We took a train from Montreal to Ottawa. That wasn't as frightening as the plane, but I was still scared. I'd never traveled faster than our sled could go.

"Telephones and radios—I can't tell you how terrifying they were. Voices came out of nowhere. I thought little people lived inside them.

"Cars were easier, but they were so noisy. Everything was so noisy.

"I'd heard about trees, but I'd never seen one or electric lights or water coming out of a tap. I'd never imagined buildings bigger than the trading post. I'd seen buttons and zippers at the trading post, but I didn't know how they worked. I had to learn how to dress myself.

"I'd never even heard about toilets or bathtubs. Washing was a new concept. And I had to learn about modesty. There are no secrets in an igloo. I didn't understand the idea of closing a bathroom door, or any door, for that matter.

"Trying to sleep alone was . . ." He shook his head again. "I tried. My whole family always slept together in the snow house or the tent. I'd never been alone in my entire life. I slept with Marcia until I learned how to tolerate being on my own.

"The list goes on and on. It helps to be adopted by an anthropologist, though. Marcia understood. I was going through 'culture shock,' and she'd experienced some of the same feelings in Ungavaq. It helped me to know that."

"When she got you settled down, what did she do with you? Did you go to school?"

"No. She hired graduate students to tutor me. She taught here at Carleton. Her schedule was fairly flexible, so I spent a lot of time with her if she wasn't teaching or having an office hour. The rest of the time, I spent with the students.

"First they taught me English. They had fun helping me read the children's books they'd liked when they were little. That was the first time I found out books could have pictures too. I loved that. It opened a whole new world for me. One of the most exciting days in my life was when they took me to the public library. I got my own library card. I couldn't believe that many books existed and that I'd be allowed to read them."

Again, Jack paused in the narrative. I guessed that in his mind he was reliving that very special time.

"They taught me other things. Since they were anthropologists, I didn't get much math, but I do know statistics, and I can balance a checkbook. I learned history by studying archaeology and the history of anthropology, and art by studying the art of contemporary and past cultures. I got a lot of biology and some chemistry when I worked with the primatologists and physical anthropologists. The linguists helped me understand the structures of English and Inuktitut. Many of the graduate students were from other countries. I learned about the contemporary world by talking with them about their homes. Marcia thought I should know Canadian history, so we bought some books, and the foreign students and I learned together."

"Did you have any friends to play with?"

"No, I spent my time here in an adult world. I know how strange my upbringing was, but it was exactly right for me. I wanted to know so much, and Marcia structured my whole world to satisfy that desire. Besides, the graduate students liked to play soccer. They taught me that and to skate and play ice hockey and to ride a bicycle. I taught them Inuit games too."

"Like what?"

"We have lots of contests of strength, wrestling, the blanket toss. We make string figures. We juggle."

"You can juggle?"

"Sure. I'll show you."

He did a little demonstration with some packages of chopsticks. People at the other tables stopped talking and turned to watch. He offered to include the soy sauce bottle, but I said, laughing, "Maybe later." He got a smattering of applause when he set the chopsticks down. He nodded to the people.

"Anyway, at the end of that year, Marcia was true to her word and took me back to Ungavaq. She stayed to do some follow-up work on her previous research.

"I had a lot of stories to tell. I provided most of the village entertainment that winter. They thought Ottawa was a very strange place. I'm not sure they believed most of what I said, but my father was pleased.

"I helped Marcia with her research too. I was fluent in Inuktitut and almost fluent in English by this time. I was sort of a cultural translator since I was in between, with knowledge of her culture and knowledge of my own."

"But if she took you back to Ungavaq, how did you get back here?"

"The following spring, she returned to Ottawa, and my parents let me go with her again."

Our food arrived. The waitress made a ceremony of serving the spectacular platter of mixed sushi and sashimi, bowls of rice, and miso soup. We took a break to savor the food.

CHAPTER Eight

After we'd eaten a little I said, "Tell me what happened after Marcia brought you back a second time."

"After that I spent half of each year at home and half in Ottawa. Marcia watched the weather reports and took me to Blackwell after the first big freeze of the year. She'd go back to Ottawa, and I'd wait for my father."

"She left you there by yourself?"

"Yes."

"You were so young."

"I was eleven the first time. I probably could have walked home by myself. I knew how to hunt and build a snow house and all those things, but I didn't have any dogs, so it was safer and easier just to wait for my father. We did it that way for years. The trader, Mr. St. Clair, was a friend. He looked after me. I helped him with the trading as people came in. That's where I learned my math. I can count fox skins with the best of them. When my father arrived, I'd go back with him. In the spring, before the thaw, someone would take me back to Blackwell. Marcia or one of the graduate students would pick me up."

"They went to a lot of trouble for you and, I suppose, expense too."

"Yes, and like most kids, I never thought about it; I took it for granted. Later I came to understand the importance my father placed on me taking part in my grandfather's world. I didn't understand until much later how important I'd become to Marcia."

"Important to Marcia how?"

"I'd become like a son to her."

"Ah, I can understand that."

Now we were silent as I thought about the children I'd never had. Finally, as Jack had, I shook my head. "Where did you go to college?"

"Marcia enrolled me here at Carleton. I didn't have any of the documents you need. She pulled a few strings. We negotiated about my schedule each semester because I wanted to keep the same routine of travel back and forth to Ungavaq. It worked out OK."

"It must have taken you longer to finish, though, if you were attending only half of each year."

"Yes. Eight years to get through my undergraduate work. Of course I majored in anthropology."

"How did you become a teacher?"

"I figured out some things about myself. I realized I'd become a sort of in-between."

"You said something like that earlier. What do you mean?"

"Well, I was too worldly for the Inuit and too Inuit for the rest of the world. I couldn't see myself going back to Ungavaq and living as a hunter and fur trapper, but I couldn't see myself living away from my family permanently, either."

"You worked it out."

"The answer popped into my head. I decided to go to graduate school to major in archaeology. I wanted to be a cultural anthropologist like Marcia, but I would have had to work in a foreign culture so I could see the differences between it and my own. That meant I could specialize in any culture in the world except that of the Inuit. But archaeologists don't have that same restriction. I could study archaeology and specialize in the Arctic in general and Canada in particular."

"I don't think Marcia could have pulled strings to get you into graduate school. You must have done that on your own merit."

"My grades were good enough. I loved graduate school. I went to Columbia in New York City. For my graduate-level field experience, I participated in a dig in Belize. That convinced me I'd made the right decision. I also found out for sure this Inuit body isn't designed for hot weather."

"What then?"

"After I got my PhD, I taught for a few years at Cornell in Ithaca, New York."

"You were still going home regularly?"

He nodded. "Things had changed though. When I was a child, Blackwell was nothing but a trading post with a couple of cabins nearby. By the time I was in graduate school, Blackwell had become a large town. You've seen what it's like now. The Canadian Government pushed the Inuit to settle in permanent locations. My family settled in Ungavaq. Laura's father had started Northern Air. He flew on schedule from Blackwell into Ungavaq. I didn't have to wait for the freeze to travel home any more. I could go during the regular college vacation times. That made things a lot easier."

"How did you end up teaching at Carleton?"

"Marcia told me about an opening here for an archaeologist. My credentials were good, and it didn't hurt to have the recommendation of a senior professor."

"So you teach during the year and go home for the summer? That's wrong, isn't it? Ted Grainger didn't expect to see you until January."

"I've worked out a great schedule over the years. I'm in residence at the university from January to June, for the winter/spring semester. I work on digs and write in the summer and fall. Undergraduates take a field course and help me out in the summer. Graduate students come to Ungavaq in December for a class. It's been a dream job."

"Why didn't anyone tell me about this when I was in Ungavaq?"

"I've been doing it so long, they don't think anything of it. I'm sort of there and not there, the way I have been all my life."

"You married and had children. That must have been difficult with all the travel."

He looked down.

I'd hit a nerve.

His voice lost its animation. "I wasn't as lucky in my marriage as you were in yours."

"I'm sorry. I shouldn't have asked."

He hesitated. Finally, he said, "That's all right. It's in the past. I don't mind telling you if you don't mind hearing it." He looked at me again.

"Yes. Please. I want to know you."

He put his chopsticks down. "I did a lot of dating in college and at Cornell, but I never met a woman who cared anything about my family or Ungavaq or even, really, me. They only seemed interested in a 'different' experience with someone they thought was primitive or savage—something they could tell their girlfriends about." He looked down at his fingers and spread them out for just a moment.

I'd heard anger in his voice. I'd spent enough time with him to recognize he was taking that moment of silence to put emotion back under control. I never noticed anything like that with the other Inuit, but I'd seen Jack do it several times. I wondered if he really didn't want to tell me about this, but he continued.

"I married Kaiyuina fairly late, after I came to work in Ottawa. The people in Ungavaq knew the people in Seal Haven, of course, and knew she was marriageable. They set it up."

"Your mother told me her tattoos were to make her beautiful for your father. Were your tattoos for Kaiyuina?"

"No. They weren't. I don't talk about them."

"I'm sorry."

"It's OK that you asked. I just don't talk about them."

I guessed that maybe the tattoos had some religious meaning, but I'd seen no other men in the village with facial tattoos. I let it go. "Well, I interrupted you. Tell me more about your marriage."

"The first years were good. We had Michael and Grace."

"You didn't give them Inuit names."

"We did, but when they came here to college they decided they wanted 'more Canadian' names so they would fit in better. I didn't agree with them, but I honor their wishes."

"Ah. What are their Inuit names?"

"Michael's name is Miteq and Grace's name is Pamioq."

"I like those."

"Anyway, Kaiyuina hated the life in Ottawa. I had my work; she had nothing. She was so lonely. The faculty wives seemed to feel about her the way my dates had felt about me. One day she just refused to go, so I had to leave Ungavaq without her. After that, we spent time together in the village or in the field, but, ultimately, she refused to go on the digs with me too. She did a good job with the children, but after a while, we didn't have anything to talk about any more or, really, any reason to be together. We stayed together, though. We weren't angry at each other. Neither of us wanted to marry anyone else. We just didn't share much. Then she died."

Maata had told me that when Kaiyuina died, Jack had been saddened, but not devastated as I'd been about Robby. I hadn't understood. Now I did.

He paused to see if I wanted to ask anything. When I didn't, he said, "Well, that's it. I told you, a long story. That's my life."

"Your life so far, at least."

"Yes." He smiled.

"Thank you for telling me."

"It's strange. This is the first time I've told anyone that story from beginning to end. Only my family and Marcia knew the whole story before."

"I'm honored. I'm glad you told me."

"Now maybe you'll tell me about your life."

"Yes. Sometime. Not tonight."

We finished our dinner and sat quietly savoring our fresh cups of tea. Neither of us felt the need to fill the space between us with talk. I felt easy and comfortable with him.

After a while, we decided to go, so Jack paid the check. He turned down my offer to pay my share.

As we left the restaurant, he put his hand on the small of my back to guide me though the Friday evening crowd. I could feel his warmth and the strength of his hand through the thin fabric of my dress. I thought, *I wish he'd caress me. I wonder what he'd do if I turned and put my arms around him.* I was flooded with the desire to feel his body against mine.

When he took his hand away to open the car door for me, I thought, Oh, Lord. Where did that come from? I have to get some control here.

I was still unsettled when he opened the door on the other side and slid onto the seat. I'm not shy. I'd been faithful to Robby all the years of our marriage, but I'm not afraid of men. I'm not afraid to flirt when we both know it's for fun. But this relationship was too new, and in a short time, Jack, and the people in Ungavaq, had become too important to risk losing everything because I wanted to feel a man's touch. I didn't want him to think I was like those women he dated, turned on because he was "different."

To redirect my thoughts, I said, "Well, Professor, you've probably published quite a bit. Have you written anything I could understand? Remember, I haven't had an anthropology class in a million years."

"There's a textbook, Introduction to Archaeology."

"I'd like to read it. I've seen some of your world of Ungavaq. It would be fun to see your other world."

"I have a copy at the office. We can swing by and pick it up."

We parked in the same place we had before. The campus was nearly deserted. The students were on break before the first summer session. We repeated our walk of the afternoon. When we reached his office, he turned on the light, walked to one of the packed bookcases, and pulled out a book. I stood beside him, conscious of the warmth of his body. I counted. There were seventeen other books with his name on the spines.

"Jack, this is impressive."

"It's publish or perish in this world. I haven't perished yet." He chuckled. "Some people think I'm pretty wordy."

We walked slowly back to the car in the warm twilight. "I hadn't felt this good in a long time. I was still thinking about kissing him, touching him, holding him. I hadn't felt that kind of desire, even with René.

We drove back to my place. Jack parked the car and walked me to my door.

"I don't have much in the refrigerator," I said, "but I can offer you a cup of tea."

"That would be nice. I'm not ready for this evening to end yet."

We sat on my sofa, sipped tea, and talked. Jack told me about his career—about some of the digs he'd participated in and some of the more interesting things he'd found. I told him about my sisters and my parents and what it had been like growing up in San Diego.

We spent a lot of time talking about classical music—what we liked and various concerts we'd attended. Jack had never been to an opera, so I told him about my experiences with that. *Tosca* is my favorite, and, even in a bad production, the music is so glorious it always moves me to tears. I'd bought a small CD player and some CDs, so I put on a highlight disk, and we listened for a while.

"I wouldn't mind another cup of tea," he said. "After that I wish you'd tell me about my grandfather. My mother and sisters didn't ask. They wouldn't have. They take life as it comes, but I've been trained to be curious about the past, and I'm more comfortable asking questions than they are."

"Tea won't keep you awake?"

"No."

"I'll make you another cup, but if I have another, I'll be up all night."

He followed me into the kitchenette and leaned against the counter while I put the kettle on to reheat.

"I don't actually know that much about Brendan. Our research turned out to be a lot more difficult than we anticipated. I do know some things. Robby's mother told him a bit, and Robby had an older cousin, Tommy, who grew up with his father."

"Anything you could tell me would be more than I know," Jack said. "My grandfather is a mystery to me."

"Well, Tommy said Brendan was smart. Brendan's father had one of the first cars in Pittsburgh. Brendan completely dismantled it. He took apart everything that could be taken apart. His father just about had a heart attack over that, but Brendan reassembled it without any trouble.

"He was also somewhat of a brawler. He didn't mind a fight. He was Protestant Irish. Tommy said he often got in fights with the

Catholic Irish boys in school. I guess they brought the old country's battles to America with them.

"He was artistic. I have some pencil sketches he did and a silver-backed dresser set he engraved for Robby's mother, Isabelle."

"I can add something about his artistic talent," Jack said. "He was a skilled ivory carver. He did some of those carvings on the shelves in my mother's living room. I'll show you which are his when we go back to Ungavaq."

"Who did the others?"

"My father liked to carve too. He taught me how to do it. Tell me more about my grandfather."

"He lived with his parents in Pittsburgh. We found his name in the newspaper when he graduated from high school and in the city directories from when he turned eighteen until he was twenty-two. That's when he came to Canada. Now I know he joined the army here and that he was involved in something top-secret, but we don't know what. When he joined the army, he listed Ungavaq as his home.

"Beyond that, we didn't know anything about him until he met Robby's mother. She told Robby that Brendan had kissed the Blarney Stone for sure. He could talk to anyone. He never met a stranger. He was interested in everybody."

The kettle whistled. I took a moment to pour the water into the teapot.

"I don't know how he and Isabelle met, but Isabelle told Robby that when she met him, he'd been ill and was deeply sad. I think that might have been how they described depression in those days.

"He was a farmer when they met, but when his health declined, he sold the farm. I don't know how he became a farmer. After high school, he went to college for two years. When he dropped out, he worked as a clerk in his father's bank and lived with his parents."

"He sure didn't learn to farm in Ungavaq," Jack said.

"Isabelle said that as they got to know each other he came out of the sadness. She found herself falling in love. She knew when they married his health wasn't good, and their time together might be limited, but she had no idea it would be so short. You could see in those photos I gave Maata that he was ill. He died shortly after their second anniversary. He was thirty-two years old. Isabelle told Robby she never regretted a minute of the time they spent together. That's not much information, but it's all I know."

I poured Jack's tea.

He carried it back into the living room.

We sat on the sofa again.

He stirred sugar and milk into it. "The part about his charm fits in with what I know," Jack said. "He liked to sing too."

"Oh, I forgot that part. Yes, he was musical. Robby had a mandolin that had belonged to Brendan. Isabelle said Brendan often played it."

"You know, I told you I learned English from Marcia, but that's not totally accurate. I didn't know it at the time, but I actually learned my first English from some songs Brendan taught my grandmother. She taught them to me. I have a strong memory of singing 'In the Good Old Summertime' with my grandmother in our snow house when I was about five years old. I found out later it was a popular song when Brendan came to Canada. Some other songs too. We didn't know what the words meant. I didn't even know it was English, but my grandmother told me the stories the songs told."

"I heard you singing 'Bicycle Built for Two.' Was that one of the songs Brendan taught your grandmother?"

"Yes. When did you hear me singing?"

"Oh, I don't know. At the house. You were someplace. I walked in. You were singing. I guess you were singing to yourself." I knew perfectly well when I'd heard him. He sang when he changed his shirt. I just didn't want to admit I'd stood there long enough to hear him sing that song.

"It's funny about heritage," he said. "Those songs are really special to me. They're a gift my grandfather gave me. I taught them to my children."

"You got your eyes from him too. Both you and Robby did."

"I got my hands and feet from him too. If you look, you'll see most Inuit have small hands and feet. It's a biological adaptation to the cold. I'm tall for an Inuit too. Like my father. And I have to shave every day. Most Inuit don't have much facial hair."

I had definitely noticed his hands, but I didn't say that. "Are you cold a lot?"

"No."

"I don't understand. Why are most Inuit smaller?"

"Over the generations, smaller people with smaller hands and feet were more likely to survive through the hard times. On average, they didn't have to eat as much to stay warm. You remember the Arctic hares we saw that first day."

"Yes."

"I don't know if you had time to notice, but their ears are much smaller than hares' ears elsewhere. That's for the same reason. They don't lose as much heat as they would with bigger ears, so they can survive on less food."

"Ah. That makes sense."

Jack noticed me stifling a yawn. He set his cup down. "That's my hint to get going. Thank you for telling me about my grandfather."

"Oh, no, Jack, you don't have to go yet. I'll have a little tea after all. That'll wake me up."

"No, we've had a long day. You need some rest." He stood and walked to the door.

I followed.

"When you feel like it, I hope you'll tell me about Robby too. I'd like to know about all of my family."

I had a flash of sadness. He might have noticed, because he changed the subject. "You mentioned you don't have much in the refrigerator. I could pick you up at eight for breakfast."

"That would be great. After breakfast, would you like to meet René?"

He thought a moment. "Yes, I guess I would. There's almost nothing more interesting to a professor than a good researcher. After that, we'll need to decide what we're going to do. I just had to pick up those books and files at the office. We can go back to Blackwell and wait there until Friday, or we can hang around Ottawa for a few days. I can show you the sights."

"I'd love to see Ottawa with you!"

"Then put away those high heels and wear walking shoes tomorrow. I'll see you at eight."

I had just a moment more to look into those hazel eyes. I hoped he might try to kiss me, but he took my hand, gave it a squeeze, and he was out the door—no kiss.

Should I have hinted? Too late now.

I called Carola. I couldn't wait until the next day, and it was only nine o'clock in San Diego.

"Hello."

"It's me."

"Are you home already?"

"It's after midnight here."

"Oh, I forgot about the time difference. Did you have a good time?"

"Yes!"

"Did he kiss you?"

"No."

"So are you his sister or his girlfriend?"

"I don't know, but we're having breakfast tomorrow."

"I assume that doesn't mean he's sleeping over, or you wouldn't have called me."

"Carola!"

"Well?"

"No, he's not. But I guess we're spending the week together. He asked if we wanted to stay in Ottawa or go back to Blackwell. He wants to spend time with me."

"That seems a little pushy. He didn't ask you whether you had any plans?"

"No, he didn't. But it didn't feel pushy. It just seemed natural. It felt good."

"Well?"

"Oh, Carola, I really like him." We talked for an hour.

CHAPTER Nine

WE HAD BREAKFAST AT A COFFEE SHOP—PANCAKES, BACON, and eggs.

"Most of the women I know in Ottawa pick at their food like little birds," Jack said. "It's nice to see you eat and enjoy your food."

"Most of them probably go home and eat after they leave you. Since you're my brother, I don't have to hide my eating habits from you."

He laughed, but then his mood changed. He became more serious as he said, "I hope you never feel that you have to hide anything from me."

Just as serious, I said, "I'm sure I won't."

We finished breakfast and drove to the Archives.

René's secretary didn't work on the weekends, so we just went through her office as I had done before. I tapped on his door.

He called out, "Come in."

As I opened the door, he was already crossing the room to greet me. "I missed you," he said as he took me in his arms and gave me a lingering kiss.

I'd expected a kiss, but not like this.

He glanced over my shoulder and moved to step in front of me. He almost bristled. "Who are you?"

I blushed. "René, this is my nephew, Jack O'Malley. Jack, this is my good friend, René Benoit. He's been such a help in this research." I couldn't believe I'd just said something that sounded so stupid, but in the tension of the moment, I couldn't think of anything better.

Jack stepped forward. They shook hands. When I'd said Jack was my nephew, I could see René relax a little, but now Jack looked stiff and uncomfortable. I was sure our kiss had embarrassed him.

"A pleasure, Jack," René said, although his face belied his words. "Come in and sit down."

Jack chose the single chair. That left René and me on the sofa.

I realized I'd made a mistake bringing Jack here. Both men were on edge, and I didn't know how to fix things.

"Anne, tell me about Ungavaq."

Glad for a chance to think about something else, I outlined what I'd discovered about Brendan.

When I finished, René made an effort to be a little friendlier. "Jack, what are you working on now?"

"How do you know about Jack's work?"

"I guess he didn't tell you. He's probably *the* expert on the archaeology of northern Canada. Anyone in academia or research would know who he is. You'd think Inuit wouldn't leave much behind since they lived in snow houses and tents, but if there's anything there, Jack seems to be able to find it."

"Thanks for the compliment," Jack said. "We're coming to the end of the work on a dig at a thousand-year-old Thule Culture site not too far from my home in Ungavaq. I plan to publish a preliminary paper on the project in the late spring or summer of next year."

"You know," René said to me, "even after we found the reference to Ungavaq, it didn't click in my mind that you could be related to Jack. This really is a surprise."

"A surprise for all of us," I said. "Anyway, we shouldn't keep you any longer. You have work to do."

"Anne, do you have time for some lunch later?"

"We've made plans to go sightseeing."

"That's OK," Jack said. "We can do that some other day."

"Of course my invitation included Jack," René said. "Jack, have you seen the Archives?"

"I've been here before, but it's been years."

"Anne, maybe you could show him around and then we could go out to lunch."

I looked at Jack.

He nodded.

Lunch was a little tense, but not nearly as bad as the time in the office. Gradually, both men seemed to unwind, and they did seem to have a lot to talk about.

After lunch, René went back to work. This time he gave me just a quick kiss good-bye.

Jack made no comment after he was gone except to say, "Well, let's go explore Ottawa."

That day we took a boat tour on the Ottawa River.

"I'd like to take you to dinner again," Jack said, "but I assume you and René have plans."

"We don't have plans. René takes care of his disabled sister. I almost never see him on the weekends. I'd enjoy having dinner with you."

After dinner, we walked. Jack was more distant than the previous night. When he took me to my door, I invited him in again, but he said he had work to do. He turned to leave, then turned back. "I'd like to see you tomorrow."

"Yes. What time?"

"I'll pick you up at eight again." He turned and left.

I called Carola. When I told her about the tension between Jack and René, she said, "Anne, wake up. You're an attractive woman. Both those men are interested in you."

"You think they're jealous of each other?"

"You bet I do."

"I don't think it could be that."

"What else could it be?"
"I don't know."
"What are you going to do?"
"I don't know that either."

Sunday morning, we rented bicycles and pedaled along the Rideau Canal. Jack was cool at first, but he seemed to relax as the day went on. He asked me if I'd ever had a canoe ride. When I said no, he took me canoeing. He said if I'd come back in the winter, he'd teach me to ice skate where we had just been in the canoe.

We had fun that day, but that night we had an experience that almost ruined the whole week. We went to a summer pops symphony concert at the National Arts Centre. Afterward, as we walked toward the parking garage, we were still in the thrall of the music. It had been wonderful.

We passed two men on the street going the other way. One of them made some kind of remark to Jack that I didn't hear. They were in their late twenties and kind of rough-looking. I could smell alcohol. I thought they were panhandling, but I realized I was wrong when I saw Jack stiffen. He didn't say anything, though. We kept on walking.

After a minute, I realized the men had turned. One of them called out, "Hey, lady. You ain't so bad. Whatcha doin' with him? You can do better than a fuckin' Eskimo."

"We should keep going," I said.

"They're following us," Jack said, in a low, strained voice. "You stay here."

We turned.

He walked toward the men.

The same man who'd spoken before said, "Whatcha think yer gonna do, Chief?"

I thought Jack was going to say something to him, but he didn't. He walked up to him. Almost faster than I could follow, he took the man's hand in his. Suddenly the man was kneeling on the ground and crying out in pain, with his hand bent back at the wrist.

Jack looked at the other man and said quietly, "You don't want part of this, do you?"

The second man looked at Jack a moment, turned, and walked away without a word.

Jack turned his attention back to the first man and said slowly and distinctly, "I can break your wrist, or you can leave."

The man said, "Leave! Leave!" He was still writhing in pain.

Jack let go.

The man got to his feet and ran.

Jack watched him go and then walked back to me—face flushed with rage, hands tightened into fists.

I was shaking.

He said, in the same low, strained voice, "I'll take you home, now."

We walked to the car, but before he started the engine, I said, "Jack, please. I don't want to be alone. Would it be all right if I stayed with you a while? Could we go sit by the canal where we were today?"

He nodded and turned the key.

In the dim light from the instrument panel, I could see a muscle in his jaw twitching. He had his teeth clenched. From what he'd told me about the Inuit and emotion and from his behavior of the last few minutes, I knew that he'd been humiliated twice—once by the words and the second time by losing control of his anger.

We drove a while and then pulled into a space in the parking lot near the canal. Jack had pointed out the building where he lived when we were there earlier in the day.

"Do you want to talk about it?" he said quietly.

"No. I just want to sit here with you for a while. Could we listen to the radio?"

Jack turned on the classical station and then reached over and took my hand. I could feel his tension. I suppose he could feel mine.

Gradually, we relaxed. We sat for about forty-five minutes saying nothing, listening to the music, watching the lights reflected on the water. Moment by moment, as I relaxed, I became more aware of his hand—warm, strong, gentle. That led to thinking about his body and, finally, him. I didn't understand what I was feeling. Desire, but more than that.

It had been so long since I'd had to deal with these kinds of emotions. I didn't know what to do. I didn't want to make a mistake. I thought maybe I ought to go home, but I didn't want to leave him. I could only think to say, "I'm feeling better now. I wouldn't mind a cup of tea."

"This late?"

"Yes."

"OK," he said.

The next day was beautiful—in the 70s and sunny—so we spent a lot of time walking and talking. At first, he didn't bring up the topic of the confrontation, so I didn't either. Then he said, "I want to apologize."

I'd spent a lot of time in the night thinking about him and what had happened. I knew immediately what he meant.

"I accept your apology, but I don't think it's necessary. Am I right that you're apologizing for letting your anger show?"

He looked at me with surprise. "That, and the way I treated you last night."

"Well, I understand from what you told me before you don't like to show your emotions, but that man's behavior was so awful and unexpected. We didn't deserve that."

"He was talking about me, not you. You didn't deserve that."

"No, he was talking about us. We're family."

We walked a few minutes.

"We should decide not to let that experience poison our day," I said.

He nodded.

Somehow, my saying that cleared the air between us. We went on to have a pleasant time.

I met René for lunch on Tuesday, and I walked back with him to the Archives.

"Come up to my office," he said.

He closed the door, turned, and put his arms around me. "I couldn't do this the other day." He kissed me until I was dizzy.

"I've missed you, Anne. I have things scheduled the rest of this week. I can't cancel any of them. I won't have a chance to see you again before you go back on Friday. I don't have any claim on you, but I don't want you to forget me."

"No. I won't forget you. I couldn't."

He kissed me again.

Carola had certainly been right, at least about René.

Jack took me to the Parliament Building, the Canadian Museum of Contemporary Photography, and the Central Experimental Farm.

We went to Byward Street Market on the one rainy afternoon of our week. We were caught in a downpour that didn't let up for almost twenty minutes. People ran for shelter in all directions, and we ducked in under the blue plastic awning of a flower seller's booth. The rain trapped the saleswoman in the other half of the booth across an open walkway, so although she waved, she didn't bother to come see whether we were serious customers

Flowers surrounded and enclosed us—hanging baskets of scaevola, million bells, petunias, geraniums, bougainvillea, and fuchsia and buckets of calla lilies, sweet peas, carnations, and roses. We were alone in a sea of flowers. It was magical.

"This is so beautiful," I said.

"They're more beautiful because you're here."

My heart leapt. I hadn't expected that from him. Oh, Lord. I felt like I was sixteen again. "What a wonderful thing to say."

In the next booth, a woman rushed to put her supplies under cover. A tattoo artist, she did temporary tattoos with henna. She had dozens of exotic designs hung on the support posts of her booth and in an album I could see on a table.

"Jack, look at that. Would I look better if I had tattoos like your mother?"

He stiffened.

"Jack, what is it?"

He turned to face me. "Are you mocking?"

"I'm asking," I said softly.

I could see him relax. "All right. Yes, I'm old-fashioned. I like the tattoos."

"I do too. Shall I get one?" I pointed to the other booth. "She could do those five lines on my chin. It wouldn't be the right color. The henna's brown. Would it be OK for me to have a tattoo even though I'm not Inuit?"

"A tattoo? On your face?"

"Yes."

"We're in Ottawa, not Ungavaq."

"What does that matter?"

I saw the smile spread across his face like the sun coming out. "Yes, I'd really like that."

When the rain let up, we ran to the next booth. The woman looked surprised. I think we were older than her usual customers.

"I'd like to get a tattoo."

"I'll do it for you if you want it, but I'm just closing up," she said. "Once they're dry, the tattoos will last about two weeks—you can wash and everything—but they really need to dry at least two hours before you get any water on them. I'd advise against it for today. Can you come back when the weather's better, maybe tomorrow?"

"Yes, we'll try," Jack said.

We didn't get back, though. We spent almost the whole day at the Canadian Museum of Civilization in Hull, across the Ottawa River. The museum had a large section on the history of the First Peoples of Canada—the Inuit and the Indians. Jack explained each item in each display, and I noticed more than one display had a card saying "On loan from Dr. Jack O'Malley."

Friday, we caught the earliest plane to Blackwell. Jack had emailed Laura, and she'd delayed her takeoff to Ungavaq. This time, I had more luggage. With Jack's guidance, I bought things I needed: jeans and warm shirts, a warmer jacket, a wool hat, gloves, and lots of bug repellent—Ungavaq was rich in mosquitoes and biting flies. Jack also helped me select fabric to take back as gifts for his mother and sisters.

When we finished that shopping, I asked him to take me to a bookstore. There, I headed for the children's section and selected a tall stack of my favorite books.

He'd been browsing in another section. When I met him by the checkout stand, I could see the question on his face.

"These are the favorites that I always had in my classroom," I said casually. "I'm going to read them to the children in Ungavaq."

In all this time, it hadn't come up in our conversation that I'd also been a teacher. I'd been hoarding that little bit of information. It was worth it to see the look on his face.

He laughed heartily. "Touché."

At the last minute, I remembered to buy a couple of throwaway cameras. I hadn't brought a camera to Canada. I hadn't thought it would be the kind of trip where you took photos, but I'd been wrong.

I'd begun to feel I understood a little of Inuit culture. Every once in a while, though, I got a reminder of how far I had to go if I wanted to be with Jack and the family.

We were checking in at the Ottawa airport. The woman at the counter asked for a photo I.D. I reached into my purse, and in the process, dropped it, and many of the things in it fell out onto the floor. "Oh, damn!" I said.

I saw Jack stiffen as I'd seen him do before. Again, I could see him make the effort to relax.

I knelt.

He bent down to help me gather up my lipstick, comb, and other items. He didn't say anything.

As we walked to our gate, I said, "I know I did something wrong there. Would you tell me what?"

"It's all right. It's just me. I've sort of shifted into the mindset I have in Ungavaq."

And I was amazed to realize that his speech had shifted back into the softer, gentler rhythms of Inuktitut. I found myself slowing and softening my words a little when I said, "It isn't all right, because I'm going back to Ungavaq too. Please tell me. Was it because I swore?"

"Not the word. The emotion."

"Irritation?"

"Yes, anger."

"Ah. What would I have done if I were Inuit?"

"You'd have giggled and said, 'How funny.'"

"Would I have felt irritated inside and covered it up?"

"No, because your body would have given away the emotion, even if your words didn't."

"That's difficult."

"Yes."

"Do you think I can learn?"

"I don't know."

"You said if I showed emotion, it would make people uncomfortable. They wouldn't want to be around me. Did I make you feel that way?"

He looked away. "No. . . . Yes, a little."

"I'm sorry. I don't want that."

"I don't want it either. I make people feel that way a lot." He couldn't hide a sadness in his voice. "I think sometimes I make you uncomfortable."

I quickly shook my head. "No." I laughed. "Well, yes, a little."

He laughed too.

"I see you watching me," I said. "I wonder if I measure up."

"Of course you do."

"I do wonder, sometimes, if people are just tolerating me and wishing I'd go away."

"It's not like that at all."

"Really, I know. I just wonder. But I think Maata wouldn't have invited me to stay longer if that were true. Still, if you were my teacher, I don't think I'd be getting an A in your class."

He really laughed now. "Well, you've put that into words we can both understand. I think you'd be getting maybe a $B+$."

"Ah, you're generous."

"My other students don't think so."

"I won't tell."

In Ungavaq, Jack and I spent time together, but mostly I was with Maata and his sisters. They'd decided they were going to make a seamstress out of me, so we plunged into a graduate-level course in sewing. I'd certainly never be any competition to any of them, but I loved the camaraderie of sewing with them. Other women from the village often joined us, or we went to their homes. We worked on clothes for Inuit dolls that would be sold in gift shops around Canada.

I paid attention, and, of course, Jack had been right. Every time something happened that would have irritated me, the other woman would just laugh and say something like, "How funny. Look, I dropped the thread, and it rolled under the sofa."

There were always small children around when we had these sewing parties. When a three-year-old with greasy hands grabbed the fabric Maata was working on, Maata laughed. One of the other women said, "Look, isn't it funny little children have no sense," and the rest of them laughed too. I could see no sign that Maata and the others were irritated. This just happens in life—not worth getting upset about.

One day, when we were planning to sew at Maata's house, I came into the living room to see what looked like a large pile of animal hides stacked on the sofa.

"Perhaps you'd like to see these," Maata said.

I almost said, "What are they?" but I remembered in time. "I would like to."

Maata unfolded them. "These are Jack's clothes. I brought them out to show you. I made them."

What I had thought was a stack of leather was, in fact, a double set of clothing. Maata showed me that Jack had worn an inner set—pants and a hooded coat—of caribou hide with the hair turned inward to his skin. The outer set was worn with the hair turned outward. Inlaid strips of lighter colored hide decorated the darker hides that formed the outer coat. The outer coat had aprons front and back that came almost to mid-thigh. The outer trousers were knee-length and made of polar bear fur. They were designed to be loose fitting and worn with knee-high boots, called *kamiks*. The hand stitching was beautifully done; the tailoring was as fine as anything I'd ever seen in Robby's clothes. In most places, I almost couldn't see the seams. Maata showed me several places where she'd mended tears, but I wouldn't have spotted them by myself.

"These would be heavy to wear," I said.

"Yes, but they keep him warm."

In surprise I said, "I wouldn't think Jack would have much occasion to wear these now."

"Sometimes he wears them. Perhaps you would like to learn how to sew skins."

"Yes. I would. It looks like it would be difficult to do such beautiful work."

"I'll teach you."

We started with the lesson right then. When the other women arrived, they encouraged me with little suggestions.

I started learning about cooking too. Maata taught me about what she called "country food"—the traditional foods they'd eaten in the past and still enjoyed. One was a special treat—*maktaaq*, well-aged whale skin and blubber from either a beluga or a narwhal. Maata served some beluga maktaaq to Jack one night. She said it was something you had to learn to like and didn't offer it to me.

I always did my best to eat what was served. Maata didn't serve raw meat to me. She always cooked my portion, but usually she and Jack ate their meat raw. And no trimming fat for them. With obvious pleasure, they ate large portions of fat. Jack told me if a traditional Inuit had eaten only the protein part of his food and had left the fat, he probably would have starved to death. You just couldn't take in enough calories without eating fat. Only hearty eaters survived the cold.

When I wasn't sewing or cooking, I read Jack's archaeology text. When I needed help, I went to him. He was preparing for his next batch of students, but he always had time to talk.

And I read to the children. We had a story hour each afternoon. Even some of the older children came to join us. I read and told stories—something I'd always loved to do. The children told me stories too. It reminded me of why I'd loved teaching so much.

One night, late, long after everyone else was asleep, I heard a soft tapping at my bedroom door. "Anne, it's Jack. Come out. I have something to show you."

I slipped out of bed and put on my clothes.

Jack was waiting in the living room. "Put on your coat and hat. It's chilly."

"Where are we going?"

"Just outside, on the porch."

As we stepped out the door, I was astonished by the startling display of dancing light that met my eyes. The sky was filled with greens and reds and blues and purples and pinks and whites. Curtains of unbelievable colors shimmered, swirled, and pulsed overhead. I gasped in amazement.

"This is the best aurora we've had in a long time," he said. "It's not usually visible in the summer. I didn't want you to miss it."

We sat close together on the porch steps.

"There are two stories about the aurora," he said.

"I'd like to hear them."

"It might be that there's a storm on the sun, and electrons and protons in the solar wind are hitting our upper atmosphere and exciting oxygen and nitrogen atoms."

"And?"

"It might be that the spirits of the dead are playing football with a walrus skull. . . . People often feel they must choose one over the other."

"Hmm. I'll have to have to think about that. When you put it that way, they seem equally likely or unlikely."

"Ah, you're not ready to make a decision."

"No. Will I be allowed to watch if I don't want to decide?"

"I suppose, but just this once." He smiled.

"I guess you have a favorite."

"No. I don't choose between those stories. I can't."

"Because you're in between?"

"Yes."

We stopped talking and watched the lights.

Jack started humming.

"That's 'Frankie and Johnnie.' Is that one of your grandfather's songs?"

"It is."

"I know the words." I started singing softly. "Frankie and Johnnie were lovers. Oh Lordy, how they could love. They swore to be true to each other, just as true as the stars above. He was her man, but he done her wrong."

He smiled. "Perhaps you know the other verses."

"I used to, but I don't know if I remember them now."

"Let's see." He sang, "Frankie and Johnnie went walking." And I did remember and joined him. We sang it all the way to the end.

"Do you know 'My Grandfather's Clock'?" I asked.

"Yes."

I have no idea of how long we sat there singing. After a while, I felt drowsy, but I didn't want to go in. I was having too much fun. I rested my head on his shoulder for just a moment, and . . .

When I woke, he was leaning against the porch post. I rested against his chest. He'd put his arm around me. His eyes were closed. I wanted to stay cradled against him, so I held as still as I could. After a while, he opened his eyes and smiled at me, and we sat up. He moved his arm away.

He looked at the sky. The aurora was fading in the increasing light of day. "It's about four o'clock. You'd better go in and try to get some more sleep."

"Yes, I guess I should. What a special gift you've given me. Thank you."

"I think we'll remember this night for a long time."

When I got to my room, I thought, *I should have just kissed him*, but he'd already told me my emotions made him uncomfortable sometimes. Could he feel that I wanted him? Did that make him uncomfortable? I didn't know. I was afraid to find out.

Over the next two days, Jack's twelve students arrived.

I'd been waiting for them because I wanted to find out if Jack's speech would change into that more forceful pattern I'd heard in Ottawa. I found out that what he called his "teacher voice" was actually his "Ottawa voice." He maintained his gentle speech rhythms here in Ungavaq, even when students were present. That's not to say he wasn't different around the students. He was professorial. I watched, amazed, as he seemed to shift back and forth effortlessly and unconsciously.

Two weeks after he and I returned to Ungavaq, Jack, his brother-in-law Quipac, and the students—with what seemed like a mountain of supplies—took off hiking. They headed to the Thule Culture site where they'd work—a four-day walk from Ungavaq for the heavily laden group. Nobody ever said archaeology was for wimps.

I watched them walk away—all those young students so excited that they were going on a real adventure with a famous archaeologist. I'd talked to all of them. They were just about floating on air with anticipation. I thought probably by the end of the summer, when they came back to the village, they'd be different—some of them disillusioned over the strenuous work and hardship of archaeology and some of them even more committed to what would become their life's work. I wished them all well.

Quipac led the group. Jack was the last to leave. He'd told me that some of the less fit ones would begin to straggle after not too long. He had to make sure that they didn't fall too far behind. He'd whistle to signal Quipac when he thought the slowest one needed a break. He said he was like a little dog, nipping at their heels.

I laughed at that image.

He asked me if I wanted to walk out of the village with him.

I was so glad. I'd put off thinking about it, but this could possibly be the last time I'd ever see him. I was leaving in two weeks. I didn't know if I'd have an opportunity to come to Ungavaq or to Ottawa again. I imagined just casually dropping by his office at the University. I'd say, "Hi. I just happened to be in Ottawa and thought I'd drop by for that ice skating lesson you promised me." What a foolishness!

We walked. We didn't talk. He kept our pace slow. The students were far ahead. Finally, he turned and said, "I don't think you should go any farther. I don't want you out of sight of the village."

I felt so sad, but I didn't want my emotion to make him uncomfortable. I tried to think of our happy times together. "I hope your dig is successful. Someday, maybe I could see it."

"I'd like that."

"Good-bye, then."

He took my hands in his. "No, we don't say good-bye. We don't make a fuss."

"What do you say?"

"'I'm going now.'"

"What do I say?"

"You say, 'Yes, you're going.'"

"Yes, you're going."

He let go of my hands, turned, and walked away. He didn't look back.

I stood and watched him for a few minutes. I didn't start to cry until I turned to walk back to the village.

Two weeks later, as Maata, Laura, and I came out Maata's front door to walk to the dock, Jack was standing at the bottom of the steps. I couldn't speak. I wanted to cry and laugh at the same time. Finally, all I could say was "Jack!"

"I knew you hadn't gone yet. I'd have seen the plane."

"We'll go on to the dock," Maata said, and she and Laura walked down the steps and along the path.

"I didn't expect to see you."

"I couldn't let you leave without saying good-bye."

"You told me you don't say good-bye."

"Ah, yes. I did, didn't I." He reached up to me.

I walked down the steps and took his hand.

I touched his cheek. "I almost didn't recognize you."

He put his hand where my hand had been. "I should have shaved before I came to visit a lady, but it's difficult to do in the field."

"I'm glad to see you any way you are."

"I've come to wish you a safe journey. I'd hoped to be here earlier so I could have breakfast with you one last time."

"Oh. You walked all that distance for breakfast?"

"For breakfast with you. It's not far, but I was slower than I realized. I can walk it in two days without the students to shepherd."

This certainly made leaving Ungavaq all the more difficult.

He let go of me and said, "Hold out your hand."

I held it out, palm upward, and he set something on it. "I couldn't let my sister leave without a gift to remember us by."

I looked and saw an exquisitely detailed ivory caribou, about an inch long. It looked in motion with its body curved as if looking at something behind it. Its eyes, ears, nostrils, mouth, and hooves were carefully incised. I could even see the pattern of its coat. Part of one antler was missing.

"Oh, Jack, it's beautiful. Is this something from your dig?"

"Well, yes and no. I couldn't give you the original because it has historic and scientific significance, so I made this copy for you."

"That's even better."

"It's to keep you safe. It's an amulet that they sewed into a child's clothing. The more it's worn, the stronger it becomes. And, you know, the caribou go away, but they always come back again. Maybe this will bring you back to us."

"I don't know what to say when 'thank you' isn't enough." No one was around. Maata and Laura were busy with something on the dock. So as if it were the most natural thing in the world, I leaned forward and kissed him on the cheek. Then, I remembered. "Oh, Jack. I'm so sorry. I remember what you said about kissing in public. I'm so sorry."

"It's OK." He took my hand in his again, and we continued walking. This time, when he helped me onto the dock, he didn't let go.

As he'd taught me, I didn't say good-bye to Maata. Instead, I said, "I'm going now."

"Yes, you're going," Maata responded.

My eyes swam with tears, but I managed to control them. I hoped Maata would forgive the emotion.

Before he helped me into the plane, Jack stood close and looked at me.

I wanted him to hug me. I wanted to feel his beard against my cheek, the strength of his arms around me, the warmth of his body against mine. I wanted him to say, "Don't go."

Instead, he said softly, "I'll miss you."

"I'll miss you too."

There was nothing else to say. I climbed into my seat with my heart racing.

I'd known this man for only six weeks. I couldn't understand how he had come to be so important to me in that short time, but I remembered what it had been like with Robby. Was I falling in love? I'd joked with Carola about that, but I just didn't know. And now I was going back to René.

Laura taxied down the bay and gunned the engine for takeoff. The plane finally leveled out and circled to head to Seal Haven. Jack and Maata stood on the dock. I watched until I couldn't see them anymore.

CHAPTER Ten

I'D CALLED RENÉ FROM BLACKWELL TO TELL HIM I WAS ON my way. He was waiting at baggage claim. He kissed me, deep and long. He had clearly missed me, and I had missed him.

I'd been dreading this meeting, but I thought, I have to deal with this sometime. It might as well be now.

I waited until we were in the car. "René, I've been thinking about things while I was gone. We need to talk about something."

He was silent for a moment. "About us?"

"Yes."

He'd started the engine, but he turned it off again. His hands were tense on the steering wheel.

No more tense than I felt, though. I hadn't had a conversation like this with a man in nearly forty years. I just had to say what I was thinking. Brave thought, but I didn't feel brave. I was afraid of losing him. My feelings for René were more complicated than I had understood.

"I think we were getting to the point . . . I mean . . . I think you were going to ask me to go to bed with you."

His eyes widened in surprise. "Well, yes. I've been thinking about that, but you went to Ungavaq. Now I hear you putting that in the past tense."

"I'm not ready. You're a very attractive man. Robby's been gone a long time, but I don't feel single. I'm in a kind of limbo, I guess. I can't figure it out. I don't want to make promises I can't keep."

"You're saying you don't want to see me anymore."

"Oh, no, René! That's not what I'm saying at all. Not at all."

"You need to be clearer with me. What does this mean?"

"I really just meant what I said. I'm not ready to go to bed with you. Do you want to stop seeing me?"

"No."

"Will this change things between us?"

"I don't want it to," he said with a shake of his head. "We'll have to see. We're just learning about each other, and I guess you'll be going home soon."

"Yes."

"Do you know when?"

I shook my head.

"Let's keep seeing each other."

I nodded and breathed out. I'd been holding my breath.

He started the car again.

We settled back into our routine of research and lunch and rides home. We confirmed that Brendan had lived with his uncle in Ottawa after he left Pittsburgh and before he went to Ungavaq. René found the residency papers generated when Brendan first crossed the border into Canada. I found his name in the records of a city census from early 1913.

Shortly after I returned, René happened to mention that the second session of summer school was about to start at Carleton. I didn't have any pressing reason to return to San Diego, so I decided to stay, take a class, and continue researching.

I finally attended two classes: Canadian History and Introduction to Anthropology. I didn't register. I just asked the professors if I could audit. I ended up with more of an understanding of the time when Brendan was living in Canada, and I enjoyed the challenge of keeping up with the other students.

As I fell back into the busyness of big city living, Ungavaq came to seem more and more like a dream. It became harder to remember that time with the family or to believe Jack could have cared for me the way I'd hoped. It seemed I'd built a whole fantasy on his friendliness to a stranger.

When we were together, René continued to kiss me. The first time after our conversation, we were hesitant, confused, and, I think, scared of making the wrong move, but it didn't take us long to get past that. I still felt committed to Robby, and I still thought about Jack, no matter how unreal that time with him was coming to feel, but neither Robby nor Jack was here, and René was. My body seemed to be waking up from a long sleep. I found myself yearning for his kisses.

One night in the car, something changed, and I didn't want him to stop. He understood almost immediately. He reached under my shirt and caressed my breasts. I was so excited. It felt as if it were the first time anyone had touched me. He kissed my mouth and the hollow of my throat and the whole time his hand touched, stroked. He pushed my shirt and my bra up, leaned down, and put his mouth on my breast, kissing and sucking and caressing, now with his tongue and his hand. My body was swept with sensation—feelings I hadn't had since the last time I'd made love with Robby. It felt so good, and I wanted more.

His hand was under my skirt moving up my thigh. I was ready for whatever he wanted, until I realized that I was imagining Jack's hand, not his, on my leg. I thought about going on. I wanted to go on. But whatever compromise he might have been willing to make, this was wrong. "René, please," I said. "I have to stop. I'm so sorry."

He moved his hands away and kissed me gently. "It's OK." He settled back in his seat with a deep sigh.

I sighed too. It would have been so easy to keep going.

As I adjusted my clothes, he took a deep breath, "Anne, I'm very fond of you, but I can't offer you anything more than what we have already."

He had misunderstood.

"I'm not holding out for some kind of commitment, if that's what you think."

"No, I don't think that. But there's a barrier between us. At least part of that is my fault. I want you to understand why there won't be a commitment. I need to tell you about my life."

"You don't have to."

"I want to."

He took a moment to get his thoughts organized. "I've been engaged twice. My first fiancée was Estelle. She was my sister's best friend. They were crossing a street. A car hit them. Estelle died. Yvonne was brain-damaged." His voice had dropped. He was so quiet I almost couldn't hear what he was saying. His face showed the pain of those memories.

"Oh, God, René!"

He held up his hand and shook his head to stop me from saying anything more.

"It took me a long time to get over that. Then I met Janet. We planned to marry. My parents were still alive. She assumed that Yvonne would be institutionalized at some point. When I told her that wasn't going to happen, she broke the engagement. By doing that, Janet forced me to look at the decisions I'd made. I realized that it would be . . . unrealistic to expect anyone to share the life I'd chosen.

"Now there's you. I'm selfish. I want to keep what we have for as long as I can. You're not just a summer romance for me, but that's what I have to be for you. I won't offer you anything else. Someday someone will offer you more. That's not OK, but that's the way life has to be for me."

"Oh, René, I'm so sorry."

"I don't want you to feel sorry for me. That's the last thing I want. I have a good life. I have friends. There've been some good women in my life too. The truth is my sister can be a pain sometimes, but I love her. I want to take care of her. My parents didn't force this on me, so don't feel sorry for me. I just want you to understand. You're very special to me. I hope you'll stay in my life as long as you can."

I nodded. "Of course."

He didn't mention Jack. I was glad, because I didn't know what I could have said. I certainly didn't want to tell him the confusing thing that had happened in my heart while he was touching and kissing me.

"What do you want to do now?" I asked.

"Everything you'll allow," he said, with a short laugh.

"That's not what I meant." I laughed too. "Seriously, though, I don't want you to feel I'm teasing you."

"I know that's not what's going on. I'll trust you. You trust me to stop when you want me to."

After that, we kissed and touched and played and stopped when I needed to, until the day I didn't ask him to stop. I'd never gone to bed with a man before unless I thought the relationship would be ongoing. There hadn't been any one-night stands or vacation flings. I don't know why I changed my mind.

He stopped of his own accord, but the next day, he asked me to meet him for lunch at the café in a small hotel. When I got there, he showed me a room keycard.

"Would you like to eat here in the café, or would you like to go to the room and order room service?"

"Why did you wait till today? Why not yesterday?"

"Because I don't want you to regret this decision. Once we cross this line, I don't think we can go back. I don't want to lose you."

"You know there's been no one since Robby."

"I know this is difficult for you."

"Ah, René. I'm not going to regret anything." Maybe not, but if I was making a mistake, René was never going to know.

He led the way across the lobby and pressed the button for the elevator. We rode to the fourth floor like some old married couple, eyes front and not speaking to each other.

I looked at my wedding ring. I thought, *I ought to take it off*, but I couldn't bring myself to do it—better to feel that I was being unfaithful than to feel that I was abandoning Robby altogether.

We walked down the hall side by side, not touching. We came to the door.

"Did you bring any condoms?" he asked.

That was so unexpected, I nearly laughed. "No. I'm long past having to worry about getting pregnant."

"That's not what it's about. You're not long past getting AIDS or some other disease."

"René, are you trying to tell me something?"

"No, I'm trying to teach you. I thought this would probably be something you hadn't thought about. Maybe I'll be your only lover, or maybe I'm just the first. I don't know. But you need to know how to protect yourself. I brought condoms. You're going to have to learn about this."

"I've never even seen one."

"You will today."

He reached toward the lock with the keycard. "Now, are you sure?"

In answer, I put my hand on his and guided the keycard into the lock.

He opened the door.

I went in.

He put out the "Do not disturb" sign, closed the door, and locked the security lock.

The room had a small table and two chairs. Two places were set with a plate of sandwiches, a bowl of fruit, and a bottle of wine. The king-sized bed was turned down. A dozen red roses in a vase on the bedside table filled the room with fragrance.

"Oh, René, so beautiful!"

He came up behind me, put his arms around me, kissed my neck, and held me close against his body. "Anne, you're so beautiful, and I've had to hold back for so long."

"Hold back?"

"My feelings for you, my need, my desire."

I turned to face him. His body was hard against me. I kissed him. Then I reached up, loosened his tie, and unbuttoned the top button of his shirt. "Don't hold back any more."

He kissed me as never before—a kiss of love, not lust.

Now I understood, and for all my misgivings, this didn't feel wrong.

I didn't know what to expect, but when he undressed, I remembered how much I like men's bodies. His was lean and wiry. He had the muscled calves and thighs of a runner. I liked everything about him, and I desired him.

"This may be a little different for you," he said. "I like to talk. If it bothers you, tell me. I don't have to do it: I just like to do it."

I didn't know what he meant, and I thought, at first, it probably would bother me. But he didn't talk dirty. He just talked about what he was doing and feeling. His quiet voice in my ear, when he wasn't kissing me or doing something else, was so erotic. I think he did it so that he wouldn't lose control too soon. I loved it, especially because I found out that when I did the right things, he couldn't talk at all.

We were in bed resting after that first time. I had my head on his chest, and he had his arm around me. I felt wonderfully relaxed. I hadn't realized how much I wanted this again. And the time after spent touching and holding was almost better than the sex. René wasn't one of those men who just rolled over and went to sleep.

He kissed me on the top of my head and said, "Well, you certainly surprised me, eh?"

"Surprised you? How?"

"You were so reluctant to go to bed; I thought maybe you didn't like sex. Was I ever wrong."

"I like it a lot."

"I noticed. You're enthusiastic," he said, with a smile.

"And I like you a lot," I said. "You're very inventive, especially that last thing."

"Had you never done that before?"

"No, but I certainly hope I'll get a chance to do it again."

"I think I could arrange that. Will you come back tomorrow?"

"So soon?"

"Not soon enough."

"I'll be here."

He kissed my head again. "I want you to do something."

I was giving him little kisses on his shoulder and chest, working my way down his body.

"I'd like you to buy some underwear. There's a place you can go. I have a charge account there. You can just charge it to me."

I froze. Red flags went up in my mind. What in the world was he talking about? Why would he have a charge account at a place that sold women's underwear?

He couldn't have seen the look on my face, but he certainly felt the sudden tension in my body.

I pulled away from him and sat up.

"Anne—"

"René, are you trying to pay me or something."

"Oh, God, no! Not that. I didn't mean it that way."

Now he was sitting up too. I thought it would be too theatrical to cover myself with the sheet, so I just sat looking straight ahead.

"How did you mean it if it's not some kind of reward?"

"It's just that your bra and panties are white. I don't like that."

"I don't understand."

"It seems so medical. It makes me think of bandages. I didn't mean to insult you."

"Bandages?"

"Like when my sister was in the hospital. It takes my mind back to that terrible time."

"You've seen my underwear before. You never said anything."

"Because I was trying not to want you. I didn't want to think about you in other underwear."

"Oh."

We were quiet for a while.

"I'm sorry," I said. "I should have known that you'd never insult me. Yes, I'll get other underwear, but I'll pay for it myself."

"I don't want to make you spend what you can't afford."

"You just tell me where you want me to go."

"All right."

"What color?"

"Anything but white."

"OK."

"And, Anne, I do like lace."

I guess he did like lace. Just talking about it excited him. I moved closer. "Do you have to go back to work now?"

"No, I took the afternoon off."

I lay down again. "Well, come here then and tell me how you think I'd look in lavender lace."

I didn't know what to expect, but I'd assumed that René was sending me to some place like Mimi's Love Closet. Robby and I'd gone into Mimi's because we were curious. Somehow, the French maid outfits and bras and panties with cutouts just didn't seem like our style, so we ended up not buying anything.

I should have known better. That wasn't René's style either.

Lingerie a la Mode was definitely not like Mimi's. Small and very expensive—I could see why René had been concerned about what I might spend in this high-fashion establishment.

The woman with the French accent who waited on me was about my age, well dressed in a conservative gray pants suit, and beautifully coifed. She was the owner. She welcomed me and, after we had talked a little, asked me how I'd found the shop, since they didn't advertise.

"A friend recommended it."

"Oh, and who was that?"

"Dr. Benoit."

"Ah, yes. He's referred a number of people to us over the years. He's been a good customer ever since he and his poor sister moved to Ottawa—more than twenty years now. We help him with her. I'm always pleased he feels he can recommend us."

"I wondered how he'd know about your shop."

"Well, he has to do everything for her, including buying her underwear. Poor thing, she's just like a child, you know. He brings her here, and she's learned to trust us. We speak French to her. That reassures her. Usually he calls before they come. They come after we're closed because she's jealous when he talks to other people. I wait on them. He sits out here. We take things into the back to fit them to her. She doesn't like to let him out of her sight, though. The first time we took her into the dressing room, she had a temper tantrum. There's no other way to describe it."

"Oh, dear. That must have been difficult."

"Over time, she's learned that everything is OK—that he won't leave."

"No wonder he recommends you so highly."

"I'll have to thank him when I see him again. What can I offer you today?"

"I'd like five sets of underwear—matching bra, pants, and slip. I want them in five different colors—no white. Oh, yes, and garter belts, maybe just garters, and stockings too. Bring me your best, but it has to have lots of lace."

Maata got tattooed to please the man who loved her. The least I could do was buy some underwear.

René and I were together every weekday afternoon after that. I think he must have used up all his vacation time. Sometimes we went to the hotel, sometimes to his house, and one memorable Friday afternoon, he told his secretary to start her weekend early. When she was gone, he locked the outer door and the office door. I didn't realize what he had in mind. He held me close and said, "I want you to invade my life, permeate my life, fill my life. I want it to be so that every place I look, I'll have a memory of you."

And he made that happen that afternoon.

I'd been in Canada almost four months when the summer session at the university finished. I felt I'd looked at every record available, so I told René the time had come for me to go back to San Diego.

Our last time together was difficult. I'd had feelings I hadn't expected all through my time with him. I'd started out thinking he was a safe person to just have fun with, to explore with, to start over with. It had turned out to be so much more than that. But we'd known from the beginning that our time together was limited, and I'd known that Jack was still in my heart. Now, René and I weren't breaking up. The feelings we had for each other were still there. We were just leaving that part of our lives. I didn't know how to say good-bye to him. He had wakened my body from its long, sad sleep. Now I was walking away from him.

I didn't mention Jack, but I told him the rest of it.

He held me.

"I don't know what we are to each other," I said.

He kissed me—my eyes, my cheeks, my mouth. "We're lovers, but more importantly, we're friends. We'll always be friends. Don't look back in sadness at what we had. We'll see each other again."

Ernesto and Carola picked me up at the airport.

I'd been calling Carola almost every day, but Ernesto knew we'd still want some time to catch up. He dropped us off and said he'd be back later.

The first things I saw were the vases of flowers everywhere. Ernesto had cut them in the garden and Carola had arranged them to welcome me back. A large flat bowl crowded with roses sat on the coffee table. Their beauty made me think of that wonderful day at the flower market in Ottawa.

I went over to smell their fragrance, but I sighed when I saw the mountain of mail piled up next to them. Carola had stopped forwarding it when she knew I was coming home. The bills had gone to my bank, and the grocery store and department store sale flyers had been recycled, but the rest of this had to be dealt with.

"There's one on top you might be interested in," Carola said.

"It can't be from René already."

"No, not from René. From Ungavaq."

I picked it up.

The strong, masculine lines hinted at who'd written it. My heart did a little flip-flop.

"Oh, Carola!"

"It came today."

I tore the envelope open. I was right. It was from Jack.

I hadn't expected to hear from him while he was at the dig, and then, bit by bit, I'd stopped expecting to hear from him at all.

Suddenly, my heart was racing.

It was a short letter dated the previous week. He wrote:

> Hello, Anne,
>
> I enjoyed talking to you when you were here. I hope you might like an update on what I've been doing. I've been back in Ungavaq for almost a week.
>
> We had a productive time at the dig and actually finished what I wanted to accomplish earlier than I thought we would. The students were ecstatic to get back to where they could get hot baths, and I was glad to have a shave. If you didn't recognize me before, you really wouldn't have known me when I got back. I looked like a wild man. You should have seen me. Maybe you'd have liked me better that way.
>
> I'm cleaning and cataloguing the artifacts. I'll be working on that and on the rough draft of a paper on the dig until early December. We made some interesting finds there, including your caribou, so I plan to work that paper into a book on the site. I'll be taking a semester off from teaching in the spring to finish the writing.
>
> Another group of students will be arriving at Ungavaq in December. These five will be older. They're graduate students from different universities who are considering specializing in Arctic anthropology. I'll be giving them a four-week course in cold-weather survival.
>
> I miss you even more than I thought I would.
>
> Jack

I read it to Carola.

"Well," she said, "that's a nice letter."

I stood for a few moments looking at it. I guess I'd hoped for something different—something more. I set it down and said, "Let's go unpack."

Carola worked on one suitcase while I did the other. I put two or three things away, then stopped. I almost felt as though I was going to cry with disappointment.

"I thought maybe he'd say . . ." "But I didn't know what I'd thought he might say. "He's been on my mind from the first day I met him, but I don't have any sense of how he feels."

"He's in Canada. You're here. Does it matter how he feels?"

"I didn't think it would, but it does."

"What kind of romance can you have with someone in another country?" She unpacked my raincoat and gave it a shake before she laid it on a chair to go to the hall closet. "I thought you were just thinking about some kind of fling. You had that with René. You're home now. The thing with Jack didn't work out."

"Well, my time with René was more than a fling, but still, there's Jack. It doesn't feel over to me, but I don't know what Jack feels." I took another pair of slacks out of the suitcase and hung them up.

"You know he likes you."

"Oh, yes. We had too much fun for me not to know that—but as anything other than a sister? That I don't know."

"No sense of that at all?"

"No."

"Did he flirt with you?"

"No." I stood again, thinking about it. "Well, I'm not sure. Sometimes I thought maybe there was something. He held my hand. He said that thing about me making the flowers at that market more beautiful."

"Anne, you are wearing a wedding ring. That's a sign that you're not available."

"He knows I'm a widow. The ring didn't slow up René."

"Jack isn't René. Did you flirt with him to let him know you were interested?"

"No. I was afraid I'd embarrass him."

Carola rolled her eyes. "¡No seas tonta!"

"I'm not foolish. He's from a different culture. I don't know what the rules are for him."

"Oh, Anne, give me a break. He does live in Ottawa. He can't be totally oblivious to the signals."

The kettle's whistle saved me from having to respond. Carola left the room, carrying the raincoat with her. When she returned, she brought a tray with two cups of tea.

I stirred in sugar and milk. "I thought about really kissing him—not just that peck on the cheek."

"There'd have been no way he could have missed *that* signal. You should have done it."

"Yes, maybe I should have. Maybe I should have given him a kiss good-bye, but he told me that Inuit don't show affection in public."

"His mother and Laura were there."

"Yes."

"Then it's not unusual he didn't try to kiss you. I guess it's something that he held your hand. I'd say, judging by the way he closed his letter, he's not thinking of you as a sister. *You* may be missing some signals."

"Maybe. I sure don't think of him as a brother."

"It sounds like you think about him a lot, though."

"I think about his hands. They fascinated me."

"Why?"

"He's similar to Robby in some ways—especially his eyes—but his hands are completely different. Robby's hands were slender. His fingers were long and tapered. They were like his mother's. You remember."

"Yes."

"I used to tease him that they were piano player's hands because he could span so many keys on a keyboard." I spread my fingers out to show her.

"What are Jack's hands like?"

"They're short and broad. His fingertips are blunt, the knuckles prominent. His hands look muscular and powerful. I was surprised at his gentleness the few times he touched me. . . ." I realized my voice had trailed off.

"No, you don't think of him like a brother, do you? Just thinking about him makes you dreamy."

"Yes, daydreams. Sometimes I even wonder whether his hands would feel different on my body."

"Different?"

"Than Robby's."

"Or René's?" she said as she pulled one of my lacy slips out of the suitcase. "Wow! This is gorgeous. Is this what you bought to wear for him?"

I blushed. "Yes."

She lifted out the rest of the underwear piece by piece and inspected it.

"Dig down a little more," I said.

She did and found a package wrapped in silver paper.

"Open it," I said. "It's for you."

She opened the package carefully. "Oh, Anne, these are beautiful. But I can't wear something like this around my grandchildren."

I'd bought a powder blue lace nightgown and peignoir for her at Lingerie a la Mode. "Oh, I hadn't thought of that," I said with a little smile. "I'd sort of thought you'd wear them around Ernesto."

"You've just made him a very happy man," she said with a giggle. "And I bet you made René happy too. You and Robby were always very physical. You kissed and touched so much in public, it wasn't difficult to guess what you did in private. I think you missed that. I think it's good that you met René."

"But I still think about Jack. I imagine what it might be like with him. I feel terribly guilty, though. I feel like I've been unfaithful to Robby, and now I want to be unfaithful to René."

"Anne, Robby's gone. You're not being unfaithful. He'd want this for you. He loved you too much to want you to be lonely. And René told you what the limits were. You don't owe him anything."

"He just wants to be a friend."

"Ha! You treat your friends that way? I'm going to have to watch out when you're around Ernesto." We both laughed.

"You know what I mean. He wanted it to be casual, but it really was much more than that. We just didn't talk about that part."

"You want something like that with Jack?"

"No, It's more than casual for me already. I just don't know how much more. I feel like a teenager again, Carola—so unsure of myself. Here I am having heart palpitations over a man a continent away. It doesn't make sense."

"Well, it does make sense if you want him. Planes fly every day. Go back when he's in Ottawa. Have your fling with him. I doubt he'd turn you down. Find out what you really want. René's a complication, but you could work that out." She turned to put the underwear away in a drawer.

I sat on the edge of the bed. "It's more difficult than that. I learned enough in that anthropology class to know that different cultures have different rules about who appropriate partners are. I have no idea how Jack's family might categorize a relationship between us. We're not related by blood, but we are kin. That or the fact I'm not Inuit might make a relationship between us forbidden."

She sat next to me. "They didn't disapprove of Brendan and Ivala. I think you're just afraid. Anyway, you're not thinking about marrying him, are you? What you and he do in private in Ottawa is your own business, not his family's."

"I don't know what I'm thinking." I looked down at my rings—rings Robby had given me more than thirty-six years ago. "I do know something. I didn't take these off for René, but I have to for Jack." I took them off my left hand and put them on my right.

Carola put her arm around me. We sat quietly until my tears subsided.

"You're more serious about this than I thought," she said. "I guess you're ready to think about the future."

"I don't know if I'll ever see him again. I can't drop in on him in Ungavaq or even in Ottawa just to see how things are going."

"In fact, you could."

"But he hasn't asked to see me again. The letter seems to say he'll be too busy to see me."

"It does seem like that, except for the closing. That was a lot more personal."

"I don't know what he feels for me."

"I guess that's the disadvantage of caring about someone who's been brought up not to show emotion. But, nobody can suppress emotion entirely. He's just going to be harder to read than you're used to. You're going to need to learn how to see those signals."

"I don't know what to do."

With a shrug, she said, "At least you're relatives, so, if nothing else, you can send him a Christmas card." She chuckled.

"Ah, you're making fun of me now."

"Yes, because you sound so helpless and resigned. But you're wrong about something. Things have changed since we were teenagers. I don't think you can follow those old rules. You can't stay by the phone and wait for him to call. You need to take a risk. Let him know how you feel."

I stewed about this for a few days. I wanted to take Carola's advice, but I thought again, for the millionth time, about what he'd said about my emotions making him uncomfortable. Then I thought, *He's attuned to subtle signals. I'll try that first.*

I wrote him a sort of newsy letter telling him about what René and I'd found out about Brendan and about taking the summer school classes. I closed by saying I missed him too, and I hoped to see him again someday soon. I underlined "soon." I had another thought. I remembered what he'd said about the women who'd thought he was some kind of savage. I added a p.s.: I vote for clean-shaven.

Ten days later I had a bonanza—a letter from Jack and an email from René. Jack wrote:

Dear Anne,

I just received your letter. I'm writing this reply while Laura waits, so it will be short. I thought maybe you'd like to come back to Ungavaq in December and join my students in the four-week class. It might give you a more complete view of what Brendan's life was like during the time he was here.

You've seen Ungavaq in the summer, but the winter is very different. If you're interested, I can meet you in Ottawa and help you buy the clothes you'll need. I'll lend you the necessary equipment, including a sleeping bag, so you don't have to buy that. You'll need to register in the class so you'll be covered by our insurance, but you don't need to pay tuition. You can go as my guest. I'll take care of the formalities.

Think it over and let me know.
I miss you,
Jack

He'd included a printed copy of the course description from the Carleton catalogue. It read:

> Seminar in Arctic Adaptation - Dr. Jack O'Malley
> December 6, 2004—January 5, 2005
> Students will participate in a four-week Arctic living experience.
> Equipment and food will be provided. Students must provide their own cold-weather clothing, sleeping bags, and personal necessities.
> The class will focus on methods of cultural adaptation to a severe climate.
> Historical and current adaptations will be considered.
> For further information . . .

I called Carola.

"Well, that's some kind of signal. Is it what you had in mind?" She laughed.

"If you can't be serious, I'm not going to read my letters to you."

"Any man who wants you to survive in the Arctic must be interested in you in some way. You just have to figure out what it is. Maybe he wants someone to keep him warm. I'll bet you could warm him up."

"You stop that!" I was laughing too much at this point to have much authority in my voice.

"I don't know what to make of this letter, Carola. He hasn't exactly asked me on a date. On the other hand, he can't invite me to the movies. Still, a cold-weather survival course . . ."

"What are you going to do?"

I was used to other people making decisions for me. Robby had always done that, and Carola. She's really the one who decided I'd go to Ottawa, and even there, René was the one who decided I'd go to Ungavaq. This time, I had to decide. I guess, finally, my sense of Jack's competence coupled with my desire to see him again convinced me to accept.

"I'm going."

When I read René's email, I found I wouldn't have had to worry about how to see Jack again because René gave me the perfect excuse. He'd continued our research and had found something exciting—a record of a box stored in the military archives. The document listed it as the "worldly possessions of Warrant Officer Brendan O'Malley, deceased." It'd been in storage since 1919, to be released only to next of kin.

The Army thought Brendan had died sometime before 1919, but he was alive until 1923—another mystery! Now, despite the fact that eighty-five years had passed since that box had been deposited in the archive, they still needed the signature of the next of kin to release it. When René explained the situation, the military archivist said he wasn't in a position to decide whether Jack, as son of the elder son by blood, or I, as widow of the younger son born of a marriage, was the legitimate heir. He'd require both signatures or a court order before he'd release the box. Thank goodness for bureaucracy.

I wrote to Jack explaining the situation, accepting his invitation to go "cold-weather camping," and asking if he could meet me in late November in Ottawa to sign for the box and look at the contents.

Now, at the end of September, November suddenly seemed a long time away.

CHAPTER Eleven

THE WHEELS OF THE PLANE FINALLY TOUCHED DOWN AT THE Ottawa airport.

As usual, everything seemed to slow down as soon as we landed. All those people who stand up at the first possible moment and then wait, making the rest of us feel trapped and uncomfortable, followed their usual pattern. I could never figure out why they didn't relax and wait a few moments more until the doors were open and people could file out.

When I finally had my turn, I carried my purse and overnight bag to the front of the plane and claimed my coat from the attendant. I stepped out of the plane to a chorus of, "Have a nice day." The chilly air in the jetway gave welcome relief from the warmth of the airplane cabin.

I'd spent most of the flight thinking about the reunion ahead. Whenever I thought about what I wished would happen with Jack, I remembered him saying that my emotions made him uncomfortable. What was I going to do about him? And what was I going to do about René? I didn't have any answers.

I found my luggage on the carousel and walked over to stand in the Customs and Immigration line.

I knew Jack and René were in the waiting area ahead. They'd both wanted to meet me. I hadn't known what to do. Finally, I'd called René.

He must have heard something in my voice. "Don't worry about it. I'll take care of everything," he'd said.

In spite of my misgivings, I was eager to be with both of them again. It seemed to take forever to get through the processing.

They stepped forward as I came through the doorway. Jack came up to me, half a step ahead of René, and said softly, "Clean shaven, as requested," took my hand in his, and touched it to his cheek.

"Very nice," I said. I felt my cheeks redden. I had to remember to breathe.

Then he hugged me!

That hug felt just as I'd imagined a thousand times it would. He was warm and strong. His skin was smooth. I was aware of every inch of his body. He smelled wonderful, not of cologne or shaving lotion, but just of himself. I forgot about all the people brushing past us rushing to gates or taxis. I stopped hearing the echo-y announcements on the p.a. system. For a moment, I even forgot that René was there.

I didn't know what the hug meant, though. Jack didn't ask questions in Ungavaq. He did in Ottawa. Maybe the hugging was like that. Maybe it didn't mean anything. Maybe it was just Ottawa manners, but I hoped it was more than that.

René started to give me a big kiss, but he felt me pull back a little, so he toned it down. When he stepped back, he said, "What a beautiful necklace, Anne. Is that Inuit ivory?"

I was wearing the ivory caribou on a fine gold chain. "Yes. Jack made it for me."

René's face fell. I might as well have just slapped him. He looked at me for a moment, nodded, turned, and said, "Jack, that's beautiful work." Before I knew it, they were deep in a discussion of the problems of carving walrus ivory.

I didn't want it to be this way, but René had just shown me how he wanted to handle it. No regrets. He'd told me before that that's how it had to be. I had no choice but to follow his lead.

"Ahem, you two. I don't want to interrupt this fascinating discussion, but I do have some suitcases to take care of."

René smiled. "OK, OK." He turned to pick up my suitcases. "What's this?"

"That's my coat."

He picked it up from where it had been lying on top of a suitcase. He and Jack looked at it.

"Didn't you bring a warm coat?" René asked.

"That is my warm coat."

"Ah. I don't think so," he said. "Warm in San Diego and warm in Ottawa are two different things, eh? It's cold out there, and the wind's blowing."

"Let's walk to the Tim Horton's over there," Jack said. "If you two don't mind waiting, I want to get something from the car."

I chose a table that didn't look too sticky. René offered me tea, but I'd had some on the plane. I cleaned off the napkins and soda cups the previous occupants had left and sat. He strolled over to the counter to buy himself coffee and a couple of honey crullers. He was one of those people who could eat endless amounts and never put on a pound. When he got back, he gave me half of one of the crullers, and then we just talked about my flight and the weather until I said, "I was wondering. . . ."

"What?"

"Oh, never mind." I was fiddling with the little packets of sugar and sweetener, lining them up with the labels facing the same way. Suddenly, my palms were sweating. I couldn't look at him.

His chair creaked as he leaned forward. "What?"

I finally managed to say, "I was going to ask you what you and Jack have been talking about." I raised my eyes from the table.

He looked nonplussed for a moment. Then he settled back into his chair and looked at me thoughtfully. "Ah, Anne. Not about us, if that's what you're worried about. . . . You and I are friends. We're going to need to talk about this."

"René, I don't think you want to hear this."

"I need to hear it."

I just looked at him. I knew I was hurting him, and I didn't want to.

"Look," he said. "I knew someone else would come along. I was hoping it wouldn't be quite so soon. You must know I love you."

"I never thought we'd say the words."

"Well, I am saying them." He shook his head and smiled. "I made a mistake. I don't allow that to happen. I usually spend time with women with whom that won't be an issue, but with you . . ." he shook his head again, "my heart conquered me."

I looked down again. I didn't know what to say.

"Anne, look at me," he said gently.

I looked up. He took my hands in his and kissed them tenderly.

"We're not children. We knew how things were. I wouldn't have been willing to give up the joy of loving you to avoid this. And there's no way to avoid it, because, no matter what I might want, I still can't offer you anything more than friendship. I think if I were to offer you more, you wouldn't say yes, but I can't afford to be jealous of Jack. I can't make the choices I've made in my life and be jealous of the choices other people make."

"Oh, René." I started to cry.

"Let's just talk. Tell me what you're thinking right now."

It took me some time to calm down enough to talk. I was afraid I was embarrassing him, but he obviously didn't care what passers-by thought. He handed me a handkerchief, and I blotted my eyes.

"I don't know where to start. I'm still so confused. This whole business with Ungavaq and Jack has just turned me upside down."

"I knew there was something. When I met you in May, you were so sad and quiet. We had fun together, but there was always that undercurrent of sadness, eh? When you introduced Jack to me, I could see that things had changed for you. That's good. I want you to be happy. But I'll miss you, and I'll be here if things don't work out with Jack."

"René, I don't know what to say."

He just nodded. "It really is OK."

"Why did you think things were different after I came back from Ungavaq?"

"Because you were different. You were really different when you came back at the end of July. You were happier, but at the same time,

I could see there was something else, some kind of turmoil. You didn't say anything. I didn't think I should ask."

"But you still kissed me, and you made love to me."

"Why wouldn't I? I like kissing you. I like making love to you. If I get another chance, I'll kiss you again, and I'll do whatever else you'll let me do. I'm a gentleman, but I'm not a fool."

"René, I've been so lonely. It started even before Robby died, when his health began to fail. I thought if I loved him enough, he wouldn't leave. I knew that wasn't true, really. Still, I felt like I'd failed him somehow."

"Life isn't that easy," he said quietly. "If love were enough, my sister wouldn't be the way she is."

"I'm sorry. I'm being self-centered and thoughtless."

He shook his head. "How do Jack and Ungavaq fit in with this?"

"I want something. I want a family." I shook my head. "I don't know what I want, but I feel, again, like I'm failing Robby. It's as if I'm saying to Robby that what we had wasn't enough."

"Was it enough—what you had with Robby?"

"It was then, but when I went to Ungavaq, I felt like I'd come home. They seemed to like me and want me. And there's Jack. I don't know where my life is going." I hadn't meant to say all this to him, but once I started, I couldn't seem to stop.

"Has he said anything to you?"

"No. I don't even know if he could be interested in a non-Inuit."

He thought for a few moments. Then, he said, "You can afford to wait. You're not alone anymore because you have me, and you have that family, no matter what. The worst that could happen would be that Jack would only be your friend."

"Just wait? But what about Jack?"

"You've spent a lot of time with him. Has he ever mentioned another woman?"

"No."

"Just wait. See what happens."

"Carola said I shouldn't wait; I should take a risk."

"I don't know what she had in mind, but somehow spending four weeks in survival training seems to fit the bill. I think you need to let things develop."

"It's what I've been telling myself, but it's difficult."
"Yes," he said, "it is."

Jack was gone about ten minutes. When he came back, he carried a large plastic bag. "I came prepared for any possibility," he said and handed the bag to me.

I wondered if my eyes were all red and puffy, but he didn't comment.

I opened the bag and took out a coat—a hooded parka—teal blue, almost the same color as the dress I'd worn when Jack and I'd gone out for dinner that first time.

"I didn't think you'd know how cold it would be when you got here. If you don't like it, we can always return it, but at least it'll get you from here to the car. Try it on."

I did. It fit perfectly. I did a little twirl to model it for them. René—standing slightly behind Jack—nodded.

"How did you know what size to get?" I asked.

"I just described you. The saleslady figured it out."

"It's perfect. Thank you for being so thoughtful."

René said with a chuckle, "I guess it's safe for us to walk from here to the car now, but you're going to have to do something about those shoes too." He pointed at my high heels. "Jack, you don't happen to have a few pairs of boots in your car, do you?"

Jack laughed. "No luck, there." We walked toward the exit.

When I got out at my hotel, René said, "We were hoping you might be free for dinner tonight. Do you happen to have an open space on your social calendar?"

"I can probably work you in."

"We'll be back at seven."

René arrived first, a few minutes early. He called from the lobby. I went down to meet him.

"Is Jack here yet?" he asked, as he looked around.

"Not yet."

"Come with me."

He took me to the little alcove off the lobby where the pay phones were. It gave us a little privacy. There, as he'd said he would, he kissed me, and it was the kiss he hadn't given me at the airport. He held me in his arms for a long time. We didn't say anything. Then, he gently brushed the tears off my cheeks, and we went back out to the lobby.

He had his arm around me when Jack arrived. As Jack walked up to us, though, René stepped back.

After a moment's hesitation, Jack stepped forward and offered me his arm.

We walked the short distance to Le Seine, a restaurant they each liked.

The temperature had dropped to near freezing. I was glad I had my new coat.

We had a good French dinner. We sat in a high-backed booth that gave us a feeling of privacy. The *coq au vin* was a nice change from the mystery-meat sandwich I'd had on the plane.

My mind just whirled through the whole meal. Being single was a lot more complicated than I'd remembered.

The next morning, as I waited for Jack to pick me up at ten, I was tense wondering what time alone with him would be like.

It turned out to be like spending time with your brother. He was friendly—he did hug me—but nothing more. He reminded me of our fictive relationship and teased me about being sensitive about my age.

The military archive was in the same building where René worked. All that time he and I'd been working together, that box had been down in the basement waiting for us.

We met him in his fifth-floor office. It looked much the same as it had before, except that a huge Christmas cactus in full scarlet bloom had replaced his usual orchid.

My mind whirled, as it had the night before. I hadn't anticipated that going into his office would remind me so strongly of the kisses and other intimacies we'd shared there.

We headed down to pick up the box. I wondered if Jack felt as tense as I did. This could be the answer to all our questions, or it could be nothing. I didn't see any tension in him, but maybe I wouldn't recognize it if I saw it. I had goose bumps.

In the basement, Jack and I showed identification and signed the release. We were handed a well-worn cardboard box, sealed with ancient, yellowed tape.

We returned to René's office and set the box on the worktable. René slit the tape with scissors. .

We could see several official-looking documents and a water- and-mud-stained old-style canvas backpack. The first document was a much-faded carbon copy of a receipt showing that articles had changed hands in Germany in 1918 from the Germans to the British. It also stated that the items had been found at the site of a plane crash in Germany in 1917.

The Germans had found one body, that of the pilot, in the wreckage and had assumed the things found at the site belonged to him. The artifacts were handed over to the British under his name. The British archivist had done a careful inventory and realized these had to be the possessions of not one, but two people. He finally tracked down enough information to state that the plane also had a passenger—Brendan—then listed as "missing in action."

The English pilot's family had picked up his possessions. The remaining items took months to go from England to Canada. Archivists had created documents each time they changed hands. One of the documents changed Brendan's status from "missing" to "presumed dead."

I'd been looking for a plane crash. The documents solved that mystery and created many more. What happened to Brendan after the crash—and before it, for that matter? If this were the crash mentioned in his medical records, he was severely injured. Had he escaped the area before the Germans found him? Who'd nursed his injuries? And what was he doing in Germany in the first place?

René lifted out the backpack and under it a rolled-up blanket and a canteen. He undid the buckles of the backpack, removed its contents one by one, and laid them out in a row on the table. They included some articles of clothing—several pairs of socks, underwear, handkerchiefs, and a shirt—a comb, a straight razor, shaving soap—dry and cracked with age—and a brush, a small tarnished mirror, a toothbrush, a can of toothpowder, matches in a tin, a coiled length of rope, several well-used maps, and a compass.

"It looks like he planned to take a long hike," Jack said.

None of this really told us anything about Brendan. I began to lose hope of finding anything of significance.

The next items out, a pistol and a cloth bag of ammunition, got my attention.

Jack checked the pistol. "It's unloaded."

"I guess it's not surprising he had that," I said. "Brendan was a soldier in a time of war."

"But it's a Luger," René said. "That's a German pistol, not a British one. Why would he have had that?"

"Maybe it's a war souvenir," Jack said.

The final item—a leather-bound pocket diary—was the prize.

"It's in a language I don't recognize, maybe a code," René said. "I don't understand why this is with the backpack. I'd have thought the Germans would have handed it over to their cryptographers to decode. How could they have overlooked it? Anne, does this mean anything to you?"

I looked at a few pages of the neatly written script. It made no sense at all, but at the same time, it was familiar. I handed it to Jack. "I don't know what it is, but I have a book with similar writing at home. Robby always kept it in his desk because it was in his father's handwriting. It came to him as part of his father's estate. He took it out from time to time to look at it, but he never was able to translate it."

Jack looked at it for a moment and a broad smile came across his face. "I guess we've found Brendan. I don't think anyone else could have written this. It's phonetic Inuktitut—not what I learned from Marcia; it's his own system, but it's close enough that I'm sure I can figure out what it says."

Tucked into the back of the diary were German identity papers. René spoke some German. He was able to translate for us. The papers were for a "Werner Schultz" and included a photo of a handsome and vigorous-looking young man. They identified Schultz as a wounded and honorably discharged veteran.

A second photo was proof positive the backpack had belonged to Brendan. I recognized the man and woman in the photo as Brendan's father and mother because I had a duplicate of it in our family album in San Diego.

Wheels began to turn in my mind. "Werner Schultz" was Brendan. The photos I'd previously seen of him were like the ones I'd given to Maata. They'd been taken after he'd married Robby's mother, Isabelle. By that time, he looked ill and gaunt. It saddened me to think of the things that must have happened to this handsome young man in the seven years from the date on the ID card to the time of the photos I'd seen.

I told Jack who the people were. He gazed for a long time at his grandfather and great-grandparents. He was going to put the photos back in the box, but I told him to put them in his pocket to show to Maata and his sisters.

At first, I couldn't think why Brendan's photo would be on Werner Schultz's identification papers, but something flashed into my mind—Brendan's secret military promotion. I reminded René and Jack of that. "I think there's a possibility Brendan was a spy."

"I can't think of any other reason why he'd have false identity papers, especially German ones, in a time of war," Jack said. "The answer may be in this pocket diary. I'll work on translating it into English. We'll see what we find."

René had a new archival storage box. We shifted the blanket, canteen, backpack, and documents into the newer box and took it with us when we went to lunch.

CHAPTER
Twelve

We had lunch at the same coffee shop where René and I had often gone—memories everywhere.

As René rose to return to work, Jack said, "We'll call you as soon as the translation is finished."

René leaned over and kissed me on the cheek. "I'll look forward to it."

After he left, Jack said, "Well, we have to find something to do with you."

"I suppose I'll just go back to the hotel."

"You can't sit in that hotel room until I finish the translation. Come spend the day at my condo instead."

My heart rate shot up. "I'd love to."

"I arrived yesterday too. I didn't have time to get groceries. Let's swing by the store and get a few things so I can at least offer you a cup of tea."

We stopped at the supermarket and spent the next forty-five minutes selecting a lot more than tea.

As we picked over some mushrooms, he said, "When I first came to Ottawa, I wasn't used to eating much in the way of fruits and vegetables."

"I didn't see much you could eat in Ungavaq, other than berries."

"A special treat was caribou intestine with the contents included, but that was about the extent of my exposure to produce."

"Oh, Jack. I'm trying to be open-minded, but caribou intestine—ugh!"

"What's the matter with intestines? You eat them."

"No."

"I've seen you eat sausage."

"Yes."

"Sausage casing is intestine."

"No!"

"Yes."

"Oh."

"What we eat is just sort of a vegetable sausage."

"Tell me more about it, like what it's filled with."

He looked at me quizzically for a moment, then sort of shook his head and said, "Whatever the caribou ate: lichens, grass, moss, just about anything green, and maybe a rock or two." He stopped, looked at me again, and then smiled. "Ah! I just figured it out. You're not asking questions."

"I'm trying not to."

"You started at the airport, now that I think about it."

"Yes. I thought asking questions might be one of the things I do that's uncomfortable for you. I think it must be hard enough to be with me. I just thought I'd try to make things easier."

"You're not hard to be with. You've never been hard to be with. Don't think that."

"I think I should do it. Not ask questions, I mean. It's difficult, though. I have to watch what I say every minute."

"Do you want to know a secret?"

A question! "Yes."

"All the education I got was to train me to ask questions. That's what scientists do. It's not easy for me to avoid questions, either, and I've been practicing for sixty years. When we're together, just the two of us, let's not worry about it. In Ungavaq, we can do it, but not here."

"You really mean that?"

"Yes."

"OK. Can we talk more about food? I guess you had to be open-minded when you came here. I'll just have to try harder when you talk about things like vegetable sausages."

"I wasn't open-minded at all. Food was a big problem. There wasn't much in Ottawa similar to what I considered home cooking. In the village, I'd tried a few of the canned foods Marcia brought for special occasions, but it took her a long time to convince me to try things in Ottawa."

"What were you willing to eat?"

"Raw beef—it looked enough like caribou—raw fish, raw eggs, berries. I liked sweets, especially ice cream, but I was resistant to other things. Maybe 'stubborn' is a better word. I didn't make things easy for Marcia that first month. I think if it had been possible to send me home, she might have done it."

"But she didn't."

"No, and I liked most things when I finally did try them. I can get fruits and vegetables in Ungavaq now, but it's the limited selection Laura brings in each week. One of my greatest pleasures here in Ottawa is the abundance of fresh fruits and vegetables. I never pass up a chance to try something new."

We spent a long time talking over the merits of the assorted produce, and we enjoyed every minute of it.

Things were going smoothly until Jack bent down to pick up a bunch of radishes I'd dropped. When he straightened up, I saw that he was wearing something on a chain. It had slipped out from under his shirt.

"Jack, is that an amulet like mine?"

He looked embarrassed. "A little different." He tucked it back under his shirt.

I didn't say anything more.

Jack's condo was like his office—compact and simply decorated. Again, there were the floor-to-ceiling bookcases filled with books and artifacts. These flanked a large south-facing window that framed a breathtaking view of the Rideau River. I could see Carleton University and the Rideau Canal where we'd gone canoeing in June. Jack said he could walk to work along the canal-side path, or even skate to work on the canal in winter.

The living room furniture was upholstered in bright, warm colors—reds and yellows with a touch of green—not surprising since he was usually here during the cold, dark winter months. The window took maximum advantage of the winter sun.

"Have you lived here long?"

"Eight years. It's my second bachelor home in Ottawa. We lived in an apartment during the first years we were married. When Kaiyuina decided not to come to Ottawa any more, I moved to a smaller place that didn't have memories connected to it."

"Ah, you did love her, didn't you?"

"Yes." His voice had softened. "But she could never feel that way about me." He shook his head, clearing away those sad memories of the past. "Anyway, I bought this condo to share with the children when they started college. It's actually bigger than it looks. It has a large kitchen, a separate dining room, and three bedrooms. When the children got older, they decided they'd rather share apartments with friends, so I'm on my own again. I use one of the extra bedrooms as an office and one as a guestroom. Would you like the ten-cent tour?"

"I'd love it."

He showed me through the condo. His bedroom was simple—a double bed, two bedside tables—one of them stacked with books—a chair, a big chest of drawers—nothing else. The bed was covered with one of those beautiful Hudson's Bay point blankets, creamy white with one broad stripe each of green, red, yellow, and indigo. I laughed at myself when I wondered how many women had slept under that blanket and whether I'd ever be one of them. I'd come a long way from that day in May when I'd been so shocked by René's kiss.

"This is so different from the way you live in Ungavaq. Do you get lonely here?"

"I do. But there are compensations. I can't go to a concert in Ungavaq or to a library. In a way, I have the best of both worlds."

We went back to the kitchen and put the groceries away. He prepared some tea. We sat at his kitchen table drinking it.

"I've been waiting for the right moment to give you something." I reached into my purse, pulled out a box, and held it out to him.

He took it, opened the lid, and lifted out a pocket watch and chain.

"It was Brendan's," I said. "His father gave it to him when he turned twenty-one. He left it to Robby. I know Robby would want you to have it. We had it cleaned on a regular basis. If you want to wind it, I'm sure it'll work."

Jack cradled the watch in his hand.

"You should see what's inside."

He opened the front cover. A portrait of a young Inuit woman was engraved inside.

"I think Brendan engraved it, and that's your grandmother."

Jack didn't say anything. I could see he didn't trust himself to talk. After a while, he said, "Yes, that is my grandmother. I remember her. She was an old woman, but her face hadn't changed much."

"What happened when Brendan didn't return?"

"She married again—twice, in fact. An Inuit woman had to be practical. A woman with a child could never survive without a husband. But I think Brendan was the love of her life. She never talked about him. Mother said it made her sad."

"Her life was unhappy?"

"I don't think so. I think that just made her a little sad. Life can be hard, you know. You just make the best of it."

"Tell me more about her."

"My mother told me her second marriage was unhappy. Her husband beat her, and he beat my father. When she gave birth to their daughter, he put the baby in the cold to die. He didn't want daughters."

"Did she rescue the baby?"

"No, that wasn't an option for her."

"Oh! How awful."

"Yes. She wasn't with him long, though. My grandmother had a widespread reputation for the quality of her sewing as well as her other skills as a wife. Her third husband took her away."

"Took her away?"

"Yes, by force. He fought for her."

"By force?"

"Yes, if a man could take a woman, she was his."

"I thought Inuit don't fight."

"They don't fight about little things. A wife was not a little thing."

"Because of the sewing."

"Yes. Men didn't fight much, but when they did, usually someone died."

"Was there a death this time?"

"Yes, so they had to leave the area for a few years until the anger of the second husband's family had cooled. Her third husband was a good father. He treated my father like his own son. My grandmother had three children with him: my aunt and my two uncles. When her third husband died, they came to live with us. My father was an excellent hunter and could support all those people."

"So the gap in your knowledge of your family is Brendan."

"Yes. I'm glad we're doing this research. I don't hold out much hope, though, that it'll answer the questions I really want answered."

"What questions?"

"Why did he abandon her? Why didn't he come back? Did he ever intend to come back? I've wondered about that all my life. My father did too."

"Are you thinking, maybe, that he didn't intend to come back because she was Inuit?"

He looked down and said, very softly, "Yes."

"I don't think that can have been it."

He looked at me. "Why do you say that?"

"I didn't know Brendan, but I did know Robby's mother, Isabelle. She would never have loved a man who would do something like that."

He sat quietly for a minute or so. I guess he was thinking about what I'd said. He shook his head. "Well, I'd better get to work. Thank you for the watch."

He went to his office to start the translation while I looked through the books in the bookcases. I selected Peter Freuchen's *Book of the Eskimo* and settled down on the comfortable sofa to read.

After an hour or so, I took Jack another cup of tea. I could hear him singing softly to himself. He was sitting at his desk with the diary in front of him, the watch sitting open next to it. I could hear it ticking. I put the cup down.

"Sit a minute. I want to read something to you. It's the first entry in the diary."

I sat in the easy chair next to the desk.

He swung his swivel chair around so he could face me. "*Tuesday, March 16, 1915*—I was sworn in today. Now I'm a soldier. This is the proudest day of my life. I'm an American and don't have a dog in this fight, but I'll become a Canadian when I spend my life with you, my dearest wife, Ivala." He stopped.

"Ah, Jack. There it is, first thing. He did love her. He did intend to go back. She was his wife."

"Yes. The diary is a love letter to her."

"It's so sad that she never knew." Oh, emotion. I can't seem to avoid it.

"Yes. . . ." He changed the subject. "I guess I'm not a good host. I walked away and left you on your own. What did you find to do?"

"Oh, I've been poking through your book cases. There's a lifetime of interesting reading there."

"I'm beginning to think I'll either have to get rid of some or move to a bigger condo." While he was talking, he rolled his shoulders a few times.

"Is your back tight?"

"A little."

"I can help with that. Swing around again."

He turned the chair so his back was to me. I walked over and started to massage his shoulders. The muscles were tight and knotted. *Why is he so tense? Am I making him uncomfortable again?* I kneaded his muscles and worked on the knots. As I worked, I murmured, "Jack, come on. . . . Relax. . . . Let me soothe them. . . . Just let go."

His shoulders continued to resist. But after a time he relaxed and leaned into my hands, almost as if he'd given himself to me.

Always before, it had been him touching me.

I softened the pressure and allowed myself to be more aware of how his body felt under my fingers. My hands were calm, but my mind wasn't. The more I touched him, the more I wanted to touch him.

I thought about reaching across his shoulder and sliding my hand down under the front of his shirt—touching his skin. It would have been so easy. I knew he would be smooth and warm and silky . . . and I knew I shouldn't.

I thought about running my tongue around the shell of his ear and taking the lobe between my lips and tasting him, and I wanted to do it. Oh, I wanted to, and I knew I shouldn't.

It was all I could do to keep from leaning over and kissing the back of his neck. I had no idea how he'd react if I did.

I stopped moving my hands. For a moment, I couldn't bring myself to take them off his shoulders. But I had to.

I sighed. "While you work on that, maybe I'll . . . make some dinner for us."

He took a deep breath—in and out. "That would be nice."

Reluctantly, I walked back to the living room and waited for my heartbeat to slow down.

When I'd calmed down, I poked through his kitchen cabinets to see what I could put together without my recipes and with the ingredients at hand. The kitchen was remarkably well stocked for someone who didn't cook.

I finally settled on making an omelet with a mushroom sauce, a tossed salad, and steamed broccoli. We'd bought a baguette and some frozen peaches. I made some garlic bread and used the fruit to make a cobbler for dessert.

The whole time I cooked, I thought about what I'd wanted to do to him and what I wanted him to do to me. I kept telling myself I just couldn't go on this way, I had to calm down, and then I'd think of him again.

I put the food on the table and called him to eat. I was pleased to see he was impressed. He had seconds of the cobbler. I gave myself a silent pat on the back.

As we cleared the table, Jack asked, "Do you want to spend some time with René tonight? You didn't have any time to be alone with him this morning. Maybe you'd like to call him and plan something."

I guess I looked blank.

"It's OK," he said. "I could take a break in the translating and drive you back to your hotel if it's inconvenient for him to pick you up here."

"We're going to see him tomorrow, aren't we?" Then I understood. "Oh, I get it. You think René and I are dating or something." *Oh, wow. What do I do now?*

"Yes. Aren't you?"

"No, René and I don't go out in the evenings. He takes care of his sister most of the time." *Well, sort of true.*

"You don't ever go out?"

My mother said you go to Hell for lying. I hope not. "We've gone out to dinner a couple of times, but it's difficult for him because he has to get someone to stay with her. He told me she's sweet and nice, but I think there's more to the story, because, for whatever reason, he's reluctant to leave her with anyone else. He and I don't date. We're friends."

"But I've seen how he kisses you."

No you haven't. "Oh, Jack. He's a Frenchman. He's exuberant. It didn't mean what you thought." *Forgive me, René.*

Jack looked at me for a moment.

Did he believe me?

"I guess I misjudged the situation," he said. "I'm glad. I mean, I'm glad he's your friend."

He went back to his translating while I put away the leftovers and cleaned up the kitchen.

I can't say I've never told a lie before, but I don't usually. I wondered, have I made a mistake? Maybe he won't trust me anymore. Maybe I should tell him the truth. God, I'm such a coward!

I put on some classical CDs I'd found and settled down to try to distract myself with more of *Book of the Eskimos*. I had trouble concentrating, though. I'd read a page or two, and then Freuchen would say something that made me think of Jack. I'd stop reading, and my mind would jump back to when I had my hands on him.

That went on for a long time. I must have dozed off. The next thing I knew I felt Jack gently stroking my hair and saying, "Anne, time for bed." I'd fallen asleep with the book open on my lap. When I heard his voice, for just a moment, I thought I was still in my dream.

"It's late," he said. "Why don't you just stay here tonight?"

I was half-asleep as he led me down the hall to the guestroom. There, he hugged me and kissed me gently on the cheek. Then he went off to his own room. Well, that was certainly more than "Ottawa manners."

He'd laid one of his shirts on the bed for me to use as a nightgown. As I lay in the bed wrapped in his shirt, drifting off to sleep again, I thought about that kiss. I thought about just walking down the hall and tapping on his door, . . . but I didn't dare.

The next morning, I woke up confused. It took me a while to realize where I was. It was still dark outside, but the sun rose late in November. The bedside clock showed 7:45. I got up, dressed, and went to the kitchen. I could smell hot butter and apples, and I could hear Jack singing "Oh, What a Beautiful Morning" all the way down the hall.

"Well, you certainly sound happy this morning."

"I am."

"Ah, you're cooking!"

"Well, I didn't expect you to do all of it."

"Your mother said you don't cook."

"She thinks I don't. Men don't cook in the village, but, of course, we always had to prepare our own food if we were hunting or traveling without women."

"Oh, I see. Your life is different here in every way."

He nodded.

"Those smell delicious."

"They're just camp food—apple pancakes."
"I'm glad I'm going camping with you."
"I'm glad you are too."
"Tell me about the diary."
"Well, what should I tell you? It's quite a story. It does carry us a few steps further in the search. Let's have these pancakes, and I'll read it to you."

We set the table and sat.

Jack read between bites.

CHAPTER Thirteen

He started the diary when he began his army basic training in Ottawa. He was twenty-four. Judging from the date on one of the archive documents, he made the last entry on the day before the crash.

"It took me longer than I expected to work out the translation. So many words and concepts didn't have Inuktitut equivalents. He worked out his own vocabulary by combining words. For example, we had no word for airplane, so he used something as simple as 'sky sled.' Some of them were harder, but I used the context to figure them out.

"I couldn't translate some of the words at all, though. They seemed like nonsense. I finally figured out what he did. When he wanted to use words for which there was no way to work out an Inuktitut equivalent, he reversed the English syllables and added Inuktitut syllables at the beginning and end and between the syllables of the word. I had a good laugh when I finally stumbled on to that trick.

"I've marked some passages to read to you. We'll read the whole thing later."

"It's exciting that I'm going to hear Brendan's own words," I said.

"Well, it's partly his words and partly me. That's the problem with translation. He originally thought in English. Then he translated it into the written Inuktitut he created. He was an American writing more than ninety years ago, and language changes. Now I've translated it back again, but I'm a Canadian of today. You really can't keep the translator out of it.

"Anyway, here we go. He was faithful in his diary keeping. He wrote almost every day, but I'm going to skip days as I read."

Tuesday, March 16, 1915—I was sworn in today. Now I'm a soldier. This is the proudest day of my life. I'm an American and don't have a dog in this fight, but I'll become a Canadian when I spend my life with you, my dearest wife, Ivala. I'm sure this war will be short and glorious for our side. The cowardly Hun will turn tail and run. I'll be home to you by next winter, or at the very latest, the winter after that, I'm sure. I've never kept a diary before. I'll do this so in future I can tell you what I was doing while I was away. I can put down my most private thoughts for you.

"Jack, is it OK for us to be reading this? He wrote this for her. Is it an invasion of their privacy?"

"I've thought a lot about that. There are things in here that are personal, but I do think if my grandfather were alive, he'd tell most of these stories. I told you about those songs. This is his legacy to us too—to you as much as to me."

"What about René?"

"I think it's OK. I don't think there's anything here for my grandfather to be ashamed of, certainly not how much he loved my grandmother. Let's read it. Then you tell me if it would be better not to

show it to René."
"All right."

Wednesday, March 17, 1915—I don't report until tomorrow. I'd forgotten what a city was like. Now I remember why I left Pittsburgh and Ottawa. I can't stand the noise and bustle. I'll write to my parents tonight. The recruiter gave me an address where they can write to me. What will they think? I wish I could write to you too. If I could have seen the future, I would have tried to teach you to read. But that's a vain thought now.

Sunday, March 21—After church, I had time for private reflection and remembrance. My heart is heavy. I miss you so much—the feel of you, the taste of you, the sound of you. I miss holding you in my arms. Oh, Ivala. There are times when I begin to think I've made a mistake. I didn't know how lonely I'd be away from you. When I come back to you, I'll never again go to the trading post without you. I couldn't stand to be separated from you for the weeks that would take.

Wednesday, March 24—Ivala, I long for your touch. I hope you can understand why I needed to go. Will you wait for me? Others in this company have surely left loves behind, but that's cold comfort. Some of them have photographs of their sweethearts. I'll have to keep your image in my heart.

"He really missed her, didn't he?"
"Yes. She was never far from his mind. Listen to this part."

Sunday, March 28—I took time to engrave your dear face inside the cover of my watch.

I clapped my hands with delight. "We were right!"
"Yes," he said with a big smile. "Here's how he did it."

I asked the base dentist if I could have some worn-out dental picks. He was kind enough to oblige me with two. I was able to sharpen them in the machine shop. I sat here thinking of you. Your face was as easy for me to see in my mind's eye as if you were here. I'm pleased with the likeness.

Monday, March 29—I've made a friend, Henri, a French Canadian from Montreal. He saw me engraving my watch and was interested. I was worried before that he might want to steal it—but not now that we're getting acquainted. He's like me, different from most of the other men.

Wednesday, March 31—Henri has agreed to teach me French, and I'll teach him how to engrave. We started today with some vocabulary. He taught me a few simple sentences. We've set a goal of carrying on our conversations in French as soon as I'm able. He gets tired of speaking English.

Saturday, April 3—Henri makes me work hard with the French. He has told me that tomorrow he'll no longer speak to me in English! I hope he doesn't mean it. I may have to learn pantomime. We walked into town to buy drawing pencils and paper. I was going to teach him engraving, but I found we have to do some of the basics first. He's never tried to draw before and doesn't understand the use of the pencil yet, nor how to shade or draw perspective.

Tuesday, April 6—I had a letter from my father today. I expected him to be angry. Instead, he said I'm doing the right thing. He and Mother are proud of me. They think America should be in the war. He says that in the army I'll gain knowledge of life and that I'm in for a great adventure. They're praying for my safety and good health. They expect me to do my duty and bring honor to myself and to the family. I'll do my best. I'll write to them tonight to tell them about my experiences so far.

Saturday, April 10—I've completed four weeks of basic training. So far it has been hard work and disagreeable at times, but overall not as bad as I expected. I'm able to do most of the drills and exercises without too much trouble. Tomorrow Henri and I plan to buy a French-language newspaper so I'll have a different way to practice my new skills.

Sunday, April 11— There's irony in the fact that I used to fight with the Catholic boys in school, and now my best friend is Catholic. Henri asked why we'd been fighting. It was just because they were Catholic, and we weren't. How foolish. I dreamed about you again last night, Ivala. You were lying on the caribou skins. I was touching you, loving you. How I miss you. Sometimes I dream that I'm a bird flying to you, and I can't fly fast enough. Know that my mind and my heart fly to you even if my body can't.

Saturday, April 17—We spent the whole day today being tested, with written exams in the morning and measurements of our physical abilities in the afternoon. I had not realized my life in the north made me so physically fit. Though I'm older than the others, I did better in all the physical challenges than they did.

Sunday, April 18—We bought another newspaper today. The news is no better in French than in English.

"Here's something a little different," Jack said. "He hadn't mentioned this before."

Wednesday, April 21—For the third night in a row, those men in the mess hall harassed us. They've heard us speaking and called us "dirty Frenchies." I picked the one I thought was the leader. I stood nose to nose with him and said, "I've killed a bear with a lance. It wouldn't bother me at all to kill you. Leave us alone." Time will tell whether he'll back off. I'm ashamed of my bragging and threatening.

"Wow! Do you think he really killed a bear?"

"I thought you'd find that interesting," Jack said. "Probably, although if he did, it's unlikely he did it by himself. Bears aren't all that easy to kill with a lance. People usually worked together to do it, but if he was the first one to strike, he'd be the one credited with the kill, and he'd get the best part of the skin."

"Jack, have you killed a bear?"

"Yes. More than one."

"With a lance?"

"Yes."

"Oh."

"I'll read some more."

Thursday, April 22—My commanding officer called me in. I thought my threat had been reported, but it was something else quite surprising. I've passed my tests with extremely high marks. They want me to go to Code School—thirteen weeks of learning to decode intercepted messages. After that, I'd be promoted and sent to England. He gave me twenty-four hours to think it over.

Friday, April 23—I talked to Henri. He's happy for me and said I'd be a fool to turn it down. A promotion would mean more pay and might put me on track to become an officer. I'll be sorry to part company with him. He's a good friend. It's an important assignment, though. I accepted the offer.

Tuesday, April 27—I moved to a new barracks. Henri and I still meet in the mess hall. He asked about the bear. That's probably the most dangerous thing I've ever faced, but not the most frightening. Telling your father I wanted you to be my wife was worse. I'm glad he finally decided to allow it. And I'm glad you didn't put up too much of a fight.

Wednesday, April 28—Henri asked me why I wanted to live with the Eskimos. I told him I first went because I wanted adventure; I stayed a second year because of misadventure; and I want to go back again because of you. Of course, I had to tell him all this in French. He encouraged me to try to send you a message through the trader, so perhaps you will hear something of me after all. I've sent a letter, asking him to translate it and read it to anyone from the village who comes to trade. Maybe, with luck, the message will get to you sometime in this next winter. Are you thinking of me as much as I think of you?

Thursday, April 29—I'm enjoying Code School. I have to learn German and about code. Maybe my head will burst with all this learning. This is important work. I had a letter from my mother today. She enclosed a photograph of my father and her. She asked me to send them a picture of me in my uniform.

I rose from the table and refilled our teacups. "I guess he never got around to sending that picture, or else it was lost. It would have saved us a lot of research if I'd known he was in the Canadian army."

Jack continued. "I'm going to summarize here. Brendan continued school for another five weeks. His French and German improved steadily. He found working with codes easy and fun—like playing a game of chess. You had to outsmart your opponent, the person who'd designed the code.

"Then he had a problem. His sergeant saw him writing what looked like code in the diary. Brendan told him that he was writing in Inuktitut. He was confined to barracks. The diary was confiscated."

Wednesday, June 16—They've managed to find a man who speaks Inuktitut—an officer who was on a whaling ship as a young man. He's verified that it's as I told them. The captain knew I was doing well with German. He asked whether I spoke other languages. I told him my father had taught me Gaelic, and I was working with Henri on French. They sent me back to duty with instructions to tell no one about what has happened.

Thursday, June 17—Back to German. I have a lot of work to do to catch up with the class. No time to write.

Saturday, June 19—The captain's office again. This time, several people were there. They asked if I'd consider spying on the Germans. I'm a candidate because of my ability with languages and because I've shown adaptability in living in the north. I'd be sent to England for training to learn how to pass as German. They warned me if I were caught, I'd be shot. They gave me a day to decide.

Sunday, June 20—I've accepted the assignment. I'll be fighting the Kaiser, but not in the way I expected. It appeals to my sense of adventure. At the same time, it sounds like a big game. They've truly put the catnip in front of the cat. I can't resist it.

"Ah! So he *was* a spy," I said.

"Yes. He was promoted to corporal and said his good-byes to Henri. He was given ten days of leave. He went home to Pittsburgh since there was no way to join Ivala in that short time. On July 1, he reported for duty with a contingent of soldiers being dispatched to England.

"His voyage to England was unpleasant. On the first day of travel, he wrote, 'Too sick to write.' He didn't write for the next nine days. In spite of a decision he made at the end of his first week of diary keeping to write 'only when something notable happens,' he'd never missed making a daily entry before, except when the diary was confiscated for those few days."

Saturday, July 10—Southampton. I'm told we had to dodge U-boats the whole way across, but I knew nothing of that or anything else. I've been dreadfully ill for ten days. I don't know how I'm going to get home when this war's over. I don't know if I could face that again. An army officer met me. I'm now in a manor house in a small village outside London. Everything I brought with me was taken away. It'll be returned when I return to England—or sent to my parents if I don't return. I didn't give them the diary. I said I'd left it in Canada. That's wrong but, Ivala, I'm not willing to give up writing for you. I'll miss your likeness in my watch. I looked at it every day. I'm going to draw it on a piece of paper.

Sunday, July 11—This house is enormous. I'd guess it has more than a hundred rooms. Most of it's being used for wounded soldiers and their caretakers. These are men who've received all the care they need in a hospital, and now need rehabilitation. It's frightening to see them. They've been horribly injured. Many have lost limbs. Others have been hit by shrapnel or burned. Their faces are destroyed. They struggle so to achieve some sort of normal life.

Monday, July 12—I'm ensconced in rooms set up like a typical German house—two bedrooms, a kitchen, a living room, a dining room, a study, and a small private garden. I have three teachers. One of the two men stays in the second bedroom. They'll alternate weeks so I always have someone to turn to within our rooms if I have a question or a need (and perhaps to keep an eye on me). The third, a woman, comes in every day except Sunday to clean and cook for us. She teaches me the domestic side of German life—how a German man would behave toward women. The three of them speak German in my presence. My teachers say it's better that I not know if other spies are being trained here, because if I'm captured and tortured (!) the less information I have to give, the better.

Tuesday, July 13—Training began today. We're focusing on language and behavior. I need to learn to pass as a German workingman, so even my smallest gestures need to be analyzed and adjusted. Later, when my German is fluent, I'll be trained in the methods I am to use to extract and transmit information. I've been promoted again. I'm now a sergeant with a concomitant raise in pay. I don't know who decided this, but I'm told it's because of the hazard of my assignment. I won't see the money. It's banked in Canada.

Wednesday, July 14—I found myself yearning to hear some English. As if by magic, my wish was granted. It turns out I get time off on Wednesdays. My teacher asked me if I'd like to go to the pub in the village. I jumped at the chance. I'm going in the guise of a wounded English soldier. I have a brace to wear on my left leg, which causes me to limp slightly. They've given me a cover story to account for my American accent. I'm English. My mother was widowed and married an American, so I grew up in the United States, but I heard the call to arms, and like the loyal subject to the King that I am, I came home to join up. We switched to speaking English when we got outside our rooms. We walked to the pub and had a couple of pints of bitter and some supper, bangers and mash, which turned out to be sausage and potatoes. My teacher asked me to try not to talk to anyone at the pub but him, but he finally realized it was like asking the rain not to fall. I played a game of darts, I had fun, and I stayed in character as an English soldier. He said I did well. I finally realized, though, that this time off isn't a kindness on their part. They want to see how I behave when I've had something to drink.

Thursday, July 15—I may have stayed in character, but evidently my dart playing embarrassed my teacher. A dartboard has materialized in our quarters. I'm getting lessons. I assume they play darts in Germany.

Friday, July 16—This training's quite difficult. I'll have to be able to go among Germans and not stand out as a foreigner. There are many, many details that have to become second nature.

Saturday, July 17—My teachers and I play a sort of game. We elaborate the life history of my German character. My teachers write down anything we decide, so I can be consistent in building the story. We'll go over these details many times as part of our language study. I work in the garden every day so that I can get an introduction to the German words for plants and tools and acquire a few calluses. My German alter ego was a farmer by trade before he was wounded in the war.

"Ah, there's the farming," I said. "He had to pretend to be a farmer for his role."

"Yes, but it doesn't seem enough training for him to actually buy a farm when he came back to the United States. It was make believe. It wasn't part of his spying, just part of his background story."

"Does he mention it again?"

"No."

Sunday, July 18—The chaplain came in to talk and pray with me this morning, as he will do every Sunday. Anything I say to him will be held in confidence. Nothing will be reported to my teachers. I'm allowed to speak English to him, but he does speak German. They've asked me to speak German to him if I can manage to take care of necessary spiritual matters in that language. After that, more work. I do a lot of exercising. We don't know what the physical challenges will be in Germany, so they want me to be generally fit. We go walking every day. I need to be in condition to walk long distances.

Wednesday, July 21—Another day off. The woman went with me to the pub. I took some teasing from the other dart players. They were envious because she's actually quite pretty. I did better at darts this week.

"The next part's a lot more description of his daily activities and progress. I'm going to skip over a lot here. I'll read the part where he gets his assignment."

Friday, December 10—My teachers say I'm ready to go. I knew this day was coming, but in a strange way, I'd forgotten what I was working toward. I'd started to feel I was going to spend the rest of the war in this funny play-acting world. It's a shock to realize this is going to change.

Saturday, December 11— How good has my training been? Will I be able to pass as German? I have no way of knowing. I spent a good portion of last night awake. This is the first time I've had trouble sleeping. I'm excited and frightened to realize that the time has come. I hope I get used to the idea I'm finally going into action. I don't like missing sleep.

Sunday, December 12—The chaplain knows I'm to be activated. He gave me Communion today. I talked to him about my fear. It helped.

Monday, December 13—I don't like going day to day. I asked my teacher. He said we're so close to Christmas, it's likely I'll be sent a few days before. Even in war, things slow down for Christmas. It's likely people will be friendlier, busier, and less alert right before the holiday.

Tuesday, December 14—We're all on edge. My teachers have much invested in me, and we like one another. It would be impossible to hide if we didn't. We talk about how I celebrate Christmas in Germany. We're deciding what kinds of gifts I'm giving my mother, my father, my sister, and my three younger brothers. I also have to think of a gift for my fiancée, Katrina. I don't have a lot of money to spend because I'm a wounded veteran who's just been released from rehabilitation. My family lives in a small village about forty miles from the city where I'll be assigned. I worked on the family farm, but farming's too strenuous for me now because of my injuries. I can't be with them at Christmas, because I'm looking for a job. The money I have is my mustering-out pay and a small bonus for being wounded. My other life—my life in Canada and the United States—has receded into the background. I've sent a letter to my parents telling them I have an assignment that prevents me from communicating with them for the foreseeable future.

Wednesday, December 15—I went to the pub with the woman. I told her what I'd been thinking. I've been saying whatever was on my mind (except about the diary) since I talked to the chaplain on Sunday, and I realized this might be the last time in a long while that I'll be able to tell anybody the truth about anything. When we returned from the pub, I found out I go tomorrow. I have to make a decision I've been putting off. What do I do with this diary? I've been careful not to let anyone see it. That's the first time I disobeyed an order since I joined the army. Now, I'm going to do it again. I'm taking the diary with me. I wrote before it would be a long time before I'd be able to tell anyone the truth about anything, but I can write the truth in the diary. Playing a role has been disorienting. The diary will help me keep in touch with reality. I suppose I should worry about them finding it when I'm in Germany. I'll take my chances. If they catch me, I'm a dead man, diary or no diary. I'm unwilling—it almost feels that I'm unable—to voluntarily lose my connection to you, Ivala. This war's going on longer than I thought it would. I thought I'd be home with you by now. I didn't realize the Hun would put up such a fight. Our boys are having a tough time of it. I guess I was naive. I don't know if you're waiting. It's been almost a year since I've seen you, but my commitment to you is as strong as ever, my darling. I won't leave this book behind.

"That's amazing," I said. "We see him making a decision as he writes. We see his mind at work."

"Yes. This marks a shift. He starts writing a lot more about his feelings."

"Could he have gotten in trouble taking the diary?"

"I think so. He was disobeying an order. He'd written he wouldn't put anything in it that would compromise his military responsibilities, but I'm not sure he knew how much the Germans might have gleaned from his writing. If nothing else, it would narrow down the kinds of questions they would ask him under torture and what kinds of answers they would accept. I think he was right. He was naive. He could have been severely disciplined by his superiors if they'd known about it, but that didn't happen."

Friday, December 17—Thank God, I'm on dry land again. I'd forgotten how awful the sea could be. The water's bad enough on a normal day, but there's a gale blowing over Europe. I thought I was going to die. I opened my orders today. As I expected, I won't be spying on an individual or organization. I'll be spying on the people who stay in a certain hotel while they attend decision-making conferences at a military base. Some of them will be transitory. Others will stay long term as they fulfill temporary assignments at the base.

Saturday, December 18—Traveling across France by truck. Mostly wind at this point, not much snow. The roads are open.

Sunday, December 19—Still traveling across France. Everything

I'm carrying in my haversack is used. I'm wearing the same clothes I wore through training. Even the maps have been folded and refolded enough times that they look worn. They want me to look "poor, but honest." I thought the leg brace was just for the pub on Wednesdays, but I find I have to wear it in Germany. I have to look too crippled to be reassigned to an army unit, but not too crippled to work hard. There are many servicemen who were wounded and are now recovering. I'll be one of thousands, and I won't stand out. So many men have gone to fight the war that I shouldn't have too much trouble getting a job, either. Employers are desperate for workers.

Monday, December 20—I was flown into Germany today. My first airplane ride. It wasn't pleasant. I got as sick as I had been on the boat. The storm ended yesterday, but it was still plenty cold, especially in an open-cockpit plane. I may never be warm again. We landed on a deserted road just after sunrise. I jumped out, and the pilot took off and was gone. I'm ashamed to say that I had a moment of panic as I watched him fly away. My panic subsided along with my nausea, but I was still mighty frightened the first time my language skills were tested. I was able to get a ride with a farmer who seemed to accept me at face value. I'm camping off the road for the night.

Tuesday, December 21—Another day of travel. I was lucky in picking up rides today. I see other men tramping along as I am.

Wednesday, December 22—I arrived at Stuttgart at midday. I checked into a working man's hostel and got cleaned up. My orders were to apply for a job at a certain large hotel. There's a large military base nearby. I got a job as a bellboy. They're concerned about whether my injury will prevent me from working, but they're desperate, so they decided to take a chance. I'm to live in a worker's dormitory at the back of the hotel.

Thursday, December 23—First day on the job. Since I'm newly hired, I'll have to work through Christmas and the New Year's while people with more seniority have time off. I'm glad I'll be able to work into the job when things are slow. My first task is to learn my way around the hotel.

Friday, December 24—Christmas Eve. No new guests today. No bags to carry yet. A co-worker got the passkey and showed me the various rooms in the different sections of the hotel, where to put suitcases, where to find extra towels, and how to provide the other little services the guests expect. I'm listening carefully to the local accent. Mine isn't too far different, but I'll work on getting the local sounds so my speech will be less noticeable.

Saturday, December 25—Merry Christmas. Still no new guests. The hotel put on a tasty lunch for the employees who have to work through the holidays. I'm getting acquainted with my fellows. They seem nice.

Sunday, December 26—Another quiet day. We were given time off for church if we wanted. This isn't usual, but things are so slow, management allowed it. I went today, but I won't again. I'm ashamed to pray with people I'm working to defeat.

Monday, December 27—We've had some new guests in the hotel, civilians and military officers who have business at the base. I received my first tips today. This evening I did my first bit of spying. Saturday night, when the employees on duty had had a little wine to celebrate the holiday, I managed to filch the passkey. I made a copy with a file and one of the key blanks I brought and returned the original to the desk while the deskman dozed in the early morning. Today was my first chance to see if my copy worked. It did. I read through some papers when my target went to dinner and copied the information I thought was important. I'm not here to follow a particular individual, but to find out what intelligence is being used by the people at the base to make decisions. I'm a spy and a spy catcher. I need to find where the enemy's intelligence is coming from. I thought my heart would jump out of my chest while I was reading. I have to find a place to hide things outside my room in case it's ever searched. It must be a place where I'd normally go when I'm on duty so people don't wonder what I'm doing there.

Tuesday, December 28—I was excited by what I did yesterday. Today, I feel let down. We've had some more guests check into the hotel. They also have business at the base. I'll have to see if I have another opportunity.

Wednesday, December 29—I was busy yesterday with hotel duties when my current target was out of his room, but I went in today when he'd gone to dinner. I'd barely entered the room when I heard a key in the lock. I hid in the wardrobe. He walked over to the bedside table and left. I realized he'd come back for his digestive tablets. They were gone from where I'd seen them before. I've learned how to observe so I can put things back as they were. It wouldn't do to alert a guest that someone had been rifling through his possessions by leaving them disarranged. It took me a long time to calm down after that little episode, but I did manage to copy down the information I wanted. Now I feel giddy, almost as if I've had a lot to drink. It's a good feeling. What a day!

Thursday, December 30—I have that let down feeling again today. I wonder if it will always be like this with these ups and downs or whether I'll get used to this.

Friday, December 31—New Year's Eve. Most of our guests have checked out again. They've gone home to celebrate the New Year with their families. Nothing to do today but honest work. I spent the evening writing my first letter to my "fiancée."

Saturday, January 1, 1916—The hotel's practically empty. We had a drink last night to celebrate the New Year. I'll have to be careful. I don't want to give myself away when I've had something to drink. I certainly don't dare get drunk. My first report will go out in the mail Monday. I wonder what they'll think of it. They're going to send me a letter from "Katrina" every week. I'll have to wait to see.

"I'm going to skip five weeks," Jack said. "He continued working and spying. Then there's an interesting series of entries."

Saturday, February 5—What a day! My day off. I went to the rathskeller for a couple of beers, some supper, and a game of darts. I was standing waiting for my turn with the darts when two drunken soldiers came in. They asked why I wasn't in uniform. Before I could reply, one of them called me a coward and a slacker and took a swing at me. It's been a long time since I've had a serious fight, but my instincts were functioning. I ducked his punch and gave him a blow under the heart. He dropped like a rock. His pal jumped me. I managed to push him off and drop him with a tap to the chin. My fellow dart players threw them into the street. A few minutes later, police came in. Everyone denied any knowledge of a fight. I made friends tonight. They were impressed that I was able to handle myself in spite of my handicap. I'm happy I didn't forget to stay in character. My hand's so sore, though. I'm lucky I didn't break a bone.

Tuesday, February 8—I've reaped a reward out of Saturday night. I've been invited to join the poker game after work. It goes on every night. Whatever I lose will be well-invested because I'll be able to pick up gossip.

Wednesday, February 9—I was right about gossip. There are all sorts of tidbits, such as what kind of "extra" services the regular guests like. It'll be handy to know which guests are likely to be drunk after a certain time of night, who's likely to have a woman in the room, and who's likely not to even be back in his room before the early morning hours. I don't know how some of these people get any work done!

Thursday, February 10—Another success. I'll have a lot of information for my report this week.

Saturday, February 12—Ivala, I debated about whether I should write this down, but my whole life here is a lie. I can't start lying to you too. Ha! Don't I sound noble? It's self-serving blather. I know I don't have to read this part to you when the time comes. I still wish I had your pardon, though. I had a couple of beers at the rathskeller. Greta, one of the barmaids, asked me to help her with something. She led me out the door to the back. I saw the other dart players winking at one another, but I wasn't prepared for what happened. Greta had seen the fight last week. She was impressed. One thing led to another. We ended up in one of the storerooms with the door shut and the lights out. It's been more than a year since I've been with you, Ivala. My resolve to be faithful to you was not as strong as I thought.

Sunday, February 13—Some of the other bellboys knew about my time with Greta. The hotel workers are a small closed society. Everyone knows everyone's business. I've been told Greta's one of the friendliest of the barmaids. I'm, by far, not the first to enjoy her favors.

Monday, February 14—I'm still thinking about the episode with Greta. I hadn't thought about such a possibility, so I hadn't planned what to do if something like that happened. I let my lust and a couple of beers lead me into something that might have been very dangerous. I need to think out what I'm going to do in the future. I can't afford to be involved with a woman because of my feelings for you, Ivala, and for the sake of my mission, but I recognize I'm lonelier than I realized, for companionship and for bodily comfort.

Tuesday, February 15—I wasn't prepared for how lonely this job could be. Though I can't befriend them, I like many of the people I work with. They're decent folk. They don't seem any different from the people I met in England or Canada or knew in Pittsburgh. There are some I don't like, but it's not because they're German, it's because they're obnoxious. Most of the people I meet are pleasant and interesting, and yet, many of them are actively working to defeat England and Canada. People just like these are probably shooting at Henri.. War is foolish and useless. It's sad people are dying for something that seems so pointless. I don't know what to do.

Wednesday, February 16—Today one of the guests gave me a large tip as he was leaving and thanked me for my service. I doubt he would appreciate the irony of tipping the spy who'd been going through his papers in the night. Oh, God. What am

I going to do?

Thursday, February 17—I know what I'm going to do. I'm going to stay true to my mission. I'm going to carry on doing my duty as I agreed to. No one told me this would be easy. They just didn't tell me how difficult it would be to betray people I've come to like. I'm going to have to put up with the loneliness. I can't trust myself in a friendship, and I can't have a true friendship based on lies.

Friday, February 18—I did something I shouldn't have done. Last night at the card table, they talked about a guest who starts drinking at about 4:30 when he comes back from the meetings and usually has to be helped to his room, undressed, and put to bed because he's too drunk to manage on his own. He gives one of the bellboys a big tip every day. I hadn't been in his room before because he never seemed to go out. Now I know why. I went to his room and let myself in. He was there, snoring in drunken sleep. I got the information I wanted. I was so excited I couldn't sleep for the longest time. Today, I feel elated, though I must admit I'm sleepy. Doing that was foolish. I'm sure my bosses wouldn't like it. I won't do it again.

Jack set down the typed pages. "Brendan started writing a lot about not sleeping well. He seemed to have more of those low days. He often seemed to give himself little written pep talks. It's clear he was writing for himself now, not my grandmother."

"Why do you say that?"

"He was writing about the morality of what he was doing. It bothered him a lot to be spying on people he liked. I think it would have been impossible for my grandmother to follow what he was saying. There were so many concepts in what he was writing that just wouldn't have been translatable into Inuit ideas."

"You mean the spying?"

"Yes, and the whole concept of war, the rules of war, the morality of war. It would have just been too alien to her understanding of life. Certainly when he writes about his sexuality. My grandmother wouldn't have expected him to be faithful. That's a moral decision on his part that just wouldn't have been relevant among the Inuit. They didn't have the Victorian strictures about sex that my grandfather did. Men and women were expected to be sexual beings. His fidelity wouldn't have been an issue for her. No, he was writing for himself, for his own sanity."

"So he was struggling."

"He'd been in Germany too long. He had no one he could trust. He wrote that he was so lonely that he'd speak to himself in English, just so he could hear it. I doubt that his handlers would have been concerned with his emotional health. What he writes in the diary sounds like he's depressed, but I don't think that would have showed up in his reports. He took a lot more risks than he had at the beginning. He often went into people's rooms when they were either sleeping or drunk. It seemed to give him a high, to lift him out of the depression for a while. Maybe it gave him an adrenaline rush. He almost seemed to dare them to catch him. I think he was so depressed he was suicidal."

"You think it was that bad?"

"There are clues. He'd continued to have sexual encounters with Greta when she was available and with prostitutes when she wasn't. He wasn't proud of those episodes, but he felt the physical relationships helped him deal with the loneliness. After a while, though, he quit doing that. He said he'd lost interest. He quit playing cards and going to the rathskeller too. He wrote about being tired. I think he was in big trouble. Finally, after he'd been there more than a year, everything came to a head in January 1917."

Friday, January 12—I've received a telegram notifying me that "Katrina" is seriously ill. They've asked me to come home immediately. It's a warning that the authorities are beginning to search for a spy here. I have four days to get to a rendezvous point. If I can't, they'll make a second attempt to pick me up at dawn on the fifth day. After that, I'm on my own. It'll be up to me to try to hike out to Switzerland. I thought about not going. It seems like so much effort. I could just go to sleep and wait for them to come. But I must go. It's my duty.

"That doesn't make sense," I said. "He'd be executed if he stayed."

"That's one of the clues about the depth of his depression. At this point, he's on the edge of being suicidal, but he still does his duty. That's what keeps him going."

Saturday, January 13—Thank God I was able to finally dispose of that brace. I assume they'll be looking for a man with a limp, so I'll make it harder for them. I hitchhiked today, but I won't any more. I don't want people to know which way I'm going. It's dusk. I barely have enough light to write this. I'm taking a rest now. I'll walk more before I settle in for the night.

Sunday, January 14—Cold and windy. I stopped and took a nap in a sheltered place beside the road. I'll try to walk most of the night.

Monday, January 15—I won't make the day four meeting. I'll rest most of tomorrow and meet the plane the following morning. I don't know what I'll do if he doesn't come. "Katrina's" address will be abandoned by now. I have no one to turn to.

Tuesday, January 16—This has happened too fast. I'm confused and dispirited. It's hard to feel I have a place anywhere that I belong. I don't know how long it'll take me to get back to you, Ivala, and I don't have any idea what they'll do with me now. Maybe I'll be sent to fight. I'm so tired. Maybe they'll let me rest first.

"That entry was the last one. The next day the plane crashed."

Chapter Fourteen

"Well, this isn't what I expected. I thought he'd have a quiet life someplace, maybe on a farm in Canada."

"He was so young," Jack said, "twenty-six when he headed for the rendezvous with the plane. My son's that age. And it ended so suddenly." Jack stopped. He looked at the papers in his hands.

I had enough sense to just sit quietly.

"He wanted to come back to my grandmother. Why didn't he?"

"I feel so sad for him." The words were out of my mouth before I realized I was talking about feelings yet again. I stammered, "I'm sorry. I don't want to make you uncomfortable."

"Anne, don't be sorry. I hear the caring in what you said. You said you'd never hide anything from me."

"Yes, I remember."

"I took that as a promise."

I didn't answer. I thought of my lie about René.

We sat quietly for a few moments to allow things to settle between us.

"Maybe our questions will be answered in the book in San Diego. I'll call Carola. It's too early now, though. They won't be up yet."

"So, do we read this to René?" he asked.

"I think so."

We finished our tea. Jack washed the dishes while I called René to let him know we were on our way.

"Well, Anne, you were up and out early this morning," René said. "I called you a while ago."

"Ah, . . . no. I wasn't there. I had breakfast with Jack." *It wasn't exactly a lie.*

He ushered us to the seating area. Jack and I shared the small sofa. He sat in the chair.

Jack handed him the watch, open so he could see the engraving.

He held it reverently. His love of history was obvious. "Jack this is really something."

It took us almost two hours to read the entire translation. We took turns reading aloud, Jack first. I was second. While René was reading I was, for the most part, looking at him, but I happened to glance at Jack, and he was looking at me. He dropped his eyes for a moment, then looked at me again and smiled. Just his smile was enough to send my heart racing.

"That's quite a story," René said when he looked up from the last page. "Your grandfather was an amazing man, Jack. He spoke English, Gaelic, and Inuktitut and was learning French and German. At the same time, he was creating this diary language. It's no wonder working in his father's bank wasn't stimulating enough for him. It's easy to see why he might've wanted the challenge of learning to live with the Inuit and the even greater challenge of the spying. When you read about his activities, it's almost as if he needed to have danger in his life. Where do we go from here?"

"I think the book I have at home might possibly be a continuation of this diary," I said. "I'm going to call Carola and ask her to send it."

"Use my phone," René said. "I can't wait to see it."

THE IVORY CARIBOU

"Why don't you get her to send it to my place?" Jack said. "I see no reason why you shouldn't stay there instead of at the hotel until we go back to Ungavaq."

I knew this had to hurt René. I didn't want that. I had lied to Jack about my relationship to René, and even worried at the time whether that lie would come back to hurt me. Now it had come back to hurt not me, but him, and I couldn't see any way to mitigate it. If I told the truth now, I think René would be even more hurt to realize that I had denied him—that I had denied the importance of our relationship. I just said, "OK."

I called Carola. She said she'd send the book priority mail. It would arrive in a day or two.

"I still don't understand why the German cryptographers didn't manage to translate it," I said.

"We don't actually know for sure that they didn't figure it out," Jack said, "but my guess is they didn't. They never managed to figure out what the Navajo Code Talkers were saying in World War II. It's the same sort of problem. Given enough time, you might be able to figure it out logically, but probably not. Either you have someone on staff who recognizes the language or you don't. His unique spelling of a spoken language and his little trick of reversing syllables just made it harder."

"I guess it must have," I said.

"We've taken up enough of your morning, René. We should let you do the job you get paid for," Jack said. "Keep your copy of the transcript in case you want to look at it again. Anne and I have some shopping to do. She's going to need some gear for our 'cold-weather camping trip,' as she calls it. As soon as the second book arrives, we'll give you a call to let you know if it's part of Brendan's story."

As we walked toward the car, Jack said, "On second thought, rather than shopping, I'd like to take you to meet a friend of mine."

"Who?"

"Marcia."

"Oh. That's a surprise."

181

"Why a surprise?"

"Well, I had sort of assumed she'd died. Isn't she a lot older than we are?"

He chuckled. "Marcia's eighty-three and as tough as old boots. I don't think she's ever going to die. But, after a lifetime of roughing it in various remote locations while she did her research, she decided to take her retirement in comfort. She lives in a retirement community here in Ottawa. If you don't mind, we'll go there now."

"I'd love to."

Marcia's apartment was about a twenty-minute drive from René's office. Jack rang the bell. The door opened.

"Marcia," he said, "I've brought a friend to meet you," and he turned to usher me in.

I don't know what I was expecting, but Marcia was definitely not it. She was small—barely five feet tall—slender, and old. Beyond that, she bore no resemblance to any stereotype of a little old lady. She was dressed in a bright caftan made of an African print. Her long gray hair was tied up in a no-nonsense knot on the nape of her neck and fixed with an elaborate silver barrette. She wore no make-up, which made her bright blue eyes even more noticeable. She managed to look casual and sophisticated at the same time.

The strength of her personality hit me the moment she opened her mouth. "Well, Jack, here you are."

He had to bend down to kiss her. I saw tenderness in his face I hadn't seen before.

"Marcia, this is Anne O'Malley. She's my aunt, but we're telling everybody she's my sister because," he said in a stage whisper behind his hand, "she's a little sensitive about her age. Anne, this is Professor Marcia Black."

I blushed, and Marcia laughed loudly.

"I just love kinship stories. How is it you're Jack's aunt? Come in, and I'll fix you some tea." She glanced at her watch. "Oh, no. It's almost lunchtime. I don't have any seal in the freezer, Jack. You'll have to take us out," and she laughed again.

"I'm honored to meet you, Professor Black."

She offered me her hand. "Call me Marcia."

That was my introduction to the force of nature that was

Professor Marcia Black.

She got her coat. "There's a new Moroccan restaurant not too far away."

"Sound's good," Jack said. "Marcia did some of her field work in North Africa," he added for my benefit.

"Morocco?" I said. "I thought you were an expert on the Inuit."

"I was, but I was actually more focused on women's politics in small-scale societies in general. After I'd done all that I thought I could do in Canada, I went farther afield to Morocco and Kenya, and finally, when I decided I could do with less adventure, to some small villages in Switzerland. But enough about me—tell me how you two are related."

Jack and I outlined Brendan's story and continued with the diary narrative at the restaurant, answering as many of her questions as we could.

Jack handed Marcia one of the transcripts. "I thought you might like to read this."

"I would. I'd like to see the original too."

We finished lunch, Marcia's treat. Jack drove us back to her apartment. When we got there, Marcia said, "Jack, why don't you make us some tea, while I talk with Anne?"

We went into Marcia's elegant living room. It was decorated in the same reds and golds Jack had in his office. The heavy drapes were of an African pattern, and souvenirs of her African travels were everywhere.

Marcia invited me to sit next to her on the sofa. "How are you getting along with your newfound family? I understand you spent five weeks with Maata."

This hadn't been mentioned at lunch, so I realized Jack had told Marcia about me before today.

"It was difficult at first," I said. "It took me a while to—oh, I don't know—I guess to get a sense of the rhythm of their lives. At first I was sort of straining at the bit, but once I figured it out, it was comfortable for me."

"How did you spend your time there?"

"We sewed. I'd never done much of that before. They seemed to take a special interest in teaching me."

"Ah," Marcia said and nodded.

"I enjoyed it, and I was grateful. While I was home in San Diego, I bought a sewing machine and made a blouse for each of them. I wanted to show them their teaching hadn't been wasted. I was going to send them at Christmas, but I brought them now, instead."

She smiled broadly. "Oh, my dear. You are a natural anthropologist. It took me the longest time to learn what you picked up in just a few weeks. Your gifts for them will be exactly the right thing.

"You know, unlike Jack, they're pure Inuit in their outlook. None of them, except Quipac, has ever been farther afield than Blackwell, even though Jack's lived in Ottawa all these years. But, for that matter, Jack is still Inuit at his core, in spite of his other experience in the world. If you want to be with Jack, you need to remember that. You need to let him be who he is. It won't be easy. His wife couldn't do it."

I didn't question her assumption that I wanted to be with Jack. I just said, "I don't understand."

"Right now, he's just showing you the part of himself he thinks you'd be willing to accept, but you have to accept all of him. He has to know it's safe to share all of himself with you."

"The other day, we were shopping," I said. "Something he wore on a chain slipped out from under his shirt. He didn't let me see what it was, and he was embarrassed."

"I know what you're talking about," Marcia said. "It's a polar bear tooth, an amulet. It's to keep him strong. Maata sewed it into his first set of clothes when he was tiny. He's worn it ever since. In some ways he's much more adapted than his contemporaries, but some things he holds on to more than they do. That's one of them."

"It gives him a feeling that he belongs somewhere—to his family—to his heritage?"

"Ah, so you do understand. Yes. Exactly."

"Why was he embarrassed?"

"That tooth isn't just a good luck charm. It's an important symbol of his belief system. Perhaps you didn't realize, he's not a Christian. His family didn't convert as most did. He's afraid you're going to think he's primitive, uncivilized."

"But he gave me this." I showed her the caribou.

"He wants you to be safe."

"He said that, and he said it would bring me back."

"Yes. Maybe he was a little dishonest with you," she said. "He didn't tell you that it was much more than a gewgaw, a little gift of friendship. Did he put it on the chain?"

"No. I did that."

"It undoubtedly means a lot to him that you wear it. That's one way to show your acceptance."

"I'm not sure how else to show him that I can accept all of him," I said, "but maybe I can find out. I'll try."

"Good. Sometimes I wonder if I did Jack any favor by bringing him here. I don't think educating him was a mistake—someone in every group is going to be the first to learn new ways when two cultures come in contact—but in coming to Ottawa and being around us, he's become a volatile person."

I wondered if she was serious. "That certainly hasn't been my experience of him," I said, but as I was saying that, I remembered his saying he made people uncomfortable.

"Oh, I don't mean by our standards. I mean by Inuit standards. They highly value evenness of temperament and abhor emotionality. When Jack's home in Ungavaq, he's able to maintain Inuit decorum, but at a cost. You can see the effort he puts into controlling his emotions. His family does see it. He's willing to pay that cost because his family's so important to him and because he needs the stability they represent.

"On the other hand, I think he has the opposite problem in Ottawa, although most of his relationships here aren't as close as family. We may not see it that way, but we are so openly emotional here. I think that's the reason his wife finally refused to come to Ottawa any more, although they weren't well suited to each other in other ways. We were just too emotional for her."

"Jack he was an 'in-between.' I didn't fully understand what he meant."

"Quite simply, it means he's never at home any place."

"Oh."

She rose from the sofa and walked to a corner table that held framed photos of various sizes. She picked up one and brought it back. It was a picture of a boy in Inuit clothing. I realized it was Jack. He had a broad smile, and held a book in front of him with both hands as if he were offering it to the person with the camera.

"That's when I first knew him," she said. "Did he tell you how he and I met?"

I handed the picture back to her, and she set it on the coffee table. "He told me you came to Ungavaq to do some field work, and he was curious about your books. He said once you explained to him about how reading and writing worked, he wouldn't let you alone until you taught him to read."

"You know he came with me and stayed almost a year in Ottawa?"

"Yes."

"Did he tell you what happened after that year?"

"He talked about the graduate students who taught him."

"Well, there's a story you may not have heard. When I took him back to Ungavaq at the end of that first year, we didn't think he was going to come back to Ottawa again, so he gathered up the books and paper and pencils I'd given him and took them home with him.

"I stayed for six months to do some follow-up on my previous study. I hadn't been there more than a couple of weeks when I noticed I wasn't seeing much of him. I decided to look around to see what he was doing. He and Quipac had built themselves a little snow house. Jack was teaching Quipac how to read, and not only that, but how to read English. They were doing all this by the light of one of those blubber lamps. I don't know if you've seen one of those, but they don't give out much light. He was a natural teacher. I didn't say anything; I just watched for the rest of the time I was there.

"In the next few weeks, his sisters joined the class, and one day I found out he was teaching Maata. If you have any sense of the workload of an Inuit woman living in the traditional style, you'd understand it was almost a miracle Maata would make time for that, but she was motivated, and Jack was a good teacher.

"A few weeks before I was due to leave, I talked to Maata and Piuvkaq about the possibility of bringing Jack back to Ottawa again. Piuvkaq knew about the reading. He was aware that the trader, Mr. St. Clair, could read too, and that reading seemed to give him a lot of power. He and Maata talked it over with the other members of the village, and they decided to let Jack come back with me. They had the foresight to see that although Jack was just teaching children's stories, which could have been taught orally, there was more potential in reading than that. Now, all the older adults in Ungavaq who read do so because Jack taught them, and he made them ready for the teacher when the government finally sent one. I think they put their hopes in him, and he's done well for them, but as I said before, it came at a cost."

"Was that fair to Jack?"

"I think if he could have seen the outcome he'd still have made the same choice—contact with the white world and education, with the problems it included. And make no mistake. Ultimately, he's the one who made that decision, not me, not his parents. I don't think he's a tragic figure. I mean he's lonely in a fundamental way. There isn't anyone else like him."

"Would he mind you saying these things?"

"Jack knows me. He knows I say what I want. Anyway, he didn't bring you to meet me because I'm his doddery grandmother who'd just say sweet things about him. I think, my dear, you should know how important you are to him. You are *new* family for him."

"Yes, a new sister."

"I think, perhaps, more than that."

"I really don't know."

"Well, his wife refused Ottawa. His other 'friends' have refused Ungavaq. That's something to keep in mind." She paused. "I see you've recently removed your wedding ring."

I looked ruefully at my left hand. The indentation made by my ring during almost four decades was still plainly visible on my third finger. I wondered if Jack had noticed.

"I hope you'll pardon my bluntness for asking, but was it a happy marriage?"

"Why are you asking?"

"I'm a little protective of Jack. I'm not going to interfere, but I would like to know."

I didn't like to talk about things like this, but something about Marcia made it OK.

"Yes, we had our ups and downs, but on balance I was happy.

I've had a difficult time adjusting to his death. I've been lonely. I didn't realize how lonely until I started this research about Brendan again. This has saved my life, but it's turned out differently than I anticipated."

"In what way?"

"At first, I thought the research might be a way of holding on to Robby. Instead, it's come to feel like a way of saying good-bye to him. I don't know how that transition happened." My eyes started to tear.

Marcia took my hands in hers. "All marriages end in tragedy, my dear. They end either in divorce or in death. It's what comes before that's important. You were blessed, but it's reasonable and essential to move on. You know your Robby would want you to."

"I think I'm coming to understand that."

"Do you have other family?"

"My parents died many years ago. I have two older sisters."

"Well, sisters. Do you see much of them?"

"No. They're married and have children and grandchildren. We've never been close. I was an unplanned third child. My sisters were ten and twelve when I was born, too old to play with me, too young to want to mother me. They just didn't seem to notice me."

"What about your parents?"

"My mother was somewhat distant too, so my real family was my father. He was the glue that held us together. When he died, we drifted apart."

"Do you have children?"

"No." I looked down.

"I'm sorry. I can see that's a painful subject for you."

"Yes. Robby didn't want children."

"And you agreed."

"Yes."

"It sounds like that was difficult for you."

"Yes, but I taught first and second grades for a few years, until Robby asked me to stop. My students became my substitute children."

"That was enough?"

I hesitated. "It wasn't completely satisfactory, but it helped fill part of the gap. The rest of my life was so satisfying and Robby was so loving that I learned not to be . . . discontented."

"How did you learn that?"

"I guess we just focused on each other. Maybe we were more involved with each other than was good for us. He was an only child. We had no other relatives to take our attention away from each other. When Robby retired, I guess we turned even more inward."

"No wonder his death was so difficult for you."

"When he was dying, we made financial plans, but neither of us thought about how I'd manage emotionally after he was gone. He'd been my whole life for so long. He'd been my best friend. Still, we assumed I'd be OK." I shrugged. I could feel tears starting again. "I guess we were wrong." I could hear Jack's footsteps and the clink of teacups. "Well." I swallowed, determined not to let the tears fall. "I am rattling on. I don't know why I told you all that."

"I've had a lifetime of encouraging people to tell me things. It's perfectly all right."

Jack brought in a tray.

I was embarrassed. But Marcia just patted my hand and turned Jack's attention to pouring the tea and more discussion about Brendan while I regained my composure.

Jack had brought in the archive box from the car. We showed Marcia the contents, and he showed her the watch. She looked at the diary and smiled, as Jack had. "This certainly brings back memories."

Jack also showed her the photos of Brendan and his parents.

"Yes, the resemblance is there, especially in the eyes," she said.

"Robby had those same eyes."

"I guess my grandfather had strong genes."

"Marcia, may I ask something of you?" I said.

"Certainly, my dear."

"Do you have any photos of Piuvkaq?"

"Yes."

"Do you think you could have a copy made for Maata? She's never had a photo of him."

Marcia rose, walked over to the table that held the framed photos, and came back to us. "I can do better than that. Take this to her." She handed me a photo of an Inuit man of middle age. He stood next to a sled. I saw a seal tied on the load. The man held a harpoon and smiled with pride. His hood was up, but pushed back enough that you had a clear view of his face. I could see his resemblance to Jack.

"I'll get some tissue paper," she said. "We'll wrap it to protect the glass."

She left the room. When she returned, she wrapped the frame carefully and handed it to me.

I thanked her and slid the gift into my purse.

"You certainly have an interesting story," Marcia said. "Are you going to keep researching?"

"There may be a second diary. Robby had a book he inherited from his father. No one's been able to translate it. It's in San Diego. My friend's going to mail it to us."

"I'd like to see it when you get it," she said.

We promised we'd show it to her. We stood by the door. Marcia hugged me. "I hope to see you again soon, my dear. I don't often get to talk about my star pupil behind his back."

Jack laughed.

CHAPTER Fifteen

"What exactly did Marcia say about me?" Jack asked as we walked to the car.

I thought a moment. "Part of me says she wouldn't mind if I told you, but part of me says she shooed you out of the room before we talked, so I think I'll just keep it to myself for now. It's easy to see you're more than just her star pupil, though."

"Marcia's my second mother. She didn't intend for that to happen. When she taught me to read, I started out being her little homage to the gods of education, and maybe a little bit of an experiment, but she made the most basic mistake in science."

"What's that?"

"She lost her objectivity. She told me that when she brought me back to Ottawa she thought I'd stay a year and go home, end of story. She didn't plan on a lifetime relationship. She'd been married and divorced before she came to Ungavaq. I think she wanted to marry again. It didn't take her long to figure out, though, that not too many men would be interested in a woman with an Inuit kid in tow. Finally, I think she decided she just didn't care."

He turned the key and started the engine. "We need to decide where we're going. Would you like to check out of your hotel and stay at my place until we go back to Ungavaq? I didn't ask you whether that was OK when I suggested it, but it does seem sensible. If you want to, we'll still have enough time to go shopping for some boots for you afterwards. What do you say?"

"I say yes."

We headed for the hotel, where it took me a few minutes to repack my suitcase and check out. Then we drove to the store where he usually bought his cold-weather gear.

"We'll just look at boots today," he said. "We have several more days we can fill with other shopping."

One of the salesmen offered to help us, but Jack said, "I'd prefer you just act as our runner and bring things out from the back that my friend selects. Unless you've done a lot of back country hiking, I'd rather do the fitting."

Our rotund salesman definitely looked like a non-hiker. He readily agreed with Jack's suggestion.

The concept "snow boots" is a little hazy for someone who's spent most of her life in Southern California. I hadn't realized there were so many decisions to be made. We selected five styles Jack said would be appropriate, and the salesman brought the boxes to us.

I was wearing my California version of winter shoes, dressy ankle-high black suede boots with high heels. I sat down, slipped them off, and pulled the legs of my slacks up to my knees. Jack sent the salesman for a pair of socks and asked me to take my "California-thin" socks off.

When I did, Jack stood transfixed, looking at my feet.

"What?" I asked.

"Nail polish."

"Yes. It's called 'Arctic Dawn.' I thought it was appropriate. Do you like it?"

Before he could say anything more, the salesman returned. Jack took the package he held out, knelt on the floor in front of me, and slid one of the thick, warm socks onto my bare left foot.

Suddenly, I became aware of his hands. The touch of his fingers was like silk brushing my foot.

He slid the second sock onto my right foot.

I ordered myself to relax.

Jack held my left foot gently in his hand and slid the first boot on.

I held my breath.

It was immediately obvious the boot didn't fit, so he pulled on the instep with one hand as he slid his other hand down my calf to push the boot top. He let his hand rest on my bare calf for a moment longer than he needed to.

I had such a flash of heat and desire I thought I might faint! I was astonished at myself.

Jack never looked up, but the salesman smirked.

I spent the next half-hour trying to focus on the qualities of various types of leather and styles of boots—and not having much success. I finally ended up agreeing with Jack's suggestion and buying the pair he selected.

I decided the next few days were going to be more difficult than I'd anticipated. I didn't dare think about the four weeks after that. I was really going to have to exercise some self-control. I didn't want to embarrass Jack or myself.

I thought Jack hadn't noticed anything, but he was quieter than usual in the car on the way back to his place.

That evening, as we shared the duties of preparing dinner and cleaning up the kitchen, we slipped back into our brother/sister teasing. I was relieved. And disappointed.

I thought maybe I was back to my normal, more restrained self, but after dinner, we went for a walk to begin breaking in my boots. When we got back to Jack's place, he asked me to sit on the sofa and take the boots and socks off. Again, he knelt down in front of me—this time to see if the boots had caused any rubbed spots or blisters.

He took some lotion and gently and slowly massaged it into my feet. I watched his hands. He never looked up.

When I went to bed that night, I, had—for one of the few times in my life—an erotic dream. It started out with Jack touching my feet. I woke early and couldn't find sleep again.

That day, we bought more clothes, a powerful flashlight, a sleeping bag, and a hiker's backpack for me, and equipment for the camp.

We took another walk. I wore my new boots to continue breaking them in. Again, Jack inspected my feet and rubbed them with lotion. I was more prepared this time. I slept more soundly. The dream didn't recur.

Early the next day, the book arrived from San Diego. Jack said it was another part of Brendan's story. He called René as promised and said we'd probably see him the next day.

This translation took less time than the first one because Jack had figured out the system and remembered the vocabulary. Still, it took most of the day.

When he finished, I fixed some tea. We sat on the sofa in the living room. As before, he read parts of it to me.

Chapter Sixteen

Thursday, March 22, 1917—My dearest Ivala, I've decided to write again. For a long time, I've been too ill to consider it. When I could, I thought it wouldn't be sensible to write anything that might be used against Genevieve if we're arrested. Now, however, my desire to put my thoughts down on paper has overcome my caution. I still need this connection to you. I long for the day when we'll be reunited. It's been two years now since I've seen you. I feel lost and disconnected from everything I knew. Perhaps if I write things down, I'll have a chance to think about them in a useful way.

Friday, March 23—I've been here for more than two months. I remember that I was supposed to meet a plane. That must have happened because I woke up in a shrub about twenty feet from a crashed plane. I think I was aboard and was thrown clear. People were standing near the wreckage. I almost called out. Then I saw who they were: two men who looked like farmers, a police officer, and two German army officers. I could barely see them through the branches of the shrub, which meant they probably couldn't see me, either. I was so thirsty. I wanted to take bits of snow off the branches, but I didn't dare move. I drifted out of consciousness again. When I next became aware, those people were gone. Two soldiers stood guard at the wreckage. This time, I managed to stay awake. Two men arrived in a wagon. They made so much noise in their arrival I was finally able to shift my position. That was a mistake because it caused a pain so intense I nearly cried out. My leg was broken again. The two men, with the help of the soldiers, extracted the pilot's body from the cockpit of the plane and loaded it into the wagon. They also loaded a small heap of items that had been on the ground. I saw my haversack, and with it my diary, disappear. My heart fell because I'd lost my connection to you, Ivala. I'm too tired to write any more.

Saturday, March 24—Each day I feel stronger, but I get so terribly tired. Today, for the first time, I'm strong enough to go for a short walk outside—not by myself; Genevieve has to help me. It's a week since I've been able to sit up in a chair. It's cold but sunny today. The pain's bad, though, so now I'm sitting for a few minutes, getting sun and fresh air. Genevieve doesn't want me to stay here too long. She's afraid I'll get chilled or that somebody might see me.

Sunday, March 25—After the wagon left, I heard a car leave too. It passed through my line of vision, so I could see that both of the soldiers were in it. One is always grateful for small things. I guess everything of importance had been removed from the plane, so there was no further need to guard it. While I'd been waiting, I formed a plan. I started out by cutting some branches out of the shrub with my knife. I pulled myself out on the side away from the plane. I think the crash was in the early morning, but the sun was halfway down in the sky by this time. I ate some snow, but that didn't slake my thirst. It only made me colder. I struggled out of my coat. I was so stiff and cold; I almost couldn't do it. I took off my shirt, put my coat back on so I wouldn't get more chilled, and cut strips of cloth from my shirt. I set the two broken fingers on my left hand with some small sticks and a strip of cloth. I could no longer feel blood dripping from the cut on my head, so I left that alone. I had to deal with my leg. I'll not write anything more about that, except that I stabilized it as best I could with two sturdy sticks and more strips of shirt. I don't remember much else, except pain.

Monday, March 26—I'm stronger today. My leg hurts, but maybe not as badly as it did yesterday. Some days I think it's getting better. Some days I'm sure it isn't. I'm drinking a fairly steady diet of Genevieve's homemade wine to take the edge off the pain. Genevieve tells me I was delirious when she found me in her barn. I don't know how I got there or how far it is from the crash site. Genevieve says not far. She found me that night when she came to put the horse in its stall, and she suspected I might have been on the plane. She said I looked German to her. She was planning to send her son into the village to notify the doctor and the local policeman when, she says, I started talking in my delirium. I wasn't speaking German, but she could tell I was calling for my mother. That touched her heart. She thought it better not to call for the authorities. She and her son Robert, who's eleven, managed to move me from the barn into the house. I spent six days in a stupor before I was conscious enough to know where I was.

Tuesday, March 27—Genevieve and I speak French. She and the children also speak a dialect of German called Alsatian, but she prefers French at home. Every day I thank God I met Henri and that he was so diligent in teaching me. Genevieve says, however, that my accent is atrocious. I told her it's Canadian. She's going to teach me the correct way to speak. She tells me I'm in Alsace-Lorraine. I must learn to speak correctly in case the Germans, or the Boche, as Genevieve calls them, decide to come to the farm. I'm putting Genevieve and her children in unspeakable danger. If I were found here, she and her children would be shot for hiding me. I spoke to her about the danger, but she'll hear nothing of my leaving. She tells me I'm weak as a kitten and I couldn't get ten meters on my own. I fear she's right. She's told her children I'm their cousin Bertrand, who's been injured in the war and has come to the farm to get better. I don't know what Robert makes of the fact that he had to help carry me in from the barn, but Genevieve tells me not to worry about that.

Wednesday, March 28—Genevieve says it's lucky I arrived in winter. She teases that if I'd come during planting or harvest-time, she might have sent me on to the next farm. She works from morning to night. I require a lot of care, but I'm trying to do as much as I can for myself. I'm even able to do some small repairs of things around the house and farm, if I can do them sitting down. For example, almost all of the tools here needed sharpening, and I was able to do that. Robert helped by turning the sharpening stone. I use the children as my legs. The children, besides Robert, are Martine, who is eight; Felice, six; and Charles, four. They run to get tools or materials when I need them. After dark, the older ones carry a lamp for me if I have to move from room to room. My balance isn't that good. I don't trust myself to carry it. I have no trouble communicating with Genevieve, but I don't know the proper local names for the things I want, so sometimes the children and I have a good laugh over our miscommunication. I'm using my skills at pantomime honed with Henri, so we manage most of the time.

Thursday, March 29—Genevieve asked about the money that she found pinned in my clothes. I asked if she could use German money. She reminded me that though she and I speak French, we are in a part of Germany. The money is good. It's a substantial sum—all I saved from my wages and tips from the hotel. I told her to keep it. She also asked me about you, Ivala. I'd spoken your name when I was delirious. I told her you're my wife. She showed me the drawing I'd made and asked me if it was you. I had thought it lost, but Genevieve found it in my pocket when she undressed me. I told her how long it had been since I've seen you and how much I miss you. That brought tears to her eyes. When I looked at your picture today, I was reminded of that conversation and realized that I have never asked her about her life. When I did ask, she began to cry. She said her husband, Pierre, was conscripted into the German Army and was killed three months ago, shortly before I arrived here. I'd assumed, correctly, that she was a widow, but it never occurred to me that she was widowed so recently.

Friday, March 30—We talked more about Pierre today. The Boche took him in September, after the last harvest was in. He was killed in the first battle in which his unit took part. He grew hay, vegetables, and Riesling wine grapes. Genevieve has never done the planting and harvesting by herself. She's worried about whether she'll be able to feed her children. I hope the money will relieve some of that worry. She tells me that since this area has at times been part of France and other times part of Germany, some of the people side with the Boche. It's important I not assume anyone is safe to talk to until my accent improves. I talked again about moving on. She still thinks it's impossible. I know I'm endangering her. I considered turning myself in, but if I do that, it's probable that they would find out that she'd been shielding me. I'd like to think I could bear up under torture, but the reality is that I probably wouldn't. The details of my spying would come out too. The other option might be suicide, but as a Christian, I'm not sure that is an option. I'll have to think that over.

Saturday, March 31—We took the bandages off my leg. Genevieve, like any farmer's wife, has had a lot of experience with doctoring animals and people. I doubt the local doctor could have done any better job setting the leg than she did. Still, we think it doesn't look right. I'm over the infection, and the swelling's going down, but the shape of the leg is odd. The pain is almost intolerable when I try to walk. It'll be a long time before I can think of trying to walk on it without a crutch. I'll not give up though. I want to come back to you as soon as possible.

Sunday, April 1—Each day I walk more. To pass the time, I'm carving little dolls for Martine and Felice. When I finish those, I'll carve some carts and horses for the boys. Robert is quite interested in what I'm doing. I'll find out if he has any aptitude for this.

Monday, April 2—Genevieve is pleased with the dolls I've made. She and the girls are going to make clothes for them. The children are bringing me various pieces of wood so I can see which are the best for carving. I gave Robert a pencil and paper today and asked him to draw for me. He has some talent, and he's interested. I'll see if I can help him with it.

Tuesday, April 3—Without me realizing it, my days have become quite busy. I spend a lot of time with all four children when the three older ones return from school. They're lonely for their father. I'm not sure the two younger ones understand that he's not coming back. I walk every day, and there are still heaps of small repairs to be done around here that I can do sitting down.

Wednesday, April 4—Genevieve goes into the village for the market every Wednesday. She sells eggs, chickens, butter, and homemade pickles. She'd be able to sell my carvings if I continue to make things. She tells me there's been no hint of gossip that the Boche are looking for anyone in the area. If they were, there'd be no way to keep it a secret. She thinks they didn't realize I was on the plane. No one has seen me since I've started going outside. She's talked in the market about her injured cousin who has come to the farm to get better, in case anyone does spot me. We've made a game out of making up a life story for me. I have to learn my own new story and also the stories of the relatives Genevieve and I have in common. She has a large family of brothers and cousins, but none of them are nearby, so it's unlikely there will be anyone who will contradict us. She tests me to see if I can remember details. It's very like the training in England. I have to learn my whole life from childhood on. I have to know about games and songs and stories and a little history, and a lot of things about farming, since this cousin (me) was a grape grower before he was injured in the war. I practice the songs, stories, and games with the children in the evenings. They teach me even more, though they don't know they're doing it. I think Robert knows what's going on, but he's smart and loyal to his mother, so I accept it when she tells me not to worry about him.

"The answer to our question about where Brendan learned to farm is that Genevieve taught him," Jack said.

"I'd never have guessed any of this in a million years."

"Me, either. He writes about how he became stronger and was able to take on more work around the farm. Over a period of weeks, his health and his accent improved. In all this time, his leg never stopped hurting, but he never stopped trying to rebuild his strength. If he walked any distance, though, the pain was debilitating. I just read April 4. I'll jump to June."

Wednesday, June 6—Today was a banner day! Genevieve let me go with her to the market. She thinks my accent has improved enough that people will ascribe its oddness to the region where I used to live. I really enjoyed myself. Genevieve was right about people being interested in my carvings. I helped her with the sales, and talked to many people. I hadn't realized how much I'd missed that kind of conversation. I came home with my spirits high. I've been doing more around the house and farm. I can work sitting and standing. I can even walk a little without the crutch. I wasn't able to help with the plowing and sowing, but Genevieve managed it with Robert's help. We've reversed roles. I can manage a lot of the housekeeping, and I'm learning to cook, so when Genevieve and Robert come in from the field there's a hot meal waiting for them. I've learned to milk, separate the cream, and churn the butter. I find there are many things I can manage to do sitting or leaning on something.

Thursday, June 7—Pierre had a workshop. I've rigged a system so I'm able to reach everything I need to fix things. I no longer have to send the children for tools, but I still send them if I need anything from the cellar. I don't trust my leg on those stairs yet.

Saturday, June 9—When I was working at the hotel, I told everyone that I wore a brace to help myself walk. Maybe now I can make another one that would really do that. I'll try.

Sunday, June 10—We went to Mass today. Genevieve says if I'm well enough to go to the market, I'm well enough to go to church. I didn't take communion. She assumed I refrained because I hadn't gone to confession. She was surprised when I told her I'm not Catholic. She's afraid people will gossip if I don't participate in the ritual. We're afraid of gossip, because it might travel to the authorities. Even more than that, she's afraid of the sin if I take communion without being confirmed. We'll have to solve this problem somehow.

Monday, June 11—I've started work on a brace. The fabricating is the easy part. The difficult part is trying to figure out what needs to be supported to ease the pain. I'll try something and see if it works.

Tuesday, June 12—Still working on the brace. There's a lot of old leather harness in Pierre's workroom. It's still usable and has buckles. I have to figure out what to use for the frame.

Wednesday, June 13—Market day. Genevieve and I have talked again and again about how to solve the problem of going to Mass. Today, she told me we are in an impossible situation. She's decided to go to confession and talk to the priest. I hope it's not a mistake, but I didn't try to talk her out of it.

Thursday, June 14—Father Étienne has come to visit me! We had a strange conversation because I didn't know what Genevieve had said to him. I didn't want to give him any information he didn't already have. He understands our position and sympathizes. We have come to an agreement. Every Wednesday, I'm going to go to the church for an hour of instruction while Genevieve is at the market. Father Étienne says that on Sundays I can come to the altar with the other communicants. He'll take care of what needs to be done. He told me that the United States has finally entered the war. The American Expeditionary Forces have just arrived in France. I hope this means I'll be able to go home soon.

Friday, June 15—I have completed the brace. I wore it for part of today, and it relieves the pain. I wasn't as tired in the evening as I usually am.

Saturday, June 16—Today was my first full day of wearing the brace. It really makes a difference. I'm going to have to make a few adjustments because it rubs in a few places, but otherwise it's fine.

Sunday, June 17—I went to Mass today. It's comforting to be back in a church, even if it's not the one I'm used to. I went to the altar with Genevieve. When it came to be my time to take communion, the father simply pantomimed putting the wafer into my mouth and he winked. I told Genevieve what had happened when we were on our way home. I hadn't realized the importance this held for her. Tears of relief came to her eyes. She trusts Father Étienne, and now she doesn't feel she's leading me into sin.

Monday, June 18—Genevieve and I have been talking about how I can get home. We can't see a way. My leg's still not in good enough shape that I can hike anyplace. We don't know exactly where the front lines are or much about how the war is going. We hear rumors, but we don't know how much credence to put in them. There's no way to notify my superiors that I'm still alive. We don't know anyone who can smuggle me out of here, considering my physical condition. In any case, I'd be useless now and for the foreseeable future either as a soldier or as a spy. I'm going to have to be patient. I do worry about what my parents are thinking. I don't know what they will have been told. Meanwhile, Genevieve's glad I'm staying longer. There's so much work to be done here, and I'm finally able to pull my own weight.

"Why do you think they knew so little about the progress of the war?" I asked. "He doesn't discuss it at all."

"Commercial radio, and the news it brought, didn't exist yet. They were out in the country. They probably didn't even see a newspaper very often. Unless the front lines moved in their direction so that they started seeing refugees, they just wouldn't have heard that much about what was going on. Father Étienne told Brendan about the American troops. What information they had was probably announced from the pulpit at Mass. I think the church had a network for disseminating news. Other than that, they would have depended on rumor."

Tuesday, June 19—I've never described Genevieve and the children to you. Genevieve is my height, about ten years older than I am, and has brown eyes and long blond hair that she wears in braids when she works. In spite of being outdoors a good part of the day with the farm work, her skin is pale and smooth as she always wears long sleeves and a hat when outside. For a long time, she never seemed happy. Her life was full of worry. Since the plowing and sowing have gone so well, she's become a new person. I often hear her laugh. Robert has now had his twelfth birthday. He's a son any man could be proud of. I'm sorry Pierre won't know what a help he's been to his mother. He stepped forward and became the man of the family when Pierre was taken. It's been a burden to him, because he's still a child. I've tried to ease his burden where I can without making him feel I'm taking things away from him. He looks like the picture I have seen of Pierre, with dark hair and eyes. Martine, Felice, and Charles are like little versions of their mother, blond, brown-eyed, and pretty. They also are children to be proud of. The two girls together take almost total care of the chickens—a major responsibility because the chickens and eggs add so much to the household budget. The girls water and feed them daily, collect the eggs, and clean the pens when necessary. Charles is still the baby, though he'll soon be five and will have to work harder around the farm. He's already learning how to help set and clear the table for meals and to do other small jobs. He sometimes helps his sisters with the chickens, and I give him little tasks whenever I can.

Wednesday, June 20—I had my first meeting with Father Étienne today. I've decided that it would be foolish not to trust him. He knows enough already to turn me in if he wants to. I spoke to him about my thoughts of suicide. As a priest, he has a bias against it, but he took my concern seriously. He believes that God has sent me to Genevieve and to him and that I must trust God in this matter. He also thinks a suicide might do harm to Genevieve and her children. He pointed out that, especially for the children, I've become a member of the family. He asks me to think about the fact that they've already lost their father. I've agreed with him. I hope I'm not being self-serving in this matter.

"He writes about suicide, but he doesn't sound depressed any more, does he?"

"I don't think he is depressed," Jack said. "He's simply trying to balance the obligations he sees in his life. He's aware of his duty as a soldier to survive and return to his lines, but he also has a duty to Genevieve at this point. She was technically an enemy. But he never considered her that, and he wasn't willing to sacrifice her. He was an honorable man."

CHAPTER Seventeen

"NOW THERE'S A LONG SECTION WITH EVERYDAY STUFF," Jack said. "I'll skip most of it. Brendan continued to get stronger. He did everything he could to learn more about farming so that he could help Genevieve and, at the same time, become more deeply embedded in the role of 'Cousin Bertrand.'"

Thursday, September 20—We're harvesting hay. We'll have some to sell, and some to keep for the milk cows and horses for the winter. Our neighbors have come to help, thank goodness, because it would certainly be more work than we could do. Genevieve explained what needed to be done, and she and Robert give me little prompts when I need them. I seem to be a quick study. At least none of the other men have indicated through their attitude that they think I'm anything other than a farmer, and they don't show any resentment when I have to take my little rests every hour or so to allow the pain in my leg to abate. I have learned the rhythm of the scythe. It's very pleasant. We walk through the fields in a line scything down the grass. By the time we finish cutting the last field, the grass in the first fields will have dried enough, if we don't have rain, that we'll gather it into the hay wagon. Genevieve has told me ours are the first fields to be harvested and that I need to husband my strength, because Robert and I will, in turn, help our neighbors with their fields.

Friday, September 21—The wives of the other farmers help Genevieve prepare dinner and supper for us all. It's a pleasant social time. I'm getting acquainted with our neighbors. In turn, Genevieve will help cook at the other farms while Robert and I work. The last of the grapes were harvested and sold a few weeks ago. I'm so glad I have become strong enough to do this work. There's joy in work, and even the fatigue that comes at the end of a day is pleasant. We've been harvesting vegetables right along. It seems Genevieve has canned hundreds of jars of pickles. She'll pickle anything. I don't dare stop too long in the kitchen in case she starts eyeing me to be put in a jar. These jars of pickles are stored in the cellar. She'll take them to market next year. She has a widespread reputation. People come from long distances to buy her products.

Saturday, September 22—We continue with the work. I'm getting so dark from the sun I don't think my parents would even recognize me, and I've developed calluses in places where I really need them.

Sunday, September 23—A day of rest. We went to early Mass. This noon we are going to the neighbor's farm for Sunday dinner. This is our first formal social event since I came to the farm.

Monday, September 24—Yesterday was an interesting day. After we ate and sat a while over our coffee, our neighbor Paul asked if I'd like to see the plane that crashed on his farm. It still sat in a field they'd decided not to plant this year. Genevieve told me the plane had crashed nearby, but I'd never realized how close. It turned out to be in a field that abutted one of the fields where the horses and cows graze on Genevieve's land. I guess my mind's still working slowly. I finally realized our neighbor and his son were the two men I saw with the policeman and army officers on the day of the crash. We went out to see the plane. Under the pretext of relieving my bladder, I walked behind the shrub in which I'd hidden. I could still see the signs of my occupancy—the broken branches and the stubs where I'd cut sticks to brace my broken bones. To tell the truth, I haven't been sure how much of what I remembered was real. I was relieved to find I hadn't imagined that experience. When I see how far it is from here to Genevieve's barn, though, I realize I must have crawled. I couldn't have walked at all, but I just can't recall. When I came back from the bush, Paul told me a story of coming back a few days after the crash to salvage some metal off the plane. He said that behind that very bush where I'd just relieved myself, he'd found a trail in the snow that headed toward Genevieve's farm. He'd followed it to the fence, but no farther. He said this happened shortly before I came to Genevieve's to get better from my war injury, and then, he laid his finger on the side of his nose and winked.

"So the neighbor knew."

"Yes, and kept their secret. Brendan's life goes on like that. His health improved. His life settled into a comfortable routine. The family worked hard during the day and played in the evening. I'm going to jump from September 24 to mid-October."

Thursday, October 18—At last, the harvest is finished. The hay's in the barn. The grapes are sold. The vegetables, except for the turnips and rutabagas still in the garden, are canned or in the root cellar. Now we're working on getting firewood stockpiled for the winter. Robert and I use the two-man saw to cut up logs. Later, we'll split them. Robert's a hard worker, and he and I work well together. He's been practicing his drawing in the evening and is developing his skills.

Friday, October 19—We're enjoying our evenings more. Now that the harvesting is finished, we're not so tired. We spend time storytelling. I have started to tell the children a series of stories about a man who grew up in a city and went to live with the Eskimos. Genevieve understands I'm telling her my life story. Telling the stories benefits me. I've realized over time that this pain in my leg isn't going to go away. My leg's never going to be strong enough for me to walk back to you, Ivala, or to do the things required to take care of you as my wife. Returning to you is an impossible dream. I might as well have died in the war. I have died for you. This breaks my heart. Memories are all I can have of you and of the life I loved so much. Sharing the stories with Genevieve and the children eases my pain and sadness. I discussed this with Genevieve after the children were in bed. She's sad for me.

Saturday, October 20—As I reread what I wrote last night, I realized again I'm not going to be able to tell you these stories about living on this farm. Somehow, I still hadn't understood that. Maybe I'm still holding on to hope. I'll keep writing to you. I'm not ready to stop yet.

Sunday, October 21— Before Pierre was taken for the army, Robert had been learning to play his father's mandolin. He's teaching me the chords he knows. We sing together in the evenings. I remember how I sang with you, Ivala. It's bittersweet.

"Ah. See, Jack, it was important to him too. Imagine how happy it would have made him to know you taught those songs to your children."

"Yes. I think it would have." He sat quietly for a few moments. "There's a lot more, but I'm going to skip a year here. I guess he'd come to the point that he recognized he needed the diary for himself, even though he couldn't share it with my grandmother. He is able to reconcile his grief. We'll read that later. I'm going to jump to the end of the war. Brendan had stayed with Genevieve. No one ever questioned his new identity. Since he didn't have any papers, he was careful never to put himself in a situation where he'd be required to provide identification.

"On November 11, 1918, a year and ten months after Brendan came to the farm, the Germans surrendered and the war came to an end."

Tuesday, November 12, 1918—Word has come that the war is finally over. The Germans capitulated yesterday. Alsace-Lorraine will again be a part of France. Genevieve is jubilant. This has been called "the war to end all wars." One can only hope that God will make that true. There's going to be a service of thanks in the church tonight. I can write to my parents to let them know I've survived. I'm sure they've long since thought I was dead. After I write that letter, I'll write to my commanding officer in England so that I can report for duty. I don't know whether the postal system will work yet to the United States and England, but I'll have my letters ready to go when things are finally organized.

Wednesday, November 13—I was interested to see who wasn't in church last night. I think there's going to be trouble around here when some scores are settled against those who favored the Germans. I hope things don't get too ugly. There was a celebration in the church hall after the service. We sat with our neighbors, Paul and Lili. I told them the story of the plane crash from my perspective. I thanked Paul for protecting Genevieve and me by keeping my secret. He's a good neighbor and a good friend.

Thursday, November 14— After consultation with Father Étienne, we have decided I'll keep the name Bertrand and the identity I've established for a while more—until we're farther away from the upsets of the war and the peace. It's soon enough to let people know the truth when I've received some information on how to proceed. We're afraid some pro-German villager might get revenge on Genevieve for sheltering me by turning me into the authorities as a deserter. There are some people here for whom, I think, the war will never be over. Paul and Lili have agreed to keep our secret. I wrote my letters. I found it strange to write them since it's been almost two years since I've written a single word of English. I'm almost more capable in Inuktitut than I am in English. I told Genevieve what I was writing. She was downcast. I don't know why. She won't tell me. She asked if I thought my leg would allow me to return to Ivala. I said that wouldn't be possible.

Friday, November 15—After the children were in bed tonight, Genevieve came to me. She trembled as she spoke. She said she's come to care for me, the children look on me as a father, and she needs a man to help her with the farm. She's asked me to marry her. She said she knows she's older than I am and that I might not find her attractive, but she promised to be a good wife and do everything in her power to make me happy. I wasn't prepared for something like this. I have to think. I've been completely focused on the idea of returning home when the war was over and on the remote chance I might be able to get some medical treatment that would allow me to return to Ivala. Marriage to Genevieve is a possibility I've never considered.

Saturday, November 16—We had our first little bit of snow today. I spent the day splitting logs and thinking. The work has cleared my mind. I know what I must do. This is a turning point, a choice between a dream that my leg will be better and that Ivala will be waiting after all these years, and the real world. I've been foolish and selfish. I went to Canada for adventure and found it. But even that wild life seemed to settle into routine. When I read the newspapers at Blackwell's about the war, I told people it was my duty to participate. I may really have felt that. I don't remember. What I do remember is that I thought of it as a great adventure. My lust for adventure overcame my better judgment then in the same way my lust overcame me with the barmaid Greta later. I had a good wife and a responsibility to her, which I did not fulfill. Now I've been here almost two years. I have responsibilities to these people. Genevieve risked her life for me, and the lives of her children. Her children need me, and she needs me. This time, I'll not make another foolish decision.

Sunday, November 17—Last night, I explained to Genevieve that I'd been hoping to return to Ivala, but now I know that's an unreasonable dream. Genevieve knows I don't love her, but I said I'm fond of her and respect her, and I think she's beautiful. I hope love will grow between us, but even if it doesn't, this is a good life and she's a good woman. I accepted her offer. I kissed her for the first time. Last night Genevieve welcomed me into her bed. We'll live as husband and wife from now on. I've torn up my two letters.

Monday, November 18—Today we told the children of our decision to marry. They're excited about our plans. I told Genevieve that my life with Ivala is a closed book. She said she'd no more expect me to forget Ivala than she'd be willing to forget Pierre. Just because we loved before doesn't mean we cannot love again. She hopes I'll feel free to think and talk about Ivala whenever I want. It's going to be easy to learn to love Genevieve.

Tuesday, November 19—Genevieve and I talked to Father Étienne today. Since I was not married to Ivala in the church, I'm free to marry Genevieve, but I have to be confirmed as a Catholic first. This isn't a problem. As per our agreement, I have been faithfully taking lessons with the father every Wednesday since we had our first conversation so long ago, though I must confess some of the lessons were taught over a chessboard. I understand the tenets of the faith. I'm willing to comply.

Wednesday, November 20—I wrote again to my mother and father and told them of my decision to marry Genevieve and about the children. I didn't mention becoming a Catholic. That's not going to be happy information for them. One shock at a time might be all they should be expected to handle. I think it unlikely anyone would contact them, but I asked them not to let the army know I'm still alive. I tried to tell them as much as I could about what has happened over the last few years. Genevieve added a charming greeting to them in French and invited them to visit as soon as they can. I wrote a short translation afterward for them.

Thursday, November 21—I was confirmed in the Church today. Then Genevieve and I were married. Paul and Lili stood up with us. What a joyful day.

Friday, November 22—I didn't expect to feel different after marrying Genevieve, but strangely, I do, and it's wonderful. I left my parents' home, as young men must. I was a visitor in my uncle's home, a visitor with the Inuit, in the army and in Germany, and even a visitor at Genevieve's. I've felt disconnected, lost, and alone for so much of that time. Now, I'm home. I'm happy.

Saturday, November 23—My time with Genevieve gets better and better. I don't think either one of us realized how lonely we were for intimate companionship. I don't mean just physical companionship, though that's wonderful, but the freedom to share our most intimate thoughts and feelings, good and bad. Genevieve and I were friends before we became lovers. Now we can complete that friendship in every way.

Sunday, November 24—Today, Genevieve asked me if I want children born to me. I sometimes think she must think I'm very dense. I hadn't given it any thought at all. She explained that if I don't want children, we must refrain from physical pleasure for the next few days, but she's willing to give me children if that's what I want. No man could want better children than the four already with us, but in the past, I've thought someday I might like to have a son or a daughter. She thinks we should put it in God's hands.

Jack stopped reading.

"Is that the end?" I asked.

"No. But the next part's difficult."

"Do you want me to read it?"

"No," he said. "Give me a minute."

We sat for several minutes. I could see Jack was struggling. Then, he cleared his throat and continued Brendan's story.

"Their lives were happy during those months after the end of the war. In January, though, Genevieve was ill. She threw up every morning. Brendan worried. He took over much of the cooking. Being around food upset her."

Wednesday, January 15, 1919—I've been so worried about Genevieve. For days, I've been saying I want to call for the doctor, but she refused. Today, she finally told me why. She is with child. With God's help, we will have a son or daughter in September. I'm overjoyed. I love Genevieve, and she loves me. This child is a sign of our love. Life couldn't be better.

"They lived quietly and happily until April. Then, shortly after Brendan had felt the baby kick in Genevieve's belly for the first time, when spring began to show its promise, influenza reached the village. A worldwide pandemic that killed millions, it was devastating in the village."

Sunday, April 27, 1919—Something terrible is happening. People in the village are becoming ill with influenza. We've heard rumors about this illness. Some say it's sweeping the entire world. Father Étienne spoke from the pulpit today and the health authorities were with him. They say we shouldn't come into the village except in the direst emergency. The school has been closed. We shouldn't come for the market on Wednesday or even for Mass. This is a measure of how serious things are. It may already be too late for us. Charles has been complaining of feeling ill. Genevieve tells me he has a temperature and a headache. She has put him to bed by himself and has forbidden the other children to visit him.

Monday, April 28—Charles is still ill. His temperature seems to be higher. Genevieve is very worried. He's unable to eat or even drink. She sits with him and rubs him with a wet cloth to try to cool him, but it doesn't help. I'm taking care of the other three.

Tuesday, April 29—Charles is getting weaker. The doctor's been in. All we can do is try to keep him cool and comfortable. Now Martine complains of not feeling well. The doctor told me that people are dying in the village.

Wednesday, April 30—We're all ill now. Charles is having trouble breathing and he's coughing blood. I managed to get out to the barn to release the horses and the cows with their calves into the field. We're too ill to do the milking, but the calves will take care of that. There's not much to eat in the fields yet, but they'll have to make do. I released the chickens. They can scratch for food. I hope a fox doesn't find us now. The yard dogs and barn cats will have to fare for themselves. There are lots of mice and baby rabbits for them to hunt.

Thursday, May 1—The worst has happened. Charles died early this morning. Genevieve is devastated. I rode one of the horses into town to notify the authorities. Genevieve bathed him and dressed him in his best clothes. We wrapped him in a bed sheet. They came for his body this afternoon. I thought Genevieve was going to die of grief. This can't be good for her on top of her own illness. Thank God, I'm not as ill as the others are. I'm still able to care for them.

Friday, May 2—No improvement. I made some broth out of one of the chickens, but no one can keep it down.

Saturday, May 3—I wrote that the worst had happened, but I was wrong. Martine died today. Genevieve is beside herself with grief. Father Étienne came. He's exhausted. He's been comforting the sick as much as possible, but I don't see how he can do much more without killing himself with overwork.

Sunday, May 4—Felice died today. I haven't told Genevieve. I don't think she can bear any more.

Monday, May 5—Still ill.

Tuesday, May 6—Robert died today. Has God abandoned us?

Wednesday, May 7—This morning my darling Genevieve died in my arms. I thank God we came to know of our love for each other before this happened, but I don't understand how He could be so cruel to us after all we have been through. I'll be dying soon. At least I'll be able to rejoin her and our children. I wrote a short letter to my parents today to tell them good-bye.

Thursday, May 8—God is even crueler than I thought. I'm better today. I'm in despair.

Friday, May 9—Father Étienne came again today. He tells me people are dying all over France. There will be no funerals, and not even individual graves. There are too many dead and ill in the villages.

Saturday, May 10—I finally had enough strength to go out and give hay to the horses and cows and fill the water troughs. The grass is springing up in the fields so the animals didn't suffer as much as I feared.

Sunday, May 11—I sat in this empty house.

Monday, May 12—Father Étienne came again today. There have been more than sixty deaths in the village and the surrounding farms so far. We prayed together. He's more than my priest. He's my friend. I told him of my despair.

Tuesday, May 13—Étienne came again today. We talked a long time. Suicide is a sin, but I told him that this pain is more than I can bear. I can't go on. He prayed with me. He asked me to think about whether I'd like to transfer that pain to my mother and father. He's going to come back again tomorrow.

Wednesday, May 14—Étienne came again today. He's right. I couldn't do that to my parents. I told him.

Thursday, May 15—The sun's shining brightly. It's past time to think about getting back to work, but I can't. I've written to Genevieve's oldest brother.

Friday, May 16—I can't seem to think clearly. Paul and Lili came over today to see what they could do. He's offered to help me with the farming and tending the vines.

Saturday, May 17—I spent the day walking through the house. I went into each of the rooms. I looked at Robert's drawings. I went down to the cellar and looked at the canned goods and pickles. I'm drained of ideas and desire.

Sunday, May 18—I've decided to go home to Pittsburgh. I chose to stay in France for Genevieve and the children. There's no reason to stay now. I told Étienne my plan. I'm going to leave immediately.

Monday, May 19—I've written another letter to Genevieve's brother. I'll trust him to settle the estate. I've driven the cows and horses over to Paul's and given them to him. He'll come over to check on the house and care for the chickens, dogs, and cats until Genevieve's brother comes.

Tuesday, May 20—Today, I turned myself into the French army authorities. They are in process of verifying my identity. Now I wait. I locked the house and took the keys to Paul. I'll write to him and to Étienne later. I took my personal possessions, photos of Genevieve and the children, Robert's drawings, and the mandolin to remind me of those happy times.

Jack stopped reading.

I wiped the tears from my eyes took his hand in mine, and waited.

When I was sure he wasn't going to say anything more, I said, "I have his photographs at home. We never knew who the people were. I told you before we had some pencil sketches he'd done. Now I think they might be Robert's. I want you to see them."

"Yes, I'd like that." He cleared his throat. "This is so difficult." He said nothing for several minutes. "Well, let's finish the story. I can't read any more. I'll just tell you the rest.

"The French authorities arranged for Brendan to go to England. He was sent back to Canada where he received a medal and a discharge. His work as a spy had saved many lives.

"The army helped him track down Henri. Henri had been in terrible battles, and had even been in Alsace-Lorraine, but he'd managed to come through uninjured.

"Brendan returned to Pittsburgh and stayed with his parents. He saw the best doctors in Pittsburgh, Philadelphia, and New York, with the hope that they might be able to fix his leg so that he could go back north. He didn't hold any hope that Ivala hadn't married by now, but he was haunted by the thought that she might have died of influenza. He wanted to know that she was OK.

"The doctors told him there was no possibility of improvement." His physical injuries had healed as much as they were going to.

"His father wanted him to return to the bank. He tried that for a while, but realized that wasn't the life for him. With the money set aside by the army all those years, he bought a farm. The hard physical labor seemed to be a tonic for him. He began to see some hope for the future, but he'd have relapses of sadness when he thought of Ivala, Genevieve, or the children.

"One day he wrote about meeting a beautiful woman. When he'd purchased the farm, the owner had told him he had an arrangement with the local school. Every spring, the teachers brought the elementary students to see the baby animals. The owner hoped Brendan would continue to honor the agreement. He did, and one of the classes came with their teacher, Isabelle Hartt.

"From that point onward, hope came back into his life. He and Isabelle fell in love and decided to marry. Then, another blow—he became ill. He wrote one word—leukemia. The doctors told him they couldn't give him a timetable, but his prognosis wasn't good. He offered to release Isabelle from their engagement. She refused. She said a day with him was better than a day away from him. She'd take as many days as God would give them.

"They married immediately. Soon after that, Isabelle told him they were going to have a child. You'll want to hear his last diary entry."

September 24, 1922—I've decided to stop writing today because this is the happiest day of my life. There are sad days ahead, but I won't think about them now. Today Isabelle gave birth to our son, Robert John O'Malley. She and the baby are well. He's a fine, strong son. There was sadness in my past, but I was blessed to know Ivala and Genevieve, and I'm blessed to be married to Isabelle. Someday I hope to be able to tell my son about Robert, Martine, Felice, and Charles. I may even translate this diary for him. I'll let the future take care of itself, as I've always done. I'll live in the present and enjoy it.

"We wanted to know him," I said. "It's painful to live through these experiences with him. There was so much sadness in his life. Still, he kept going, and he managed to find joy."

"He was quite a man," Jack said. "I wish my father had lived to see these. He would have liked to know that his father wanted to come back."

Chapter Eighteen

I THINK IT'S TIME FOR US TO GO FOR A WALK," I SAID.

Jack stood. "Let's get some dinner."

"Is there a restaurant we could walk to?"

"Yes. It's a ways. Wear your boots. If your feet start to bother you, we'll take a cab back."

We ate at a restaurant called Jimmy Wong's Pizza. It was good, although we didn't order the chicken and bean sprout pizza. That just seemed a little too odd. After, we ordered tea.

"We know a lot about Brendan, now," I said, as we both stirred sugar and milk into our tea, "but you've never told me about your father. The photo shows that he looked a lot like Brendan when he was young. Was he like him in other ways?"

"I think so."

"Tell me about him."

"It's hard to know where to start."

He sipped his tea, then began. "He was a good man and a good father, by any standard. He was attentive and helped me learn the skills I needed to live in our world. After I started going to Ottawa, when he knew there was a chance I might go and not come back—that he might lose me—he did what he thought was right and continued to let me go."

"Why do you think he did that?"

"Ungavaq was fairly isolated, even for an Inuit village, but I think my father saw the future. We didn't have much contact with whites since we weren't near any whaling stations or a main route to one. A few explorers visited our village. My grandfather did, and Marcia did, and, of course, they knew Mr. St. Clair, but we didn't have any major contact until quite late.

"Still, we weren't out of the loop when it came to hearing about contact in other places. It's hard to believe unless you've experienced it, but our people traveled a lot and traveled long distances. News traveled with them. We pretty much knew what was happening to our world. My father wasn't happy about much of what he heard."

"Was he trying to get you away from what he saw coming?"

"I don't think so. I never asked him directly, but I think my father expected I'd be our liaison to the white world. That's why he allowed and even encouraged me to go with Marcia. Because he was half-white, he felt an obligation to do what he could to soften the blow of contact. I've actually been able to do some of that. You may not have realized it, but my brother-in-law, Quipac, is the village leader. He has been for most of his adult life. He asks my opinion on things, and he asks for my help when he needs it."

"I didn't know that."

"It's not that he's elected to anything. We do most things in the village by consensus, but he's a man of great influence."

"Was contact a bad thing for your people?"

"I think you might get different answers to that, depending on whom you ask. You had a demonstration of one of the problems that night after the concert, but I can say that in our village we don't have to worry about our children starving, as my parents' generation did. Things have worked out pretty well for us. We're in a good hunting and fishing area, so we get enough sportsmen in to bring money into the village, but we're small and cohesive enough to keep most of the bad influences out. That's not necessarily the story everywhere. As with your Native Americans, there's a downside. Unemployment, alcohol, and suicide are big problems for the Inuit. It's a complex question. . . . But I don't think that's what you want to talk about tonight."

"No."

"I do think my father was like Brendan in a lot of ways."

"What ways?"

"I think it's obvious Brendan was a man of enormous courage. He went off into the unknown three different times: first to us, to the war when he thought he'd have to go into battle, and then on the mission as a spy. He was easy to get along with. He seemed to fit in wherever he was. He liked people, and they liked him. He always looked for what was good wherever he was. He was a loving and honorable man. My father was brave and loving and honorable too."

"You miss him a lot. I can tell."

"Even after three years. His death was so sudden. Maybe it would have been better if we'd had time to prepare for it."

I shook my head. "I don't think so."

"No, I guess that didn't help with Robby."

"What happened to your father?"

His voice dropped. "He drowned."

"Oh, how awful."

"He was walrus hunting. One attacked his boat and capsized it. He sank out of sight before any of the other men could get to him."

"I'm so sorry."

The waitress was hovering. We finally realized that we were the last customers in the place.

Instead of going straight home, we walked for hours. We talked. We held hands. We sat on a bench by the canal and watched the lights. I guess we were just walking away the sadness, and it worked. By the time we got home, we were tired, but happy.

Again, Jack hugged me and kissed me gently on the cheek before I went to bed, and again, I didn't have the courage to let him know I wanted more.

The next day, we met René for breakfast. Afterward, we sat in René's office and read through the typescript.

Again, we took turns reading.

When René started reading the part where Brendan and Genevieve heard in church about the coming influenza, I looked at Jack. His face, at first glance, had a neutral expression. Then, in some way I don't understand, something changed, not in his face, but in my looking, and I could see his tension and, more than that, his distress.

His left hand rested on the sofa cushion. I shifted slightly in my seat and moved my right hand so that it rested against his.

He moved just his little finger until it slightly overlapped mine.

I'd meant to comfort him, but now I wasn't sure who was comforting whom.

When René was on the last page, I moved my hand away.

"What a story," René said. "He used a word—bittersweet—that really sums it up. I think you should edit the two diaries for publication. I'd be glad to help. We could do the research and put this story in historical context. I doubt there would ever be another book like it."

"Well, Anne, what do you think?" Jack asked.

"It isn't my decision. This started as my project, my therapy for that matter. But, Jack, this belongs to you and your sisters now. The four of you must decide."

"I think she's right, Jack. You need to talk to your sisters."

After we left René, we went to Marcia's. I made roast beef sandwiches while she and Jack went through the diaries line by line and debated his translation of some of the words. I listened with a growing appreciation of how difficult translation is.

When they took a break to eat, Jack said, "Anne's friend René thinks we should publish the diaries because they're unique, but my grandfather wrote that he was writing in Inuktitut to keep the diaries private."

"Privacy's an important ethical issue," Marcia said. "When you choose to reveal things, you don't know what the consequences will be. This isn't a problem you run into in archaeology, Jack, but in cultural anthropology, you make your living by getting people to tell you and show you things that are normally private. You do that by living with them and earning their trust. Then you go home and publish what you learned. You have to walk a fine line. You can't let concern for their feelings change your conclusions. At the same time, you can't betray the trust they've placed in you. Your problem with publishing the diaries is similar."

"Do you think we should publish?" Jack asked.

"I think you and your sisters should think about what this might contribute to our understanding of that time in world history and also about what it says about the Inuit. Brendan's attitude toward Ivala and the other Inuit and his love for her were not in spite of the fact they were Inuit. He didn't think of them as savage. He embraced the fact that she was Inuit. He was prepared to spend the rest of his life with her."

"Yes, he was, wasn't he," Jack said. "He loved her because she was herself. Being Inuit didn't come into it."

"No, it didn't. He just loved her. This was different from the kind of exploitation that was going on elsewhere. You and I are scholars because we think this kind of knowledge is important. Your sisters may have a different perspective, though. You do have to take that into consideration."

"Would we be betraying Brendan?" I asked. "Would he have wanted these things private?"

"That's certainly the question. We can't know what Brendan's intentions were, but one thing you should consider is that, as far as we know, he didn't die suddenly or unexpectedly. He did have time to destroy the second diary. He chose not to."

That evening, Jack and I packed our purchases and cleaned out his refrigerator. We were going to catch the plane for Blackwell in the morning.

In all the time we'd spent together, we'd never really talked about

Robby. I think Jack must have recognized how emotional I was likely to get, so he'd avoided the topic. As I finished washing the dishes, I asked, "Would you like me to tell you about Robby?"

"Yes, but why now?"

"It's partly the diaries and partly something Marcia said. She asked me about Robby. She noticed I'd moved my ring to my right hand."

"I saw that too."

I took my hands out of the dishwater, dried them on the towel, and turned to face him. "I told Marcia I'd restarted my research on Brendan in order to hold on to Robby, but it didn't work. She understood. It's time for me to acquire some of Brendan's courage. I think I'm finally ready to let Robby go. What would you like to know?"

Jack leaned against the kitchen counter. "I'd like to know if he was like my father, since they were half-brothers."

"I think they were similar, but, of course, Robby didn't have the kind of demanding life your father led."

"He was a teacher?"

"He started as a teacher, but by the time I met him, he was a consultant." I turned and hung up the towel. "He told me he found his job so rewarding that he never thought seriously about marrying until we met."

"Where did you meet him?"

"At an education conference in Sacramento. He was the keynote speaker. I was the delegate from my school." I shook my head. "No one else wanted to go. They figured since I was single I had the time, so I was pressed into service.

"The morning after his speech, he led one of the small discussion groups—on the importance of the arts in education. I'd liked his talk and was interested in the topic, so I went. The discussion went so well that after we ran through the scheduled time, he invited us to join him for lunch. About ten of us did, and we continued talking about the topic we'd been covering in the session. He and I got locked crossways about a point, and we kept on talking after the others left."

"You argued with the expert. That takes some courage."

"Courage or foolishness. At least it made him notice me. He

asked me out to dinner, and to lunch the next day."

"And you started dating?"

"He took my phone number; I didn't think I'd be hearing from him. He surprised me. He called a few days later and said it just happened he'd be in San Diego the next weekend; would I like to continue our discussion? He told me later that he really came to San Diego to see me. We spent that whole weekend together. Because he traveled so much, we didn't actually see each other many times before we married, but we talked every day on the phone. And he sent me flowers. I could have built a float for the Rose Parade, there were so many. We were married four months after we met."

"You made up your mind fast."

"I do that."

"He moved to San Diego?"

"He worked for himself, so he could live anywhere."

"He was a lot older."

"That made him more than my husband. He mentored me. So many husbands I've seen seem to want their wives to be dependent, but Robby helped me to grow more independent. We talked about the fact that I might be a widow for a long time. He didn't want me to be one of those poor old women who have no clue how to handle their money or their lives without their husbands to direct them."

"What was he like?"

"Soft-spoken, calm, easy to get along with."

"My father was like that too. Did Robby like music? My father sang all the time."

"You sing all the time too, you know."

"No." He shook his head.

"Yes, you do. If you're not singing, you're humming. Robby loved music. He played his father's mandolin. He loved to work with wood too. That's what he did in his spare time. That's how Brendan's creativity expressed itself in his life. He made much of our furniture over the years."

First Marcia had asked, and now Jack, his expression intent, asked, "Were you happy with him?"

I hesitated. Instead of feeling uncomfortable, though, as I usually do when people ask me personal questions, I felt OK and even relieved. "Yes, even when we were at our worst, which wasn't often, I never doubted he loved me. I was happy with him. I miss him.

"When he died, I went into a fog. I got up in the morning and dressed and did my chores and visited with friends, and the whole time I wasn't really there. I was someplace else waiting for him to come back. I thought a lot about dying. I wanted to be with him. Then I tried to bring him back with this research. But that didn't work either, and he's getting further and further away."

I don't like to cry, especially in front of people. I started to turn away, but I'd promised Jack I wouldn't hide anything from him. I stood and tears spilled down my face.

He walked over, put his arms around me, and said gently, "Let him go, Anne. Let him go."

Just like when he'd held my hand on Laura's plane, my tension melted away. I felt such a sense of unwinding and relief. For the first time, I could start to put down the burden of my grief. I leaned against him and let my tears flow.

After a while, I said, "I don't usually get like this."

"I know."

I could feel his heart beating. It was so comforting to be in his arms. For just a moment, I thought he might kiss me. I would have welcomed his kiss. I loved him. I had since the beginning.

I wondered if I should give him a signal—touch him or kiss him. It would have been so easy. Carola had said he probably wouldn't turn me down. But that wasn't what I wanted. I didn't want a little time in bed with him. I wanted him to love me. In spite of my desires, though, I was beginning to understand that it wasn't possible for him to love me. I didn't think going to bed with him could change things.

"I think the best thing for you," he said, "would be to get some sleep. You're worn out, and we're going to get up early." He let go of me and stepped away.

I couldn't blame him for wanting to get away from my tears and, for that matter, from me. He'd been so gentle with me, but I still knew that all this emotion washing over him had to be the last thing he wanted to deal with.

I wanted to say something to him—something about how sorry

I was to be burdening him, but I couldn't think of the right words. Even if I was sorry, that didn't make me any less emotional. I was sure now, if not before, that I could never be what he wanted.

I lay in bed that night and quietly cried myself to sleep, but for the first time I wasn't crying for Robby. I was crying for Jack.

CHAPTER Nineteen

We were nearing Ungavaq.

We'd been silent through the flight.

Laura was preoccupied with controlling the plane. The weather had changed, and she'd been fighting a heavy wind since we left Blackwell. It buffeted us and then, suddenly, would stop for a moment, but she seemed to be prepared for every change. I wondered if she was worried until she said, "It's weather like this that makes flying almost seem like work." Now I could see she was enjoying herself, enjoying the battle.

The weather didn't bother me, but for the first time, I felt ill at ease with Jack.

After a quick breakfast, Jack and I had carried the suitcases and boxes of equipment to the car. We'd focused on that. There wasn't much conversation.

We didn't talk on the plane from Ottawa to Blackwell, either. I didn't want to start crying again. I felt like any little thing might set me off. I closed my eyes and tried to doze.

At Blackwell, when he'd helped me climb into the plane, I'd chosen the passenger seat in the front. I wasn't sure he'd want me sitting next to him. I didn't want to embarrass him anymore. I wondered if, instead of staying, I should go back with Laura when she returned to Blackwell, but I feared that might be such an insult to the family that I wouldn't be welcome there again.

I can't stand this silence any more. I turned to look at him. "A penny for your thoughts, Jack." Trite, but at least I'd said something.

It startled him. He'd been sitting with his head down. He looked up and smiled that heartbreaking smile.

I worked hard not to cry again thinking about what I had already lost with my tears.

"I was going over things in my mind," he said.

"I should leave you alone. You want to concentrate."

"No. Quipac tells me I think too much." He gave his head a little shake. "Let's talk. You're one of my students. I've never even asked you if you have any questions about the class. We haven't talked about it at all."

Well, one of his students. Not even his sister any more. One of the crowd. "I do have questions." I didn't really, but I didn't want to let the conversation die.

"Go ahead."

"Yes, I guess I'd better clear all my questions out of my system before we land."

He smiled again. "Well, it is a class, so I suppose I'll have to let you ask questions there too. Go on."

"Why is this class scheduled across the holidays?"

"There are a couple of reasons. I want the students to experience the winter. At any other time, they'll miss four weeks of classes. That would knock them out of a semester, even though they'd have to pay their fees at their home universities.

"Also, it's scheduled across the winter solstice. They get to experience the long nights of the northern winter. We're far enough south that we don't get twenty-four hours of dark, but still, some people can't handle it. They get seasonal affective disorder, which is a fancy way of saying they get depressed. They need to know this before they make a commitment to a life in the north."

"I've heard of that. Some people in the United States get it in the winter, but I hadn't thought about it up here."

"Once in a while we get a student who starts showing signs of depression. We have to do some counseling with them about alternative career choices. We send them home as soon as possible."

"When do the students arrive?"

"They've been here a couple of days. Laura brought them out in relays."

"Oh, Jack. Have I made you late?"

He shook his head. "We do it this way every year. The students are a cottage industry for the village. Everyone's involved in their training. Mother gets them settled in various homes. Then they have to figure out what to do for two days. I think it's a good idea to get a sense of their abilities and inclinations before they're on their best behavior for the professor."

"Do they get a grade for the class?"

"Yes, but in graduate school, students get A's, B's, or C's. Most of the students in this seminar get A's. If I give a B, it means the student is having serious problems. Once in a while I give a C, which in graduate school is a signal you'd better be considering a different career."

Ungavaq—completely different from the last time I'd seen it—showed below us. It looked like a scene on a Christmas card. A blanket of white covered everything.

Skis had replaced the pontoons on the plane. This time, Laura landed on an open stretch of snow adjacent to the village where Maata waited. The students straggled to Maata's side as Laura taxied to a stop. The four men and one woman were so bundled up, I couldn't tell them apart.

Maata came to me. She took my hands in hers. "Now that you're here, it's a beautiful day."

"Oh, Maata, it is a beautiful day. I'm so glad to see you."

Jack greeted his mother and walked over to the five students to introduce himself. I heard him tell them to carry the equipment to the dance house. He'd expect to meet them there in an hour.

No one besides Maata came over. They were probably more interested in getting the work done and getting out of the biting wind than meeting a stranger.

As Laura and Jack started to off-load the plane, Maata said, "You and I will go to the house."

By the time we got there, and in spite of my warm clothes, I was shivering. When I took off my gloves, I saw my fingertips white with cold.

Maata came over to me. "You're chilled."

"Yes. I'll have to wear an extra sweater."

"Let me help." Taking my hands in hers, she held them against her cheeks. Her hands and her cheeks were warm. We stood quietly for a few moments. "This is how we take care of children when their hands are cold. You're still like a child here. We need to take good care of you."

She was so dear. I felt loved and accepted in a way that I had never felt before in my whole life. I didn't want to go back with Laura. No matter what else happened, I wanted this family. I was home here.

Jack and Laura arrived with the suitcases.

"Make yourselves comfortable," Jack said. "Mother and I want to take a walk."

"It's awfully cold for a walk," I said.

"It doesn't seem all that cold to us."

"We'll see you in a while, but I bet you'll be covered with icicles. Perhaps people will enjoy warming up with some tea when they get back."

"We'll have tea at the dance house," Maata said. "We'll meet you there."

"Ah, Maata, I almost forgot. Before you go, I have a gift for you from Marcia." I took the tissue-wrapped package out of my purse and handed it to her. She unwrapped it carefully and looked at the framed photo. I could see immediately how much it meant to her. She took a deep breath and, in a gesture that must be universal, clasped the photo to her heart. She said, softly, "Thank you," and slipped it into her coat pocket, probably to show it to the other women.

She and Jack left for their walk.

I opened one of my suitcases and took out a sweater and some packages. In addition to the blouses for Maata, Miqo, Allaq, and Saarak, I'd brought small gifts of food for each of the women who'd entertained me at sewing parties. We took the gifts and headed to the dance house.

The simple rectangular building, with an open kitchen at one end, had folding chairs along two walls. The fourth wall contained bookshelves filled with the village library, including the children's books I'd brought. Two large folding tables covered with platters of food, plates, and tea mugs divided the kitchen from the dance area. The wonderful smell of caribou stew, keeping warm on the stove, permeated the air. Parkas and snow pants, many locally made of traditional patterns, hung on hooks by the entry door.

Schoolchildren's drawings and paintings of local animals, people in the village, and mythological characters hung on the walls. Many of the drawings and paintings were what you would expect from children, but some showed an astonishing skill and maturity for the ages of the artists listed on the labels.

The graduate students were there helping. The woman spotted me first. She walked over as I hung up my coat. "Hi. I'm Jennifer Sullivan. Weren't you on the plane?"

I nodded. "My name's Anne O'Malley."

"O'Malley?"

"Yes."

"The professor's wife?" She glanced at my left hand.

"Oh, no. Just a member of the family. I've come home for a visit." It wasn't strictly true, but I wanted it to be true, and it felt so good to say it.

The other women came over to greet me.

I distributed the gifts. Inuit etiquette required me to minimize them, so as I handed them out, I told the women what poor excuses they were for what I should have given. To Miqo, I said, "I'm without hope of ever improving as a seamstress. I'm ashamed to give these blouses to you, Saarak, and Allaq. I hope you won't think they're too awful."

The women were pleased, and Jack's sisters looked with approval at the seams and finishing I'd done on the blouses. I'd even hand-embroidered on the fronts.

"Anne, this is nice," Miqo said. "The fabric's beautiful, and the stitches on your hand-finishing are so tiny and even." Saarak and

Allaq were just as generous with their praise. I glowed with their compliments. It was plain to see they were proud of their student.

Miqo turned to show her blouse to Jennifer.

Jennifer looked. "Oh, yes, quite nice. I'm not much interested in sewing, though."

"Oh, OK," Miqo said. "We do a lot of sewing here, so we are interested."

I don't think Jennifer had a clue about the message she'd just received. She wandered off to talk to one of the other graduate students. I hoped she wasn't going to be that oblivious of her hosts the whole time she was here.

Jack and Maata arrived with many of the villagers. The children ran over calling my name—"Anne! Anne! Anne!"—like a little flock of chicks peeping around a hen. Jack's students looked up at the commotion.

One of the strange quirks of my mind is that I often have trouble remembering the names of adults I meet, but I never forget a child's name. I greeted them and sat with them on the floor out of the way of the adults' feet. They all had to tell me what they'd been doing while I was away. They wanted a story, but I looked up and saw that Jack had moved to the front of the room. "You'll have to wait a while. Jack's going to talk."

Laura saw that Jack was starting the meeting, so she waved goodbye and left.

Like my experience in the Ottawa airport seeing Jack click a switch from villager to urbanite, he had clicked another switch and become Professor O'Malley.

"Welcome to the Seminar in Arctic Adaptation," he said. "When I started graduate school, I was told that if I wasn't calling the professors by their first names by the end of the first month, I was in trouble, because in graduate school you begin that transition from student to colleague. We have only a month, so you can call me Jack from now on.

"I want to introduce my family. This is my brother-in-law Quipac. He's your co-teacher."

Quipac stood. Shorter and more compact in build than Jack, he had a weathered face. He wore his black hair in the more usual Inuit style, cut almost the same length all around, sort of a bowl cut. He didn't comb it back as Jack did. It hung over his forehead. He had dark eyes, a small nose, strong chin, mustache, and wispy goatee. He nodded to the students.

Jack went around the room and named each person as he had done for me on my first day. "This is my mother, Maata. This is my sister, Miqo, Quipac's wife. This is my sister Allaq. This is my sister Saarak. Their husbands, Portoq and Erqulik, are away hunting. You'll meet them later. This is my sister Anne."

The students looked surprised, probably because I didn't look like the others.

He continued with the rest of the names and relationships.

I think the students began to realize, as I had, that almost everyone in the room was related to one another and to Jack.

"Now you've had your first lesson in field work, although one of you is already ahead of the lesson. I understand Tom has filled the last two days talking to people and developing a kinship chart. Well done, Tom."

It was certainly easy to spot him. He was taller than anyone else in the room, and he blushed at being singled out.

"If you're going to work in small societies, you'll find that most of the people in your village will be related in one way or another through real or fictive kinship. Your work will advance more easily once you understand these relationships. Behavior that might seem inexplicable will fall into place when you look at the kinship bond.

"Now for your second lesson. Most of you have treated the people you're staying with as your valued hosts, but a couple of you seem to think they're your employees."

Jennifer and one of the men looked uncomfortable.

"I can assure you my family hasn't taken this personally. You're not the first nor will you be the last students they'll help me with. They understand that you need to learn. You thought your field experience started now, but that's not true. It started when you arrived here. I suggest you consider how your behavior from the first instant of contact will impact your fieldwork. People who don't feel respected are unlikely to be eager to share their culture with you.

"Your final lesson today is that we often have a party when people return after being away. Please share tea and food with us."

Conversation broke out. Some of the women distributed tea, stew, bread, cookies, and cubes of frozen raw meat. The food gifts I'd brought were opened and shared too, as I thought they might be.

The children told me the frozen meat was caribou. They were taking pieces. I noticed none of the other students tried it. I did. I figured if I was going to learn anything, I'd better get started. It wasn't bad. I just kept thinking "meat Popsicle." On the other hand, it wasn't great.

After we'd eaten, the children and I settled down, and I told them the story I'd prepared for them.

One by one, Tom, Syd, Nick, and Dave introduced themselves to me. They were shy about asking questions, but they were interested that I came from San Diego and didn't live in the village all the time. They didn't ask why I was here now, but when Jack gathered the six of us together for a meeting, he let them know I was going to be in the seminar with them.

I'd planned to tell him that I'd changed my mind and that I'd visit with Maata instead of taking the class. I hadn't expected him to announce my participation. I didn't want to embarrass him by publicly backing out. I had to see it through, at least for a while.

We told about ourselves. The students were working for their master's degrees in anthropology, but they hadn't known each other before they arrived in Blackwell. They were in their twenties. Jennifer, at twenty-nine, was the oldest. This four-week class, designed to acquaint them with some of the problems they'd run into if they chose Arctic anthropology as their specialty, would be their first practical experience in the field.

Jack had told me that what he'd taught me during that first week of my visit—what I'd perceptively called Inuit 101—had been the outline for this class. During these four weeks, I'd learn the same things in greater depth.

When Jack told us what we'd be doing, and especially now that I could see how young and vigorous the students seemed, I was concerned about my ability to keep up. That was one more reason why I shouldn't go. I decided I had to say something to him about what was going through my mind.

The wind had let up a little, so I asked him to walk with me. We went out to stand at the same place we stood on my first day in the village. If anything, the view was more beautiful than before. It was early afternoon, but the sun was almost below the horizon. What little daylight remained reflected off the dazzling snow. Where water had lapped in June, thick ice now hid under that same snow.

He waited for me to speak.

"Jack, I really think this is going to be more than I can manage. It might be better if I didn't go. I'll just slow you up." I could hear the sadness in my voice. I wondered if he could.

Again, I had that strange experience of looking at him and thinking that his face was expressionless. Then something changed, and I could see that I'd made him sad too.

"I want you to go. Please. I'll make it OK for you."

My heart turned over, but I said, "I can't ask you to change the class for me."

"It'll be OK. Remember, we walked a lot together during those weeks you were here and this last week too. I knew you before I invited you to try this. The other thing is, they're not nearly as vigorous as they look. One or two of them may be, but most of them spend most of their free time watching TV, not exercising. There'll also probably be a couple of smokers, who'll not be nearly as fit as they look. We don't allow them to smoke during the course, though. It would be too difficult to accommodate their needs. I'll pace the activities so all of you will survive, I promise."

I hesitated, but finally said, "All right. I guess you'll just have to nip at my heels like you did with the summer students."

At that memory, his smile came back and the sadness disappeared. He laughed. "Ah, I'd like to nip at your heels."

I laughed too. I'd thought this man was emotionless, but he wasn't at all. I just hadn't been able to see him before.

"Quipac's going to help me with the class. He'll be keeping an eye on you too."

"He helped you with the summer class too, didn't he?"

"Quipac has helped me with all my field classes from the beginning. He's been my best friend for as long as I can remember. He never had the opportunity to go to school, but he knows as much or more than I do about the digs and about our history."

"I didn't realize it would take two people to run our small class."

"It's always good to have a second pair of hands for the dogs and a second pair of eyes watching out for bears."

"Bears?"

"Oh, well, yes. We do have some things up here called polar bears. Didn't I mention that in my letter?"

"I must've missed that part. Are you serious?"

"Yes, but I haven't lost a student yet."

"Let's hope it stays that way."

"The last thing I need to mention," he said, "is that I won't be able to spend as much time with you as I've been doing. I really am working. It would make the other students envious if I obviously favored one over the rest, even if that one is my sister."

I wasn't surprised when he said that. I responded the only way I could. "That's OK. I'll just be one of the guys."

Chapter Twenty

THE NEXT MORNING, WE STARTED THE CLASS IN EARNEST. The first two weeks were going to be in the village learning the skills we'd need. The dance house would be our classroom.

The first thing we had to learn was how to avoid frostbite.

"It probably won't warm up to minus ten Celsius for the next month and could be considerably colder," Jack said. "I hope you'll be cautious. I don't want to have to amputate any fingers or toes."

"Have you ever had to do that?" Syd asked.

"Yes, but not for a student yet. I don't want to start with anybody in this class."

That was the first time it came home to me that we were embarking on something dangerous.

After they had talked about our physical safety, Jack and Quipac told about village etiquette—especially the importance of refraining from emotional expression around the villagers. They told us how difficult that would be for us, since we were not used to the kind of close contact we were going to experience in the next few weeks. It re-emphasized for me how uncomfortable I must have made him feel when I cried. I wondered if, in spite of our talk, he'd come to regret convincing me to stay in the class.

Jack continued. "I expect you to take proper field notes during the next four weeks. You're going to have to write up your experiences in the two weeks after you go home, comparing contemporary and traditional lifeways. You'll send your write-ups and the field notes to me. Anne, you have a choice of trying the assignment or auditing."

He'd said the previous day that the students got envious if they thought someone was getting favored treatment, so I said, "I'd like to do the assignment. I'll learn more that way."

This obviously pleased the others, and I saw a flicker of satisfaction on Jack's face too.

Then he gave us a forty-five-minute lecture on his standards for proper field notes—and we took notes. Now I was glad I'd taken that summer school class. I had no trouble keeping up with the others.

After the lecture, Jack and Quipac took us for a walk. Before we started, Jack explained how we were going to handle the "calls of nature." Since the Inuit had lived so closely together, privacy hadn't been an option and so hadn't been an issue for them. They felt no shame about sex and elimination. Privacy was an issue for us, but where we were going, there were no bushes to go behind. We would have to work on an honor system, with the men and women separating and promising to keep their backs turned until he or Quipac called us together again.

"Well," Quipac said, "as long as we've settled that, let's get going."

He and Jack slung packs onto their backs and then picked up rifles that had been next to the packs.

"Those are heavy-duty rifles. Are you going to be hunting as we walk?" Nick asked.

Jack took his off his back and held it up for us to see. Then he let us each hold it. It was really heavy. "We both carry Winchester 38-55s. No, we won't be hunting. These are for defense."

"Defense? From what?" Nick asked.

"Bears."

"Bears?" Jennifer said. "I thought bears hibernated in the winter."

Quipac answered. "You have to remember how long our winter

is. Most bears do hibernate. Among polar bears the pregnant sows and those with cubs go into dens and sleep a while, although they don't actually hibernate. Some of the boars do too, but most of them are out, moving around, and hungry. So, take what we say seriously. You stay near us at all times. Don't go wandering off. If you find yourself falling behind, call out. Don't be too proud to ask for help."

"Why aren't we all armed?" Nick asked.

Jack said with a smile, "Mostly because Quipac and I don't want to be shot."

As we walked, Jack and Quipac explained to us how the Inuit made a living today and in the past by hunting, fishing, and gathering in what seems like a barren land.

Although they told us the snow wasn't as deep as it would be later in the season, the walking was difficult. I could see Jack was right about my ability to keep up. We all struggled.

As I'd promised, I tried to be "one of the guys." I stayed with the pack and talked with the other students—when we weren't puffing and panting too much to talk. People in parkas and wraparound dark glasses all look pretty much the same. Bit by bit, the other students warmed up to me, and I to them.

One thing bothered me. Every time I looked up, Jennifer seemed to be at Jack's side. She was as tall as Jack and with her long legs, had no trouble keeping up with him.

We stopped to rest and eat after two hours. Jack had carried a small white-gas stove and a kettle in his backpack. Quipac melted snow and made tea for the group. He told us to watch. Tomorrow we were going to do it ourselves.

Jennifer came over with her cup of tea. "Do you mind if I sit with you?"

"Not at all. Sit here on the sofa," I said, patting the snow. "It's the most comfortable seat here."

She chuckled. "I'm sure glad we're taking a break. My legs are so tired. I'm from Florida. I didn't realize it would be such hard work walking through snow." As she spoke, she unstrapped her folded ground sheet from her pack, set it down, and sat.

"I know what you mean. We don't have a lot of snow in San Diego either."

"Why did you decide to take the class?" she asked.

"I'm doing some genealogical research. My father-in-law lived in Ungavaq in 1913 and '14. Jack suggested this class might teach me some things that would be useful in that research."

"Wow! That's interesting. Is this turning out to be what you expected?"

"I didn't have many expectations. I wanted to come at this with an open mind, so I didn't ask Jack exactly what we'd be doing. I really didn't ask him anything at all. When he suggested it, I just said yes."

"You're quite adventurous."

"I never thought I was. I haven't done anything like this before. I've never even been camping. My husband was a strict believer in hotels."

"We may all be when we get done with this. You know, it might be a good idea if we kind of hang together, since we're the only women here."

"That is a good idea. We're so outnumbered." And I really thought so. Maybe it would keep her from monopolizing Jack as she'd been doing.

We each had a pack lunch. Maata had made mine. It included two roast caribou sandwiches on homemade bread, several small hard-cooked eggs—not chicken eggs, but I didn't know what they were—a couple of apples, a piece of bread thickly spread with butter and jam, and a bag of corn chips. The others had similar lunches. Jack encouraged us to eat as much as we could. We'd need all the calories we could pack in. When I first looked at it, I didn't think I could possibly eat that much, but I managed that and a little more.

Jack and Quipac ate frozen raw fish, slightly thawed over the heat of the kettle. They held the fish in their teeth and sliced off pieces with their knives. They offered some to us. Tom and I accepted. I wasn't adept with the knife. I think I nearly cut my nose off once, but I got better with practice. The fish, Arctic char, was surprisingly good, but then, I like sashimi.

Jennifer and I talked until Quipac said we should move on.

It turned out that "hanging together" was just for lunchtime. When we started walking, she was right up there next to Jack again.

The sun set early in the afternoon. When we returned to Ungavaq well after dark, a hot dinner awaited us in the dance house. We discussed the day as we ate, worked on our notes—we were allowed to help one another—and stumbled off to exhausted sleep at the homes of our hosts.

Each of the first five days followed the same pattern.

What Jack had said on that first day about our not spending as much time together as usual wasn't strictly true. We actually spent every waking hour together; it's just that we were constantly in the company of at least six other people.

We did one thing differently from the way they normally ran the class. Jack asked me, and I agreed to have the story hour every day before dinner. I let it be known that I'd be reading again, so when we returned from our walk each day, most of the children in the village would be waiting for us. When I finished reading, as before, they'd tell stories. Now, sometimes Jack and Quipac would tell stories. Finally, even the students joined in.

I heard the story of Sedna for the first time during one of these sessions. Every myth has many versions. Quipac told us one of them:

"Sedna was the most important spirit for the Inuit before they became Christianized," he said. "She was a young woman who was disobedient to her father. She refused to marry when he said she should. To punish her, her father said that she must marry the next man who asked for her.

"A mysterious man arrived in the village, married her, and took her away to a desolate island. To her horror, Sedna found that her new husband was not a man at all. He was a spirit bird. He did not hunt for her as he had promised to do, but fed her only fish. Sedna wept in despair.

"Her father regretted sending her away. He came in a boat to take her home. They hurried to escape as fast as they could, but her husband found them when they were halfway across the water. The spirit bird flapped his wings and caused a terrible storm to arise.

"Sedna's father had trouble keeping the boat afloat. He was terrified of dying. To lighten the load and save himself, he threw Sedna overboard. She clung to the side and pleaded with her father to take her back into the boat, but joint by joint, he chopped her fingers off to make her let go. Her fingers sank into the water and became the fish, the seals, and the walruses. Sedna still clung on, so her father chopped off her hands, and they became the whales.

"Finally, Sedna sank to the bottom of the sea. where to this day she controls the ocean and the animals in it. Forever after, when a hunter catches a seal or a walrus, he's supposed to give it a drink of fresh water to show his respect for Sedna. Sedna becomes angry with the people if they fail to offer her proper respect. When that happens she traps the animals of the sea in her hair. When she gets over being angry, she can't comb her hair to release them because she has no fingers.

"In the old days, a shaman would go into a trance and go down to the bottom of the sea to find out why Sedna was angry and to placate her. He would comb her hair for her and release the animals so that they could be hunted again, and the people would no longer starve.

"Of course," Quipac said, "that was in the old days. We do things differently now."

Morale, which had been pretty low at the end of the first day, seemed to go up as people came to know what to expect and feel that they could manage the challenge.

My morale may have been more "iffy." Each day, whenever I looked in Jack's direction, there was Jennifer. During the lectures, she sat nearest to where he stood. During the walks, she was next to him. In the evenings, she always seemed to have something to say to him that required her to lean in close.

Her behavior irritated me. It took me a while, but I finally figured out that I was jealous. I hadn't felt that way since high school. Robby had sown his wild oats long before he met me. I don't think he ever looked at another woman while we were together. On the few occasions other women set their sights on him, he'd made it clear that he was interested only in me.

I'd known Jennifer's kind before. They're competitive and use their sexuality to monopolize the attention of the most powerful man in any group. We had four men younger than Jennifer and relatively powerless; we had Quipac, who was obviously happily married—we saw him with Miqo every evening when we went to the dance house for dinner—and we had Jack, powerful and possibly available.

Jennifer still sat with me during the lunches, and we spent a lot of time talking in the evenings. She told me about her life. She was much franker than I'd have been with a relative stranger. I got the scorecard on her various boyfriends' abilities at oral sex. This was definitely a lot more than I wanted to know. I chalked it up to the same thing that happens when you sit next to someone on an airplane, and she tells you her life story.

Jennifer also asked me questions. Clearly, she expected as much detail about my life as she gave me about hers, but I didn't want to share the personal details of my life.

When she asked whether Jack was single and if he had any girlfriends, it just confirmed my idea of where she was headed, and I couldn't seem to stop her. What I really wanted was to tell her to go away and leave me alone.

I found myself rehearsing scenarios in my head. Jennifer would say, "I'd really like to get to know Jack better," and I'd say, "Sorry, Jennifer. You'll have to back off. You see, I'm not Jack's sister. In fact, Jack and I are . . ." Jack and I are what? I didn't know any more. I'd never known. I couldn't fill in that blank in my head. And I didn't know what Jack wanted.

Jennifer was tall, slender, a natural blonde with big breasts—and young—all the things I wasn't. Although I couldn't see it, perhaps Jack welcomed her interest.

Of course I realized I was being illogical. How could I think that Jack couldn't be interested in me because I was an emotional kabluna, and, at the same time, think he was interested in Jennifer because she was younger and better looking than I was? I don't know how I could be that illogical. I just was.

Still, if Jack could be interested in someone like Jennifer, well, that was the real world. I told myself I was better off knowing it.

That resolve seemed to work in the daytime. But when I was alone at night, I found myself in tumult, alternating between anger and sadness. As I lay in the dark, I could feel those awful tears slide down my face

I thought about asking Maata for advice, but I couldn't imagine that she'd want to know about all this emotion. If I'd been able to, I'd have called Carola. But I was on my own here.

I finally ended up telling Jennifer that Jack was single, but that he didn't confide in me about his love life. She'd have to get the information she wanted from him. There was a noticeable cooling of our relationship after that, but none in the attention she was paying him.

Chapter Twenty-One

ON THE SIXTH DAY, JACK BROUGHT OUT A THIN, THREE-FOOT-long snow probe made of caribou antler. He showed us how to find the kind of wind-compacted, fine-grained snow used to make a snow house. We were all calling it an igloo, but Jack corrected us. An igloo was any kind of house, not just one made of snow.

When he found the right snow, he and Quipac marked out a big circle. Standing inside, they used long knives also made of antler to cut slabs of snow and set them around the edge. When they finished the first tier, they shaved it into a slope and built a spiral of blocks on top of it. They reached the end of the third tier, and Quipac stepped outside. From then on, he did the cutting. The walls got higher and higher. Quipac had to stand on snow blocks in order to reach the top. Jack helped him fit the blocks in the ever-decreasing spiral and shaved them from the inside to make them fit snugly.

Jack cut a ventilation hole about three inches in diameter in the last block and cut a doorway in the wall to let himself out. Together, they made a low-roofed porch and entry. It took them less than three hours to finish the entire house. The last thing Quipac did was to install a window of freshwater ice that he'd cut from a stream in a space on the south side near the entry. You couldn't see through it very well, but it let light in.

We all worked to fill the chinks and cover the house with additional snow. When we finished, someone started a snowball fight. Jack and Quipac stood back and didn't participate. At first, I thought they were standing on their dignity as teachers, but then I realized that this kind of aggressive play was "un-Inuit." I withdrew from the fight and joined them. They didn't say anything, but I could feel their approval.

We took a short afternoon walk. After dinner, Jack told us to get our sleeping bags and other gear. We were going to live in the snow house from now on.

When we returned, we were surprised to find him and Quipac wearing traditional skin clothes. I recognized Jack's clothes as the ones Maata had shown me. After she'd taught me how to sew caribou hide, she'd guided me in mending a tiny tear on the right sleeve. As I looked at it, I couldn't help but feel proud. My pride doubled when Jack pointed to it and quietly said, "Thank you."

While we'd been gone, they'd completed a two-foot-high shelf of snow, the *ikliq*, across the rear half of the house, using snow excavated from the front half. We'd sit and sleep there, up in the warmer air. The remaining floor space, the *natiq*, would be used for storage and work.

They'd spread the ikliq with a layer of branches and several layers of skins to insulate us from being chilled and to keep the ikliq from melting from our body heat and wetting our clothes.

The Inuit put a lot of effort into keeping their clothes dry, inside and out. In fact, when they came into a snow house, they took off most or all of their clothes. The clothes were carefully dried over the blubber lamp. If they didn't take that precaution, clothes wet from snowmelt or from sweat could freeze. It might not be possible to put them on again. That meant certain death.

We found it hard to believe people went naked in the chill of a snow house, but Jack and Quipac assured us it was true. When we were inside, they stripped down to cycle shorts. They invited us to do the same, but no one did.

"You must not feel the cold the way we do," Dave said.

"Sure we do," Quipac replied. "But we expect it, and we just don't see the point in complaining about it."

I'd seen Jack's beautiful back when he changed his shirt. Now I saw that his skin in front was as smooth as I'd imagined, except for scars: two heavy parallel lines that ran diagonally from his left shoulder down to his waist, where they disappeared under the waistband of his form-fitting shorts. My imagination followed them down. I was sliding into sexual fantasy until I saw Jennifer looking at him with an admiring smile, and I felt the now familiar, sickening jolt of jealousy.

"Jack," she asked, "what are those scars from?"

"Just an accident."

She noticed the amulet he wore. "Cool tooth. Is that from a bear?"

"Yes."

"Can I buy one of those in the village?"

"No. I think you'll have to look on eBay when you get home."

Or you can kill your own damn bear, I thought as I turned away. I didn't want to see her looking at him, admiring him, flirting with him.

Up to that point we'd been using Jack's white-gas lantern. That lantern gave off a lot of heat. Because of that and our body heat, the ceiling started dripping. The first icy drop landed right on the tip of my nose, and I gave a little squeal. When I looked up, I got the second one on my chin.

Jack looked at my nose and laughed. "It'll stop soon," he said as he gently wiped the wetness away with his finger. "The snow blocks will absorb most of the melt, and the house will actually be more weather tight. Give a little thought to what snow houses were like in the spring, though, when it was still too cold to move into the tents, but not cold enough to keep the snow frozen."

"What did you do?" Tom asked.

"We got wet," Jack said, and he and Quipac laughed.

"And we didn't complain about it," Quipac added. "It was just part of life."

Quipac lit two carved soapstone lamps, called *qulliqs,* to provide us with light and a little heat. The fuel was seal blubber and the wick was moss. "The lamp symbolizes the woman's place in the family. She takes care of her family by providing heat and light and food, and she's important because of that. On occasion, an Inuit man who was an exceptionally good hunter might have two wives. Each would have a lamp. We have a house with two women, so two lamps. Each of you must tend your lamp. I'll show you how. It's tricky, but you'll get the hang of it. In the winter, the wife rarely left the snow house. One of the reasons was that she had to tend the lamp. But they didn't have the advantage of matches. We'll let our lamps go out when we want to go out to do things."

"Did a woman ever have two husbands?" Jennifer asked.

"Rarely," Quipac said. "That might happen in an area where the hunting was so poor that it took two men to support a family. It was a difficult situation, though. Sometimes the husbands would fight and one would end up dead."

Our kitchen tables were piles of snow next to the corners of the ikliq. That's where the qulliqs sat.

We arranged our sleeping bags with the openings toward the center of the room. Although the housewife would normally sleep closest to the qulliq, Jack and Quipac took the colder positions next to the walls. Quipac said, "My sister, put your sleeping bag here," so I placed mine next to his. He'd never called me "sister" before. I didn't ask what it signified. It felt like a gift of friendship. I accepted it that way.

We were finally organized. Tom and Dave, as the two tallest, had the center positions, which had more legroom. Syd was between Tom and me and Jennifer was between Dave and Nick. While we were trying to get comfortable sitting or lying on the sleeping bags, Jack started to talk.

"I'm sure you know Inuit don't live permanently in snow houses or tents any more. Many of us now live in government-built housing. We drive snowmobiles instead of dog sleds. We send our children to school, pay taxes, and vote. But Quipac and I lived in tents and snow houses until we were adults. You're looking at where we grew up."

"Are you kidding?" Dave asked.

"No, why would I kid about that?"

"Well . . ."

"I can see how you'd be surprised. We all tend to think that what we see now has more or less existed forever. But although we'd been changing our way of life since explorers first arrived, that process didn't really speed up until the 1950s and '60s. We'll talk more about this through the next few weeks."

"So when did you stop living in snow houses?" Syd asked.

"In the late '60s."

"Wow," Jennifer said.

"How did you get to be a college professor?" Dave asked.

"That's a long story. We'll talk about that later. Anyway, at that time, when we lived in snow houses and tents, we were nomadic."

The pencils all went down on notebooks as we started writing.

"We didn't live in Ungavaq year round. We were there for the seal hunting and fox trapping, but we moved somewhere else for the fishing, and somewhere else again for caribou hunting. We moved many times each year for many different reasons—sometimes miles and sometimes just a few feet. We lived in a subsistence economy. We caught what we ate and made what we needed.

"We weren't aware of this until we were four or five. We lived inside our mothers' parkas for at least our first three years. We were in skin-to-skin contact with them nearly twenty-four hours a day. Then we had to make room for the next baby. When you have your own children, think about that.

"At about age five, we were considered to have developed enough good sense that our fathers could start teaching us to be men. That's still common in many places all over the world. Age five is when children start to take responsibility for child care, herding, or other work."

Quipac and Jack opened leather bags and showed us what turned out to be typical tools and weapons that the Inuit used.

They showed us each item, explained how it had been made, how they'd used it, and how it was stored. Wood was scarce in most of the Arctic. Some areas were rich in driftwood, but not this section of Ungava Bay. What wood the Ungavamiut people had, they'd acquired by trade. Mostly they used bone and antler as their raw materials.

These were items the family had actually used when they were living a traditional life—whips, harpoons, fishing spears, lances, bows and arrows, needles and needle cases, ulus, soapstone lamps and pots, toys, and other tools. Jack and Quipac had made some of these but Piuvkaq had made or traded for most of them.

I was fascinated. I'd seen duplicates of many of these items at the museum in Hull, but to see them here gave me a whole new perspective. They defined the problems the Inuit had faced living in this marginal environment, and they showed the skill with which they had solved those problems.

Jack finished his lecture, and we finally settled down to sleep. I'd taken off my parka and snow pants when we came into the house, but I'd felt chilly and decided to sleep in my clothes. Soon, though, I was too hot in that extra-warm sleeping bag.

Trying to be discreet, but probably not managing it, I wriggled out of my slacks and turtleneck shirt. Underneath, I wore long underwear—ankle-length silk pants with elastic at the waist and a separate long-sleeved shirt—that Jack had recommended I buy.

I was almost too warm in the underwear too, but, although I normally sleep in the nude, I wasn't going to strip down any more, even in the shelter of the sleeping bag.

We students spent most of the next day building our first snow house. The first two tries collapsed, but the third stayed up. It certainly wasn't beautiful, but Jack and Quipac said it wasn't going to fall in and it would, more or less, keep the wind and snow off.

Jennifer hadn't changed her behavior nor I my jealousy during all this time. Marcia had told me that if you were going to spend extensive time in a snow house with somebody, you couldn't afford emotionality. But that didn't stop my constant knotting up inside.

We worked hard that day. By the time we finished the story hour, dinner, and writing our notes, everyone was ready to sit or lie on the ikliq and relax. We talked, sang, and told stories and jokes.

"Hey, Jack," Jennifer said, "you haven't told a joke yet."

"Yeah, you tell one," Dave said.

"I don't know many, but there's one that's a favorite among the faculty."

"Go ahead."

"Tell it."

Syd nodded. "Yeah."

Jack looked at me. "Well, there was a professor having an office hour, and a beautiful co-ed came in. She had on a very short skirt and a very revealing blouse.

"He asked, 'How can I help you?'

"She said, 'I'm not doing well in your class, Professor. I wanted to let you know I'm willing to do anything to get a better grade.'

"'Do you mean "anything"?' he asked.

"'Yes. Anything,'

"'You really mean "*anything*"?'

"'Yes! *Anything*!'

"'There is this one little thing.'

"She leaned forward so her cleavage showed a little more and asked in a breathy voice, 'What?'

"'You could study.'"

A moment's silence and then the joke sank in. Everyone (except for one) burst into laughter. It took me a while before the light bulb went on in my head. Ridicule! Jack had just told Quipac how he disliked Jennifer's behavior.

But Jack didn't have to tell a joke to communicate with Quipac. They often conversed in Inuktitut. Was that message for me? Was he telling *me* that he didn't want her attentions? Something inside me gave a big sigh of relief, and I relaxed. I spent the rest of the evening smiling.

While I'd been so selfishly involved in my jealousy, I hadn't noticed that Jennifer's behavior had been affecting the other students too. It turned out that Quipac and I weren't the only ones who received a message from the joke. Jennifer modified her behavior—not without looking sulky—and the rest of the students seemed to relax.

From that night on, Jack and Quipac told us about growing up

Inuit—the kinds of games they played, and learning to hunt and fish with their fathers, tend the dogs, and make the tools they needed. They told us about the hard times too, when food ran short and people died of hunger or disease.

We always had children with us. They joined us in our various daytime activities, drifting away when they got bored. They didn't ask; they just did. At night, they snuggled in with Jack, Quipac, and me to listen to their own history, but they were shy with the other students. Sometimes they stayed all night. No one seemed to mind.

As Jack and Quipac talked during the evenings, I thought about Brendan—about his writing that he told stories to the children after the farm work was done. Genevieve had recognized that Brendan was telling her his life story, and I finally recognized that Jack was telling me his story in a way that he hadn't before—the story of Jack the Inuit, not Jack the student or urbanite or teacher. Now I wondered if Jack had really asked me to join the class for this. He wanted me to understand about Brendan, but had he also wanted to tell me about himself? Was this all for me so that I could know him better? I listened carefully to everything he said.

Our relationship had become intense—there was no other word for it. The more intense it became, the more confusing it was. He'd told me I was the only one besides his family and Marcia who knew his life story. Now he was telling me even more. I didn't understand what this signified.

I did understand one thing. He'd wanted to make love to me that night in his condo. I'd felt the desire in his body. But he hadn't done anything about it. I'd interpreted it as his being honorable, not taking advantage of a situation since he knew he didn't have feelings for me, but now I wondered.

I still didn't know what was possible between us. There was that side to Jack I didn't know. But in these days of the class, he was beginning to open that side to me. Was he doing this so that he could be a better brother and I a better sister, or was it something else? I just didn't know.

Chapter Twenty-Two

*O*N THE LAST DAY OF THE SECOND WEEK, JACK SAID, "PACK your gear. We're going for a long walk tomorrow. We're going to camp and live more or less as we Inuit did in the past, just to get a taste of the experience. It's going to be like one of those living history museums. You can achieve the look of the life, but you can never feel Inuit, because you didn't grow up in the culture. It's important you know this. You can't achieve the frame of mind that says, 'This is my life. Tomorrow will be the same. Next year will be the same. Forever will be the same.' You're playing Inuit the way you played cowboys and Indians when you were children, but you can still learn from the experience."

We were up early. Everyone was excited.

We loaded our gear onto two sleds, each about twelve feet long and two feet wide. Jack and Quipac looked and shook their heads. A lot of the people had come to see us go. They shook their heads too, and laughed. We were the entertainment of the day.

"Are we going to have to leave some stuff behind?" Jennifer asked.

"Well," Quipac said, "if you've got stuff you're not going to need, sure, leave it behind."

"Not really, but how are the dogs going to move that much?"

"Each of those dogs can pull a hundred pounds all day, so the team can pull a thousand. The loads aren't that heavy."

The crowd gave us suggestions on loading. Everyone had an opinion, many of them contradictory. We off-loaded and reloaded the sleds. Jack and Quipac shook their heads again, and again the people solemnly shook their heads, laughed, and made more suggestions.

After our third attempt, Jack and Quipac stepped forward and showed us how to stack and balance the loads. We finally completed the loading.

He and Quipac put the dogs in their traces in a fan hitch—each attached to the sled by a long line. That surprised me. I expected the dogs to be hitched in pairs to a central line to form a double row. That's what I'd always seen in movies. But Jack said that the double row was the style among the Eskimos in Alaska.

Quipac said, "We're going now."

Several of the people responded, "Yes, you're going."

Jack and Quipac rocked the sleds side to side to loosen them from the snow and cracked long whips in the air to get the dogs moving. They almost didn't need to. The dogs were so excited and eager.

I was astonished at how fast they were able to pull the heavily laden sleds once they overcame the inertia. We really had to move to keep up with them. We soon settled into a pace that alternated a few steps of walking with a few of jogging.

Many of the people ran with us. The adults stopped after a way, but the children went on much farther than I'd have thought they should without an adult. Neither Jack nor Quipac seemed concerned. Some were Quipac's grandchildren, so I decided if he wasn't worried, I didn't need to be either. Eventually the children headed back.

We trekked until Jack called a halt for lunch.

These were our last lunches packed by our hosts. Jack suggested we enjoy them.

Uh oh! I thought. His statement seemed innocuous, but I thought perhaps it was a hint of something to come.

After we'd finished our food and tea, Jack said, "Although we've been walking, sometimes people did ride. Do any of you want to ride awhile?"

Silence as we looked at one another.

Jack had made this offer for me, I knew, but there was no way in the world I was going to be the first to say I'd like to ride.

No one stepped forward.

"Now something more serious. We're going into an area that's heavily populated by bears this time of year. They're traveling through looking for food. I'd prefer you not become lunch. I'm serious when I say that when we stop this afternoon, I don't want you to leave the immediate vicinity of the house. By immediate, I mean no farther away than where the dogs are staked, without either Quipac or me with you. I hope you don't feel this is too restrictive, but it is important. Please, don't forget."

Later that afternoon, when I was about three steps past what I thought was the last step I could possibly take, Jack called a halt. "We'll stop here for the night. Take a ten-minute break, and we'll start our house."

There was some groaning, but most of us were too tired to complain. After a break that was much too short, we prepared our campsite. Jack reminded us that we were living as the Inuit had. They also had to prepare their campsite after each difficult and fatiguing journey.

Quipac showed us how to chain up the dogs. He started to say something, and Tom said, "We know, we know. We'll be doing it tomorrow." Everyone laughed, even Quipac. I was surprised, because in the Inuit world interrupting is even worse manners than in ours. Yet he ignored the rudeness and laughed at the joke.

The dogs, staked in a big circle around the area where we were going to build, were our first and only line of warning if a bear approached. Takoolik, the alpha dog, and Aputik, the alpha bitch, ran free as an added defense.

The dogs settled down and we started construction. First, we built two platforms up out of dog reach to store the sleds. If we didn't do that, Takoolik and Aputik would eat the hide lashings that held the sleds together. Sled dogs were notorious for eating anything they could get their teeth into.

"Why are the sleds held together by leather strips instead of screws?" Dave asked. "Screws would solve the problem of the dogs eating the leather."

"We didn't have metal until the traders came," Quipac said.

"What about pegs? A lot of furniture is held together by pegs."

"Good question," Quipac said. "You know the snow looks smooth, but isn't. You saw how much the sleds were bounced around today going over the uneven terrain. Pegs, and even screws, would pull out over time. These ties, made of bearded-seal skin, allow the sled to flex, but they don't let go. The bouncing around just makes them tighter."

We built the house and, for the first time, Jack and Quipac helped us. They could see how tired we were. It still seemed to take a long time. Finally, we were able to stop and rest inside the completed house.

"What's for dinner tonight, Jack?" Nick asked.

"Fish and tea."

Silence as news of the menu sank in. We were to eat as the Inuit had when they were traveling. At least the ones who wanted to got to cook theirs over the qulliq.

By this time, everyone was too tired and hungry to complain, so we did eat. Almost everyone seemed to enjoy the meal. Cervantes wrote that hunger is the best sauce, and he was absolutely right.

After dinner, we settled down on the ikliq, and talked about the day. Quipac quietly mentioned the incident with the dogs and reminded us about Inuit manners. I realized that he'd chosen to allow that moment of camaraderie to occur, but as a good teacher, he couldn't allow it to pass without comment. That was the first time I realized that he was able to shift between the Inuit and kabluna worlds as Jack did.

We all settled in. I could hear Jack and Quipac speaking quietly in Inuktitut, and I thought I heard my name mentioned. I wondered what they were saying and if they were talking about me. In a short time, their gentle voices lulled me to sleep.

When we left the house before sunrise, we had a treat. Stars stretched from horizon to horizon in the clear sky. The only other light was the muted glow of the lamps inside the snow house and the fingernail-moon low in the sky. I'd never seen anything like it. We were in a bowl of stars. "Breathtaking" doesn't begin to describe it.

This time we were better at loading the sleds. Jack and Quipac had to do only a little rearranging. We also harnessed the dogs. They knew we were inexperienced, and they took every opportunity to be uncooperative, but we finally managed.

"These are *qimmiq*, Canadian Inuit dogs, a disappearing breed," Jack said. "We raise them in hope that they wouldn't die out entirely."

They seemed to come in all colors and patterns—black, brown, white, gray, and all sorts of combinations. What they had in common was their strength and their size—between fifty and eighty pounds, the females smaller than the males.

"I want you all to touch them," Jack said.

The others stepped forward. I hung back. I was afraid of them. I've never had a dog. These were so big and powerful, and they were pugnacious. They snapped and snarled at each other.

"Come on, Anne," he said. "Your turn."

"But they snap sometimes."

"They won't snap at you or snarl. They know better. Come on."

I reached forward gingerly. The one I touched had a rough long outer coat and an amazingly soft undercoat that were really nice. He carried his curly tail high over his back, waving like a flag.

That done, I faced the day with a little more confidence. This day was like the previous one, except breakfast and lunch were fish and tea.

In midafternoon, but already after dark, Quipac said, "This looks like a good place to camp."

Jack concurred.

None of us could see much difference between this site and what we'd been walking through all day, but we were quick to agree.

Jack told us we could unpack the sleds. We were staying here. We were soon busy with our tasks.

We worked together to unhitch and chain the dogs, and then we started on the house.

When we had the house complete, Quipac surprised us. He unpacked the freshwater-ice window and installed it near the door. He told us the Inuit often carried a window with them when they moved, because the right kind of ice wasn't always available.

Jack gathered us together to discuss our meals. We were to alternate days cooking. We were relieved to find out we were going to get to eat more than just frozen fish on this trip. They'd brought supplies of food for us to work with.

"Usually, women did the food preparation, but in deference to more modern thinking, you men are going to get to participate too. Everybody who thinks he or she is a good cook, raise your hand." Jennifer, Syd, and I did. He divided us into three teams, each with a more-experienced and a less-experienced cook.

"Quipac and I are willing to form a fourth team," he said and smiled.

There was a moment's silence as we thought this over.

"What's the catch?" Tom asked.

I was beginning to understand Jack's sense of humor. "You'd better ask them what they'll cook."

Jack just kept smiling.

We quickly voted down their offer.

We had another surprise. They showed us a meat cache not far from where we'd built the house. Quipac had constructed it weeks before our class started. First, he'd placed a layer of gravel to keep the caribou meat and fish from freezing to the ground, and then he'd covered the food with slabs of ice to keep scavengers away.

"How did you manage to find the cache again in all this whiteness?" I asked.

"Could you find something in your own backyard?"

"Yes."

"So can I." Quipac laughed.

"Now, you go into the house," Jack said. "Do whatever you need to do to get settled. Quipac and I have a project. We don't want you to come out until we call you."

About an hour later, they invited us to come outside. There was now a second, much smaller snow house adjacent to the one we'd built. Jack invited us to look inside, and there was a potty-chair! Jennifer and I were ecstatic—no more squatting in the snow. They recruited us to help, and we soon built a tunnel connecting the two rooms.

We pitched in and put together a three-sided windbreak of blocks of snow, and Jack unpacked a small camp stove. We cooked outside because the stove generated so much heat. We all helped Jennifer and Nick, the first cooking team, prepare dinner. When we got back inside the house to eat, there was a lot of talking and laughing.

After we'd settled on the ikliq, Jack said, "We think there's some bad weather coming in. For the next few days, we don't want you going outside unless we tell you it's OK. If the snow's blowing, it's easy to get disoriented and lost, even if you're only a few feet away, and we couldn't hear you yell over the sound of the wind."

They were right. None of us, except Jack and Quipac, went outside the snow house for the next two and a half days. Gale winds howled. Snow fell. Jack and Quipac went out only to get food from the cache and to check on the dogs. When they returned they were coated with snow. They beat the snow off their clothes and hung them to dry. By the time they finished, the snow in their eyebrows and on their cheeks had melted in the "warmth" of the house.

We'd worried about the dogs until Jack said, "They're OK. Snow's a good insulator. They burrow down to make dens that protect them from the wind. They sleep through the storm."

Jack and Quipac did most of the meal preparation for those three days. They cooked over the qulliqs in soapstone pots. The wind blew much too hard for cooking outside on our camp stove.

We spent our time talking, singing, working on our field notes, and, like the dogs, sleeping. We were able to sleep hours more than we normally would. The dim light made it easy, and we were tired from the hard work of the previous two weeks.

The longer we were cooped up, though, the more irritable we students became. From time to time, we had little disagreements. At the beginning, Jack and Quipac talked to us about the kind of patience required for such close living. After that, they only had to look in our direction to quell any tension.

On the third day, the wind let up. We were delighted to be set free, although we weren't sure we'd be able to get out of the snow house. It turned out we had no problem. We expected deep snow on the ground, but in fact, most of the "snowfall" had been existing snow moved by the wind.

That day, we went together as Quipac and Jack showed us how they set a trap line for Arctic foxes, making deadfall traps of slabs of ice. They propped each slab on a stick balanced on a roundish stone. They tied the bait, a piece of seal blubber, to the stick with a leather thong. If a fox pulled on the bait, it would dislodge the stick and the ice slab would crash down.

They trapped foxes in the winter for their fur, which brought money into the village. They had dark fur in the summer, but in the winter the pelts were white and in peak condition.

Jack said fox meat was good to eat in the winter too, but not in the warmer weather. I was hoping they wouldn't expect us to try some. Of course, later, they did. The meat was stringy, tough, and extremely gamy. None of us managed to choke it down.

We'd been so busy we lost track of the days. The day we set the trap line, we'd finished our chores when Nick remembered the date—December 25.

Jack and Quipac hadn't forgotten. That night, Jack heated up some of Maata's caribou stew, and we had a party. After dinner, he brought out eight cans of peach halves. We were ecstatic. These were our first sweets since we'd left Ungavaq. After we'd finished the fruit and drunk every drop of the syrup, I rummaged among my things and brought out a two-pound box of chocolates. From the reaction I got, people still had room for more sugar. We shared until there wasn't a single one left.

Quipac brought out a drum, the only musical instrument the Inuit had. The drumhead looked like a big tambourine on a handle. He played it by beating it on the rim with a stick. We learned some Inuit songs about the winter season and sang Christmas carols too, with Quipac's accompaniment. They also taught us a dance, and we danced in that confined space by standing still and moving our bodies.

The next days passed quickly as we kept busy with lectures, discussions, and demonstrations.

We took turns going with Quipac each day to check the traps. My turn came. I'd be alone with him for the first time.

He told me walking this very short trap line out and back would take about five hours. This would be easier than the ten hours we'd walked previously. Quipac showed me how to drive the dogs, and I did that for a while. Then he took over again.

It had been dark when we started out, but the day finally dawned beautiful and clear. The wind was light. The only sounds I heard were the creaking of harnesses, the dogs panting as they pulled the sled, and the strange whooshing squeal of the sled runners riding through the snow. Aside from an occasional warning from Quipac about my footing, we hardly spoke.

I was really enjoying myself, but my mood began to shift as we neared the first trap.

Jack had explained that the Inuit are a hunting culture. It isn't realistic to think they could live any other way in this environment.

The hunters had brought back caribou when I'd visited in the summer, but the caribou had been butchered at the kill site. They didn't look like the packages of meat I bought at the store, but they didn't look like animals either.

I didn't want to see dead foxes. I knew they'd be horrible. We walked up to the trap, I with my teeth gritted.

Quipac pulled away the block of ice and picked up the fox. I expected something limp and bloody, with its head lolling and its tongue hanging out. Instead, I saw something that looked like a slightly misshapen stuffed toy. The fox was frozen.

He stood, holding the carcass.

After a moment, I said, "I should touch it."

"If you want to."

"I should hold it. I need to learn this."

The thought of holding the fox was nauseating. I'd never touched a dead animal before. We'd never had pets, and I'd managed to avoid biology in high school. Robby and Ernesto had always taken care of dead mice and birds and the one cat that had been run over in our street.

Quipac waited for me to come to him.

I was shaking a little. I took the carcass from his hands. I expected it to be light like the toy I was trying to convince myself it was. Its weight surprised me.

"You don't need to be afraid. I won't ask you to do anything that's too unpleasant for you. We won't be skinning the foxes here. Jack and I'll do that later."

"Tell me how you skin them."

He removed his glove and drew with his finger on the fox's underside where he would make his cuts. "If you want to learn, I'll let you do one."

"I don't think I'm ready for that yet." I so much wanted to say yes, but I just couldn't.

He took the fox from me and tied it onto the sled. We added more seal blubber for bait, reset the trap, and went on.

We stopped after two hours, made tea to warm ourselves, and ate raw fish for lunch. Although we'd gone in companionable silence for much of the first part of our walk, after lunch Quipac started conversation by saying, "Thank you."

"I don't know why you're thanking me."

"For being as quiet as you are."

"Oh."

"This is the first time we've walked together, but I've been watching you since the beginning. Jack asked me to keep an eye on you, so I have. You're not uncomfortable with silence. So many of the younger ones are."

"I guess some of their energy gets used up by talking. I was worried about whether I could keep up with them."

"You're doing fine."

"Hmm. Now I guess I have to be quiet for the rest of the walk."

He chuckled. "No, we'll talk. There's a purpose behind this walk, other than foxes. In this class, we do almost everything as a group, so we think it's a good idea to get each student away, to be quiet or to ask questions if they want to. Some students are almost overwhelmed by the intimacy and constant contact of living in a snow house. I've noticed you have the ability to go inside yourself for quiet when you need to."

"Sometimes when I'm inside, I'm not quiet. My mind is going a mile a minute."

"I've seen that too. You had a problem with Jennifer."

How did he know?

"She's young," he said. "She may improve with age."

Now I laughed. "That's not what I expected you to say."

"Tell me what you expected I might say."

"I thought you might say I was being undignified. That's the way I felt."

"Dignity is important to us. That's why ridicule is effective against people who break the rules. But I admired the way you handled things."

"You could see?"

"Sometimes in the night, if you were facing me in your sleeping bag, I could hear your quiet tears. You never showed them any other time. I could see you were struggling. You won. You let it pass, and it took care of itself."

"I'm surprised at this conversation."

"Yes, I probably wouldn't talk to you like this in the village, unless we were alone. It's undignified for a man to pay too much attention to women's talk in public." He smiled. "I think in private, though, it's the same everywhere. A smart man listens when a woman talks."

I laughed. "You make a joke of it, but it is like that in the village."

"Yes, we have our ways."

"I've noticed."

"You're learning to see."

"I'm trying. It's important to me. I want to learn the right way to be when I'm there."

He nodded. "Just keep watching. I've learned from Jack, though, that outsiders usually need things laid out more plainly than we would in the village. It may not be easy."

"We're not as subtle as the Inuit?"

"I guess you could say that, but you could also say you're not attuned to the level of communication we manage with body language and silences."

"Somehow you don't sound like that simple Inuit hunter you seem to be most of the time."

He laughed. "You're right. I'm not. You know I go with Jack on his digs and field classes."

"Yes, he told me that."

"We've traveled together all over Canada, Greenland, Alaska, Lapland, even Siberia. I've seen a lot of the world with him."

"Have you traveled south at all?"

"No farther than Ottawa and a few airports when we changed planes."

"Why is that?"

"Well, in many ways, I am that simple hunter. I'm content in the village, but I go where our work takes us. I just think of it as following the herds." He laughed again.

"You and Jack have been friends a long time."

"Yes. His family took me in when my parents died during a hungry year."

"Oh. I'm sorry."

"That's in the past—a long time ago."

"Did you ever want to go to Ottawa with him when you were a child?"

"I never had an urge to go. I missed him, but he always came home and told me what he was doing there. That was his life. The life in the village was enough for me, but not for him."

I looked down. "I'm embarrassed to be asking questions. I know it's not good manners."

"It's OK. For a while, you can think of me as a teacher. When we get back to the village, I'll become that simple hunter again."

"I think you might be using ridicule there, or maybe you live in two worlds the way Jack does."

"Your second thought is more accurate," he said. "But it's easier for me than it is for Jack."

"Why?"

"The teaching is something I put on like a coat and can take off again. But for Jack, it's who he is. I can stay in the village and be content, but for him to be who he is, he has to leave, and that's difficult for him."

"I've come to care a lot for Jack."

"Yes."

"Is it that obvious?"

"To me it is."

"To the other students?"

"No. They don't pay attention. They don't listen to the silences."

"Is it obvious to Jack?"

"Not yet."

"In that struggle you watched, there was one thing I didn't win. Jennifer wanted to know whether Jack was interested in any women in the villages."

"And you want to know too."

"Yes."

"I won't answer that for you," he said. "You know that's between you and Jack."

"That's more or less what I said to Jennifer. You don't like being pumped for information any more than I did."

"That's right."

"Do the other students ask you about Jack? Did Jennifer?"

"I wouldn't talk to them the way I talk to you."

"Why talk to me about this?"

"You're Jack's sister, so you're my sister. We're family. We take care of each other."

I hadn't known it would be like this—this sudden welling of joy in my heart. Jack had said Quipac was a man of influence. In this, I knew he was speaking for the family. I was going to say how happy that made me, when I saw him looking at me impassively. He was listening to the silence. He knew. And I knew the right thing to do. "My brother," I said quietly, "I thank you for your care."

He nodded.

"Will you tell Jack what we talked about today?"

"I usually do after these trips, but I won't if you don't want me to."

"When I first knew Jack, I told him I didn't have to hide anything from him. I don't want to change that."

He nodded. "Well, time to get back to work."

We shared the small amount of tea left in the pot and repacked our lunch things onto the sled.

We'd originally set the traps in a big circle. When we finished checking them, we were actually only about a half-hour away from the camp. The sun had already set. We topped a little rise, and we could see the warm glow from the lamps inside the house. We were home.

Quipac let me drive the sled into camp, triumphantly, with our load of dead foxes.

Chapter Twenty-Three

One day they took us seal hunting. We hadn't realized it, but as we'd walked during those first two long days, we'd been on sea ice following the contour of Ungava Bay. It was smooth here, but not too far ahead, we could see the ice mounded into pressure ridges. Occasionally we could hear a grumbling, grinding noise or a sharp crack as distant ice shifted and piled up upon itself.

Quipac held Aputik on a leash as she sniffed out a hole. It was so small and so well-covered with snow that I don't think we'd have ever spotted it, but Aputik could smell it. Quipac moved a small amount of snow so we could see and then re-covered it. "The seal will not come if it can see daylight."

Jack laid his harpoon down with the tip touching where the hole hid under the snow, and then we looked for a second hole. Aputik found another, more than one hundred feet away from the first. We marked that one with Quipac's harpoon and walked another hundred feet or so.

Jack told us to sit. "The sea water froze in November. The ice is probably two to three feet thick here. It won't thaw until June if the weather is normal. The seals have to breathe when they're under the ice, so they maintain a series of holes, as many as a dozen or more, where they come up for air. They keep these open using their claws and teeth. The holes are small at the surface—usually just big enough for the seal's nose, sometimes just big enough for one nostril—but they're cone-shaped as they extend down to the water. The seal has to be able to get its entire body into the hole to get its nose to the surface of the ice.

"We don't normally hunt seals until closer to February when the snow cover is thicker and muffles the sound of our footsteps. Seals have acute hearing, and ice transmits sound. I want you to sit quietly. Watch what I do. Quipac will explain it to you."

On a command from Quipac, Aputik settled down and went to sleep.

Jack walked to the hole he had marked.

Quipac quietly explained Jack's actions as we watched.

Jack put his rifle down next to him, then inserted two fur-padded harpoon rests into the snow. He placed something else where the tip of his harpoon sat, then laid the harpoon on the rests.

Quipac showed us a duplicate of what he had placed on the snow—a small piece of sinew with swansdown attached. When the seal arrived, he explained, the turbulence caused by its arrival would make the down flutter.

Jack laid down his fur-covered hunting bag, then stood on it, put his hands in his sleeves to keep them warm, and bent at the hips to stare at a spot in front of him. I'd seen paintings and soapstone carvings of this scene in gift shops and art galleries in Ottawa—the Inuit bundled in his fur parka and bent over, waiting. It was a thrill seeing it in real life.

"A seal might come to that hole, but perhaps not," Quipac said. "Seal hunters usually work in groups, with one man at each hole. Sometimes they wait for hours and still go home hungry. We won't wait for hours. Now, you stay here and watch us."

He walked to the other marked hole and positioned himself as Jack had.

We sat more than an hour. Even with much quiet shifting around, we were stiff and chilled. Jack and Quipac had made no movements I could detect.

Without warning, Jack's hand swept down. He grabbed the harpoon, and forced it with all his strength through the snow. At the same time, he gave a yell, and Quipac was up and running. At Quipac's gesture, the rest of us ran over too, and grabbed the rope attached to the harpoon. We joined Jack in a tug-of-war pulling on the line attached to the harpoon head.

After several minutes, we felt the line go slack. Quipac took an axe and chopped the hole larger. He and Jack pulled the body of the dead ringed seal out onto the ice.

Then Jack gave me a gift. He knelt next to the seal, gathered snow in his bare hand, and held it until it started to melt. He directed the fresh water down his index finger into the dead seal's mouth.

He looked at me.

We could have been the only two people there.

"I give this seal a drink of water to show my respect for him," he said. "Now, his spirit will go back and tell his companions he was treated properly, and it's OK to come here and be hunted."

Some of the others thought Jack was acting, but I knew he wasn't. I understood that this, finally, was a message for me alone. He hadn't said, "The Inuit do this," or "We do this," but "I do this." Now he'd chosen to open himself to me—to let me see some of his Inuit self, his core. Something important had just shifted in our relationship.

I nodded to him.

He smiled.

Emotions, other than those, swirled around this event. It's one thing to have an academic knowledge that the Inuit are a hunting culture. It's quite another to see the reality of that fact lying bleeding on the ice in front of us. We'd seen the foxes in the traps, but this was so much more immediate. They hadn't looked real. This seal did.

I'd never seen this seal alive, but I'd felt its life in the rope as it struggled to escape being dragged up onto the ice. I'd felt its desire to live, and I had helped snuff out that life. I felt a wave of revulsion as I thought about what I had just done. But the plain fact was I couldn't pick and choose the parts of Inuit culture I was willing to accept. The family had opened their arms to me. If I wanted to be with them, if I wanted to be with Jack, I had to accept the core values of their world. I knew I had to work this out.

We tied lines around the carcass and started dragging it back to the house. It weighed more than I'd have thought—Jack said probably close to 160 pounds.

We were about halfway back when Aputik became agitated and finally snarled and howled with excitement.

"We're not the only ones who've been hunting seals today," Jack said.

There, in the snow, were the tracks of a large animal that had walked through heading north. They crossed over the tracks we had made earlier in the day.

"What went past here, Jack? Are those bear tracks?" Dave asked.

"Yes. A big male. Now you know why we carry these rifles."

"That bear has also killed a seal," Quipac said.

"How do you know that?" Dave asked.

"If he were hungry, he'd have turned to follow our scent when he crossed our tracks. Polar bears hunt humans."

Tom stepped over to one of the tracks and made a boot print next to it. The bear's track was bigger. What had been an academic fact from one of Jack's lectures became a chilling reality.

"We won't do any bear hunting today," Jack said, "but leave our seal there. We'll backtrack."

We walked for about forty-five minutes, Aputik eagerly leading the way.

"There it is," Quipac said.

Up ahead we saw the remnants of a carcass next to a smashed-open breathing hole.

Ravens and foxes stopped fighting over scraps and formed a wary circle as we walked up to the carcass.

"Each bear is followed by a coterie of scavengers," Quipac said. "When the bear has eaten its fill, they move in."

"Lord, there's not much left," Tom said. "What is that?"

"The spine and part of the head," Quipac said. "The bear waited by the hole the way we did. He's so powerful he can smash through the ice and kill the seal with one blow of his paw. They eat mostly the fat. Sometimes that's all they eat, but this one was hungry. They can eat up to three hundred pounds at a time."

We left the remains and returned to our own seal.

When we reached the house, the other dogs whined and shivered with desire. They knew they were going to eat.

Jack and Quipac butchered the seal and brought in some of the meat and blubber to be boiled over the qulliq for dinner. Jack gave the raw seal liver to me and said, "Anne, please cut this in thin slices and serve it to the others."

When Jack asked me to serve the liver, I saw Quipac glance at me and at him. After my talk with Quipac, I'd been paying more attention to the silences. I was beginning to recognize subtle signals, even if I didn't know what they meant.

Everyone except Jennifer tried the raw liver. It was actually pretty good.

That evening, we talked about what we felt and thought about the hunt. Jack reminded us of the reality of the meat section in our local supermarkets at home. I still felt strange about what I'd seen and done, but I couldn't argue against it.

New Year's Eve arrived. This time we were expectant. Jack didn't let us down. He provided another food treat. He made those apple pancakes for us, and even had three bottles of champagne. We students poured champagne into our tea mugs and toasted one another and the New Year—Jack and Quipac toasted with water—and we all sang "Auld Lange Syne." Jack—never one to lose an opportunity to teach—told us how the Inuit thought of the cycle of their year.

The next day, I waited until everyone was out of the house. I went back in and took a birthday card out of my backpack. As I stood debating about whether to put it in Jack's sleeping bag, I heard a noise.

Quipac had come in.

I blushed and said something inane like, "Oh, hi," and that didn't seem adequate, so I showed him the envelope. "It's his birthday."

He smiled. "Yes, my sister, I know, and he's not interested in anyone in the villages."

"Thank you."

He turned to leave.

"Quipac, please."

He turned back. "I'm listening."

"Could he love me?"

He looked surprised. "Oh, yes. He could love you." He turned again and went out.

His answer took my breath away.

That night, as Jack was getting into his sleeping bag, I saw him find the card.

I'd signed it, "All my love, Anne."

I watched him as he read it in the dim light.

He smiled, looked at me, and, in a gesture that echoed his mother's, pressed it to his heart before he settled down in his sleeping bag.

I didn't sleep much that night.

Chapter Twenty-Four

I opened my eyes and looked at my wrist. My watch still wasn't there. Jack had said he didn't want us to bring anything the traditional Inuit wouldn't have had except for personal health or hygiene items. So, no watch. It sat on the dresser in Ungavaq. I didn't know whether I should wake up or go back to sleep.

I wasn't supposed to feel irritated. I was still trying to be more even-tempered, but I wasn't doing well at it.

I went into the toilet room and then returned.

I'd thought I was the only one awake, but I saw that Jack was sitting cross-legged on his sleeping bag. He'd told me that even if you don't say the words, your body language gives away the emotion. He saw, but he only shook his head and grinned. I was glad he thought it was funny. The last thing I wanted him to do was to turn his back on me now.

I wondered what I ought to do. Carola and I'd had that conversation about signals. She was right. Jack was sophisticated. I thought maybe I should give him a signal he couldn't mistake.

Previously, I'd wiggled into my clothes in the sleeping bag, but not today. I stood in front of him. Slowly and deliberately, I pulled my jeans and sweater on over that clingy silk underwear in a sort of reverse strip tease.

He watched my every move.

Let him think about that, I thought as I pulled on my snow pants, boots, and parka, and stepped quietly toward the entrance.

I crawled out the tunnel. The snow made a scrunching sound under my hands and knees.

The dogs, their backs powdered with newly fallen snow, lifted their heads and looked at me. They realized almost immediately I wasn't coming to feed them, or make them work, for that matter, so they settled down again with their noses tucked under their tails.

I stood in the muted light. We were ten days past the winter solstice, when the sun hung low in the sky for a few hours each day. Right now, it sat just below the southeastern horizon. The waning moon seemed to rest on the snow in the southwest. The clouds that had brought those few flakes of snow had disappeared. The morning was quiet and beautiful.

I'd seen Jack get off the ikliq shortly after I finished dressing. I wanted to have a few minutes alone with him. I turned to look as he followed me out, but Quipac was behind him. I'd have to wait.

"Good morning," I said.

They carried their rifles, and Jack said I could walk out a way to stretch my legs and get the kinks out of my muscles, as long as I didn't go too far.

"I think I will," I said. "The snow house doesn't give much room to move around."

I'd walked about ten feet beyond where the dogs were tied. I'd just turned around to ask how far was too far, when I saw Quipac poke Jack.

Jack called out, "Wait, Anne, and I'll walk with you."

As he said that, two things happened. I sensed some movement out of the corner of my eye. Simultaneously, the dogs near me leapt up and ran to the ends of their chains toward me. Their hysterical snarling and howling as they strained at their leashes was a shocking change from the previous profound silence.

I stood, stunned. Then I turned my head toward the movement I'd seen, as Jack shouted, "Anne, come back!" There was an urgency in his voice I didn't understand until I realized the movement I'd seen was a bear coming rapidly and silently toward me!

I couldn't believe what I was seeing. In spite of the dim light, I didn't think it possible that something so huge could come so close without my noticing, but there it was, within fifteen feet of me.

When Jack yelled, it paused and reared up on its back legs to its full height as if momentarily unsure of what to do. It towered above me, sniffing the air. It seemed to look at the sky, but I knew better. Its entire interest was focused on me like a laser.

It roared.

I started to tremble. I couldn't move. The roaring filled my head and filled my body, leaving no room for thought or will.

I could hear someone running toward me. Jack shouted something, but my brain wouldn't make sense of it. He yelled again, and something in my head clicked into place. He'd said, "Anne, drop down!" I felt paralyzed, but I put all my effort into complying. I fell to my knees as the bear continued to roar. It stood at least ten feet tall. On my knees in front of it, I felt tiny and helpless.

Suddenly, I heard the loud crack of a rifle. A small red splash appeared on the bear's chest.

The dogs stopped their raging as abruptly as they'd started it.

Jack continued firing as he ran toward me. Quipac ran close behind him.

More red splashes appeared on the bear's chest.

Jack, and then Quipac, stood between it and me.

The bear seemed unaffected by the bullets at first. It continued to stand and roar, but then it hesitated, came down on all fours, and, suddenly, collapsed and twitched, but didn't try to rise.

The world became silent again.

Jack walked over to the bear and kicked one of the paws.

It didn't move.

He turned toward me.

I was still kneeling, trembling so hard I couldn't get up. I couldn't seem to remember how to stand.

He came to me and put down his rifle. He took my hands and

pulled me up, but I still couldn't move and couldn't stop shaking.

"Oh, Anne, I'm so sorry. We didn't think he was that near camp."

Tears poured down my face.

Jack stepped close and put his arms around me. He was shaking too.

My head sank to his shoulder. We stood like that for a long time, neither saying anything, until the trembling began to ease.

He turned his face toward me and saw my tears. Tenderly, he began to kiss them away, but not in the way a brother kisses a sister.

"I thought I was going to lose you," he said, his voice hoarse with tension. Then he kissed me on my mouth. His kiss started soft, tentative. I'd worried about signals, but I must have given him the right one, because the kiss changed. Suddenly it was passionate, seeking, desiring. All the love he'd been holding back was in that kiss.

My answer was just as passionate.

It was he and I. The rest of the world faded away.

He looked at me the way he'd looked at me that first day. "Oh, Anne . . ."

We realized the others stood in shocked silence near the entrance to the house. Whatever he'd planned to say had to wait.

I watched Jack as he changed. He took a deep breath and became the professor again. "Are you ready to face them?" he asked.

I gave him a little nod.

As he picked up Jack's rifle, Quipac said matter-of-factly, "My sister has faced a bear. She's not afraid of the students."

That drew smiles from both of us.

The three of us turned and walked back toward them.

As we approached, Jack said to them casually, "Well, that was a survival lesson that wasn't on our syllabus."

The others crowded around to reassure themselves we were OK. They were all talking simultaneously. . . . But nothing was said about our kiss.

As if this were a normal event, Jack said, "Anne, I think you should join the others while we present a lesson in bear-skinning."

The skinning and butchering turned out to be as much work as you would think. Manipulating a thousand pounds of bear isn't easy, and it's bloody, messy work. Jack and I never had a moment alone together the rest of the day.

We had bear stew for dinner. Afterwards, we sat and talked about the day. Again, nothing was said about the kiss, but plenty was said about the bear. Jack and Quipac shared stories about bear hunts.

As people began to doze off on the ikliq, Jack casually said, "Nick, would you change places with Anne. She's going to sleep here tonight."

That's all that was said.

Nick agreeably moved over. I shifted my sleeping bag next to Jack's.

Then began one of the strangest and most romantic nights of my life as Jack continued his courtship in whispers. I say "continued" rather than "started" because I finally realized he'd been courting me in his quiet way since we met.

I slid into my sleeping bag and slipped out of my sweater and jeans as I'd done every night. I thought about what I had done that morning. Something that had been routine had taken on overtones of sensuality and sexual teasing. I wondered what Jack was thinking.

I leaned over to whisper to him, but he put his finger to my lips to quiet me. He put his arm around me and drew me close. He stroked my hair. We waited.

The qulliq had been turned down low. Its flame flickered gently as warm air moved through the vent hole above our heads.

The others made little noises as they settled into sleep. Their breathing at first seemed so loud, but, slowly, their sounds and their presence faded from my awareness.

When the others all seemed asleep, Jack put his lips next to my ear and said softly, "Anne, I love you. I have loved you from the first moment I saw you." He kissed the lobe of my ear, my cheek, my chin, and, finally, my lips with such passion I was breathless when we finished.

When I was able to speak, I said, "I love you too."

Those simple words changed my life, as they have changed the lives of so many others.

"I thought I'd driven you away with my crying."

"No. When you cried, you were in my arms. But the next morning, when you didn't talk to me, I thought you were sorry for letting me get so close." He kissed me again.

For the first time, I ran my hands over his skin. He felt as good as I'd imagined he would—warm and smooth and exciting.

"I've wanted to touch you for so long," I said. "I saw you changing your shirt that time. I came in just when you started to take it off. I couldn't take my eyes off you. I watched you that whole time."

"I didn't know."

"I was embarrassed. I was afraid you'd think I was spying."

"A man likes it when a woman looks at him with pleasure." He kissed me again.

"Would you tell me about your scars?"

"They came from my first bear hunt, when I was a teenager. My father stepped back so I could place the first lance in the bear, but I moved in too close. Two of the bear's claws cut through my coat and skin like knives. I was lucky, and the bear less so."

Jack had told me before that he'd killed a bear with a lance, but it still gave me a chill when he said it. I couldn't comprehend the courage that must have taken.

"May I touch them?"

"Of course."

I traced the scars with my fingers from his shoulder to the waistband of his shorts. He pushed the shorts down so I could touch them where they ended on his hip. I kissed them and ran my tongue along them. His skin tasted sweet and salty. He sighed, and I could feel his heart beat.

Dave stirred in his sleep.

We lay back, quiet, until we were sure he was asleep again.

Then Jack rolled over toward me. He kissed me and gently rubbed the knuckles of his left hand across my breast. I think he wanted to see if I'd push his hand away.

Instead, I moved closer.

He turned his hand over and touched me lightly with his fingertips.

I almost couldn't breathe. I arched up to rub my breast against the palm of his hand, and he moved his hand and put it under my shirt. He had to kiss me hard then, to muffle the moan of pleasure I couldn't hold back.

We whispered and kissed and touched far into the night. I knew, because of the students, we couldn't do what we really wanted, but if he'd asked, I wouldn't have said no.

Finally, Jack said we should think about getting some sleep. As I lay in his arms and started to drift off, I suddenly thought of something. "What will the family think?"

He laughed softly. "Didn't you wonder why my mother and sisters were so determined to teach you to sew? They were afraid I might not be interested in you if you didn't know how. They want you to be a proper Inuit woman. My mother told me the first week you were there that she thought you'd make a very good daughter-in-law. She's never said that about anybody I've taken to visit in Ungavaq" He hesitated a moment. "You know, my life is complicated."

"Yes, I've noticed. I don't want to be another complication, but I don't think I can ever be a 'proper Inuit woman.' I do think I could learn to be your partner. Would that do?"

He whispered in my ear, "That'll do just fine." and followed with a tender kiss.

We finally fell asleep snuggled together.

Long before I was ready to give up my glorious dreams, the others started stirring, and the new day began.

We packed one of the sleds with as much of the now-frozen bear and seal meat, wrapped in the skins, as the dogs could pull. Jack and Quipac cached the rest of the meat and some of the equipment for later retrieval.

As I was helping harness the dogs, Quipac said, "My sister, I am happy for your happiness."

"Is it obvious?"

"Yes, to everyone." He laughed with delight.

Jack and I were teacher and student again, though. We hardly looked at each other all day. I could think of nothing but the night before and the night to come.

That day's journey back was uneventful. We passed our previous campsite in the middle of the afternoon, but didn't stop until we were closer to the village. Now the sound of the sleds whispered, over and over, "He loves you; he loves you."

This night was a repeat of the previous, except Nick didn't wait to be asked to move. Again, Jack and I lay in each other's arms and kissed and whispered until the early hours.

When we reached Ungavaq, word got around the village rapidly that we were back. The people came out of their houses to greet us. They were delighted with the bear meat. Maata and Miqo took over to distribute meat to every person in the village according to rules I didn't understand.

As they were organizing things, Quipac said, "Anaana, Anne needs to learn how to do this. She can help Miqo."

Maata smiled and stepped aside.

Miqo smiled too, and turned to show me what to do.

While I helped with the distribution, Jack unloaded his gear from the other sled. He unloaded my things too, and carried them into his house.

Later, Jack and I sat in Maata's living room and told her of our adventures.

"Anaana," he said, "Anne will be coming to stay at my house after dinner."

Maata said, "Good."

Chapter Twenty-Five

The first pleasure of being back in Ungavaq was the chance to have a proper bath. I looked in the mirror as I undressed. A month of heavy exercise had tightened my body. I almost didn't recognize myself.

I definitely needed that bath. I hadn't realized how smoky the qulliq was. Lines of grime surrounded everything that had been exposed to the air inside the snow house. Washing my hair was a luxury.

As I relaxed in the tub, in the first moments of privacy I'd had in a long time, I had time to think about Jack. There's an old saying that you should be careful what you wish for because you might get it. I'd wished for Jack to love me. That's what I got, but I didn't yet know what that meant. Except for his telling me Maata thought I'd be a good daughter-in-law, we hadn't talked about the future. We'd been too busy experiencing the present. Laura was coming to take me back to Blackwell two days from now. I didn't know what the next two days might bring, let alone the time beyond that. But whatever Jack asked of me, I would try to give. I thought about whether I should ask Jack what his intentions were, but I decided I'd do better to follow René's advice, and let time take care of it. It turned out I didn't have to wait long.

We congregated in the dance house for a village-wide bear feast and had a fun-filled evening. Early on, Jack stood up and announced something in Inuktitut in what seemed like a fairly formal manner.

Tom asked me what he'd said.

I didn't know.

After Jack finished speaking, the other Inuit smiled and nodded their approval.

When Jack sat, Tom asked, "What did you say, Jack?"

Jack looked at me. "I told them Anne and I are going to be married." He gave me that little grin that was becoming so familiar.

Tom looked confused.

Only then did Jack realize that he'd better tell Tom we weren't actually brother and sister.

"Oh," Tom said. "You know, I wondered about that. Well, congratulations!" He turned to tell the others the news.

They crowded around and wished us happiness. The whole time they talked to us, Jack watched my face to see if he could discern my reaction. I kept my face relaxed and accepted their good wishes as calmly as possible. I wasn't about to let on that I was surprised too.

We turned our attention to the singing and dancing until things began to wind down. One by one, the "campers" went to their beds in the homes where they were billeted. After a while, Jack said, "This party's likely to go on all night, Anne. We can leave now, if you're ready."

In the calmest voice I could muster, I said, "Yes, I am a little tired."

We put on our snow gear, said goodnight to Maata and the others, and left.

Away from the dance house, the village was so dark and quiet we could have imagined we were the only people in the world. The moon hadn't risen yet, but enough starlight reflected off the snow that we could see our path.

We walked hand in hand to Jack's house, the crunch of our footsteps the only sound. The beat of my heart seemed so loud, though, I was sure he could hear it.

He opened the door and stepped aside so I could go in. The warm room welcomed us. He stepped in and closed the door.

We hung up our coats.

In an instant, I was in his arms.

"I've never kissed you clean-shaven," I said. "I need to find out if I like it, but I'm not sure how many kisses it'll take before I can make up my mind."

"Well, we'd better get started on that little scientific experiment." He kissed me and kissed me and kissed me.

After some time, I turned my face away. "Before you make me forget, did you really tell them we're getting married?"

"Well, actually not. That was for the students."

My heart went thump in disappointment.

"What I told them is that we are married. Anyway, that's what they'll assume since you're staying here tonight. If you prefer, I can tell them tomorrow we called it off."

"Is it that easy?"

"For them. Not for me."

"Where am I going to sleep?"

He pointed. "That's my bedroom. There are two others."

"I guess if we're married, I'd better sleep in there with you."

Jack kissed me tenderly. Then, taking a step back, he said, "Anne, I want to do this properly. I love you with all my heart. Will you marry me?"

"I love you with all my heart, and I will marry you."

He hesitated. "Do you remember in the diary Brendan wrote that he was glad Ivala hadn't put up too much of a fight? If this were a proper Inuit wedding, I'd kidnap you from your father's igloo. You'd fight me tooth and nail up to the last minute."

"I'm afraid that bear knocked the fight out of me."

"Come outside a minute. This anthropologist will provide at least a little bit of ceremony."

I was mystified, but obeyed.

On the porch, Jack bent down, put his arms around me, and swept me off my feet. With no noticeable effort, he carried me across the threshold, pushed the door closed with his foot, and continued into the bedroom. He set me down gently on the bed and turned on the bedside light.

We laughed. It struck us at the same time that whatever dreams of a romantic interlude we had were difficult to accomplish in snow pants and boots.

He knelt down and pulled off my boots and socks. He stopped, motionless. "Oh, Anne," he said, "Arctic Dawn."

"You remembered."

"Oh, yes," he breathed. His hands trembled as he stroked and kissed my feet. "This is what I wanted to do that first time I saw it."

Ah, if only I'd known. But what in the world would we have done these last four weeks?

We pulled off our snow pants.

I hesitated.

"Is something wrong?" he asked.

I didn't know what to say. I felt so shy with him all of a sudden. I was decades away from being a virgin, and we certainly hadn't been shy the two previous nights, but that had been in the dark. Now he could see me. I was afraid that he'd be disappointed when he saw my body—that he might think I looked old.

"Would you like me to go into the other room?" he asked.

"No. You'd better see what you bargained for."

"I already know what I bargained for. The rest of this is a bonus. Would you like me to help you?"

"Yes, please."

He unbuttoned my shirt, pulled it down my arms, and tossed it onto the nearby chair, undid my bra, and tossed it over with the shirt. Then, he cupped my breasts with his big gentle hands and stood with his eyes closed for a moment. "I've dreamed about this," he said.

He ran his hands gently and slowly over me, leaned down, and kissed my breasts.

"They're not very big," I said.

"As long as I can tell the front from the back in the dark, that's enough."

He reached for the button on the front of my jeans and undid that and the zipper and pushed them down. I stepped out of them. Now I was standing in front of him in nothing but my underpants. They were cotton, plain and pink, but I don't think he even registered those facts. He was breathing deeply. I could see in his face how much he wanted me. He pushed them down and dropped to his knees again. He kissed me and held me and stroked me.

I could feel the beat of his heart through my whole body. I trembled with desire.

He rose and helped me onto the bed.

Then, slowly, deliberately, he undressed for me.

Finally, he stood naked, except for the bear tooth on the chain. He hesitated, then reached to take it off.

"No, Jack. Don't take it off for me. You don't have to choose."

If I'd thought it impossible for him to look at me with more love than he had been, he proved me wrong.

Our bodies showed the marks of our years. Neither one of us would have won a beauty contest, but Jack's muscular body stirred me beyond anything I'd ever felt before. I was consumed by the desire to touch him. I reached out to him and drew him into the bed. Now I had my turn to lean down and kiss him.

He groaned with pleasure.

He drew me up next to him and leaned in close. "I love you, Anne," he said, and he kissed me in a way I'll never forget.

Jack was a skilled and passionate lover.

We slept, as we'd not been able to the two previous nights, with our naked bodies tightly entwined.

I woke in the morning to the sensation of Jack pressed up against my back with his arm around my waist. His hand slowly caressed my body. I moved against him to let him know I was awake.

He turned me to face him and kissed me again until I was breathless.

"I hope you never forget how to do that."

"Anne, I'll never forget how to love you. I love you so much. I meant it when I said I fell in love with you the first moment I saw you. I have no idea why that happened. I felt like I'd just been marking time all my life waiting for you, and then, there you were. As we got to know each other better and better, you seemed more and more wonderful."

"Why didn't you tell me?"

"I'd been so lonely for so long. I couldn't stand to find out you couldn't feel that way about me."

"But I did. That first week I was here, you were in my life and in my mind and in my heart."

"Why didn't you tell me?"

"I was afraid you'd think it was inappropriate because I'm not Inuit."

"And I thought you couldn't love me because I am."

"Ah. It was worse when I found out you were a college professor. Inuit culture is so important to you. I thought it made it even less likely you could be interested in me that way. When you said I could be your sister, well, that just proved it. But I wanted you. Oh, I wanted you. That first night we were in Ottawa, when we left the restaurant, I wanted to kiss you, but I was afraid."

"Of me?"

"No. Of shocking you. Of driving you away."

"What a comedy. I wanted to kiss you too. I'm glad we finally figured it out."

"Me too."

He kissed me again.

I slid my hand down his body. "I wish we never had to get out of this bed."

"You're going to have to hold that thought. You're going to be late for class. And if you don't stop what you're doing right now, the professor's going to be late too."

"I forgot about the others."

"I'll take that as a compliment, but we really have to get going now."

"Before we get up, I want to ask a question. No, no, I take that back. I want to rephrase that."

"Perhaps a woman has a statement to make," he said, smiling.

"Yes, a statement. A woman served seal liver to the other students. The teachers knew something about liver she did not."

Smiling, but in his most formal manner, Jack said, "When a hunter brings home meat, he does not concern himself with the distribution. His wife does that."

"Oh," I said, and smiled back. "A wife can get up now."

We dressed, and I fixed the first meal for my husband in my new kitchen. We managed to eat our breakfast between kisses.

When we went out the front door, I watched Jack click that switch and become the professor again. I was beginning to be familiar with the process. I tried to compose myself to follow his lead.

We spent the day with the students discussing what we'd learned in the past month. At first, it felt almost as though Jack and Quipac were letting the conversation range freely, but periodically one of them would interject a comment or ask a question and set the conversation in a new direction. After a while, I was able to see how they were shaping the discussion and leading us into an understanding of what we'd experienced.

Our last day together as a class. Tomorrow, if the weather held, Laura would arrive early to start ferrying the students back to Blackwell.

In the afternoon, they decided they wanted to build one last snow house and spend the night as we had in the field. Jack looked at me. I nodded, so he agreed. Later, when we had a moment alone, he thanked me. "This type of thing is important to the students. It reinforces their camaraderie and lets them end the experience on a high note. Some of the relationships forged here will last a lifetime."

"That's more or less what I had in mind," I said.

He leaned over to kiss me, but just then Tom showed up to ask him where the snow knives were. "We'll continue this conversation later," he said.

We laughed.

Tom had the good sense to blush a little as he and Jack went to look for the tools.

So we had one last night in our sleeping bags in a snow house. Jack stood up. There were groans from the students.

"Not another lecture," Syd said.

"No, not another lecture. I just wanted to tell you what a good job you've done in the last four weeks. I'm proud of you. Each of you younger students is getting an *A* in the class as long as you do a good job on your field notes and turn them in on time. Your work has been good. The older student," he said, looking at me, "will probably get an *A* because she has an in with the professor."

They laughed and applauded.

He sat and put his arm around me.

When he did that, I suddenly understood something. Except for the hug at the airport, Jack had never shown me affection in public. Last night, he hadn't touched me even when he was telling the other Inuit I was his wife or when he'd told the students we were going to get married. He felt comfortable putting his arm around me here with the students and Quipac present, but I doubt he'd have done that in front of anyone else from the village.

Marcia said he had to work hard to maintain Inuit decorum. In the night, with his passion, he'd shown me how much he'd longed to touch me. But now I understood that if I were going to be with him, I had to let him be who he was in the village. I couldn't ask that he behave here as he felt free to do in Ottawa, and I had to learn to modify my behavior in the village. I had to be able to switch gears with him if he were going to be comfortable with me, and I had to let him realize through my behavior that I understood. I wouldn't get it right all the time, but if he knew I was trying, that would be enough.

When I'd first come to the village, Jack had explained some of Inuit manners. He'd pointed out that when I'd come into her house the first time, Maata put down her sewing and rose to greet me because she knew I expected her to. She did that because I was a kabluna. If I'd been Inuit, she'd have continued sewing. It would have been for me to sit quietly or join her in the work. I had to learn new expectations. The family liked me and were happy that Jack and I were married, but I could remain an outsider if I chose to. I had to allow them to include me. I had to learn to fit in.

That might not be easy. Jack and Quipac had teased me about women being subordinate to men, but in fact, I was choosing to live in a patriarchal society. At least when we were in the village I was going to have to comply with that expectation.

Jack was worth it.

Conversation ran late.

I think he and I were the first ones asleep.

The next day was like the end of summer camp. We heard Laura arrive as scheduled early in the morning and again in the afternoon. There were hugs and tears as each contingent left. In spite of everything, I cheered inwardly when Jennifer climbed into the plane.

After she was gone, Jack asked me about what had happened between us at the beginning of the class. I told him about how jealous I'd been and how I felt I couldn't compete if he was interested in her.

"I guess we both worried when we didn't need to," he said. "I didn't know how to compete with Robby."

His words startled me. I hadn't realized he felt that way. "You're right," I said. "Neither of us had to worry."

Jack and I stayed another two weeks in the village. Everyone joined in a celebration of our marriage. I spent some of the time with the women and made tea in my new home for Maata and my neighbors. The rest of the time I spent with Jack. We walked—yes, even in the cold—and talked and made love. He began to teach me how to sort and clean and label the artifacts from his summer dig. I saw the original of my caribou.

I didn't say anything to Jack, but one day, when he was with Quipac and the other men, I went to Maata and asked if she would tattoo my left hand.

The other women watched as she stitched two parallel lines

about an inch apart across the back of my hand near my knuckles. She connected those lines with pairs of short parallel lines alternating with "y" shapes.

In spite of my hand being chilled with snow, it hurt a lot more than I expected.

Maata asked me if I wanted her to stop, but I said no.

I went home and showed it to Jack. He took my hand in his two for a moment and then kissed it passionately. I came to understand I could not have given him a better wedding gift.

When we got back to Ottawa, Jack took me around and introduced me to his friends and colleagues and to his son, Michael.

Marcia organized a small but more traditional ceremony for us at the faculty club. She was my matron of honor. I met Jack's daughter, Grace, when she came to help with the arrangements.

Jack asked René to have lunch with him one day. Neither would tell me what they talked about, but René told me he was honored that Jack had asked him to be best man.

I called my sisters to tell them what was happening. They offered their best wishes.

The love and joy I missed from them, I received from Carola. She was delighted. She wanted to come to the wedding, but one of her granddaughters was receiving First Communion that same weekend.

"Would you mind having our honeymoon in Pittsburgh?" Jack asked. "I want to see where Brendan and his parents are buried."

"As long as we're together, I don't care where we go."

"If you're going to hang around with an archaeologist," he said, with a smile, "I guess you'll just have to get used to visiting tombs and graves." Then he became more serious. "I'd like to go to San Diego too, to visit Robby's grave, if you wouldn't mind."

"Why?"

"Partly because Robby was my uncle, but mostly because I want to pay my respects to the man who loved you first."

That brought tears to my eyes.

Marcia took me shopping for a dress for the wedding. I asked her why she thought Jack had taken so long to tell me he loved me.

"It's easy to see why he fell in love with you," she said, "and I think I know why he waited. I hope you won't take this the wrong way, my dear, but Jack was testing you. I don't imagine he was aware of it or would even agree with what I'm saying, but he couldn't allow himself to be put in the position of having to choose between you and Ungavaq. I do think he loved you from the beginning. Do you know he came to see me in June when you and he came here from Ungavaq?"

"I thought maybe he did."

"He told me about you almost getting that henna tattoo on your chin. That meant a lot to him. I could hear his love in what he said. But if he'd admitted how much he loved you and then you'd said you couldn't stand Ungavaq or if they'd said they couldn't stand you, it would have been impossible for him. You passed the test with flying colors, even though you didn't know you were taking it. I don't think Jack will ever have to choose between you and his home. He's found his home in you."

One day, we came back to the condo to find a box waiting. When we opened it, I found an elaborately embroidered and beaded caribou-skin parka. The sleeves and hood were edged with polar bear fur. A note from Maata said every woman in the village had done some of the stitching. I felt enfolded by their love.

Glossary:

anaana -- mother

iklik – the raised portion to a snow house where people work, eat, and sleep

kamik – a boot made of caribou hide or sealskin

maktaaq – well aged (fermented) skin and blubber of a narwhal or beluga whale

natiq – the floor space in a snow house used for storage and some work.

qimmiq – a breed of Canadian Inuit dogs (endangered)

qulliq – a soapstone lamp that burns seal oil with a moss wick

ulu – a semi-circular knife; a woman's main tool

umiak – a large boat, traditionally powered by women rowers

Jack's Relatives:

Ivala – his paternal grandmother (deceased)
Maata – his mother, sometimes called Anaana (Mother)
Piuvkaq – his father (deceased)
Miqo – the oldest of his three younger sisters (married to Quipac)
Allaq – his second sister (married to Portoq)
Saarak – his third sister (married to Erqulik)
Kaiyuina – Jack's wife (deceased)
Michael (Miteq) – his son
Grace (Pamioq) – his daughter
Quipac – his best friend and brother-in-law (married to Miqo)
N.B. Many others in the village are aunts, uncles, cousins, nieces and nephews.

About
CAROLINE McCULLAGH

CAROLINE MCCULLAGH, award-winning author of *The Ivory Caribou* and coauthor of *American Trivia* and *American Trivia Quiz Book* with Richard Lederer, earned a master's degree in anthropology from the University of California, San Diego. Her diverse writing projects include five novels, a cookbook, a memoir, a student opera (under the auspices of San Diego Opera), fourteen years of monthly book reviews for the San Diego Horticultural Society, and one year as Books Editor for The American Mensa Bulletin. For the past three years, Caroline has written a weekly column for the San Diego Union-Tribune with Richard Lederer. As a professional editor, she teaches creative writing two days a week.

The Ivory Caribou, then titled *Fire and Ice,* was a past Winner at the San Diego Book Awards as Best Unpublished Novel. Caroline has won twice and has been a finalist once.

Visit CarolineMcCullagh.com

Made in the USA
Charleston, SC
12 June 2016